By the same author:

Lady with a Cool Eye
Deviant Death
The Corpse Road
Miss Pink at the Edge of the World
Hard Option
Over the Sea to Death
A Short Time to Live
Persons Unknown
The Buckskin Girl
Die Like a Dog
Last Chance Country
Grizzly Trail
Snare
The Stone Hawk
Rage
The Raptor Zone
Pit Bull
Veronica's Sisters
The Outside Edge
Cue the Battered Wife

Non-fiction
Space Below my Feet
Two Star Red
On my Home Ground
Survival Count
Hard Road West
The Storm Seekers

THE LOST GIRLS

Gwen Moffat

Constable · London

First published in Great Britain 1998
by Constable & Company Limited
3 The Lanchesters, 162 Fulham Palace Road
London W6 9ER
Copyright © Gwen Moffat 1998
The right of Gwen Moffat to be
identified as the author of this work
has been asserted by her in accordance
with the Copyright, Designs and Patents Act 1988
ISBN 0 09 478930 4
Set in Palatino 10 pt by
SetSystems Ltd, Saffron Walden, Essex
Printed and bound in Great Britain
by MPG Books Ltd, Bodmin, Cornwall

A CIP catalogue record for this book
is available from the British Library

1

By July the water had sunk so low that the remains of the drowned village had started to appear. The field walls had been visible for some time but they always showed in a dry summer and this was the driest for forty-five years.

The dam was built in the fifties, five miles below the village. The people were relocated elsewhere, most of them preferring to stay in the county. Some accepted other hill farms, a few moved into town, two families emigrated to Canada. The authorities breathed a collective sigh of relief when the evacuation was over; Orrdale had always been a headache, isolated as it was at the end of a minor road, difficult to administer, impossible to supervise adequately. Doctors and the Church, Highway departments and the police, all considered it for the best that the village should pass out of existence. Some even welcomed it unreservedly, trusting that the waters of the new reservoir would erase the memory of little Joannie Gardner as effectively as they covered her remains, wherever they were.

Memories stirred with the reappearance of the village. As the water continued to recede Orrdale's old residents were fascinated by the image on their television screens. All the same no one went up there – with the exception of Isaac Dent who grazed sheep on the fells above the reservoir. There wasn't much to do with the sheep after shearing but he drove to the head of the dale several times a week to keep an eye on things. The drowned village was proving a tourist attraction. Tourists broke down walls and their dogs chased the sheep. Isaac kept a shotgun in his Land Rover.

In this corner of the Lake District farmers were rumoured to shoot loose dogs on sight. The ramblers knew that, so the party setting out from the dale to the south of Orrdale were critical of the lone girl who'd caught them up. She was accompanied by a collie, running loose. They pointed out that it made no difference that the dog was fat and scared of sheep, but they'd needed to come on quite heavy before she put him on a length of baler twine. She slipped it off as soon as she left the hikers. She could grab the dog if a farmer appeared. Now that was a joke. Once the others had gone the world was empty of people.

She hadn't noticed at first. What with getting away from the Mondeo guy and racing after the hikers the background had been just that, background. It had stayed that way for a time even when she was alone again; she'd taken one glance at the view, such as it was – a skin of thin grass and all the rest sky – and she'd shut it out. A couple of miles, they'd said: keep to the path and she'd come out above Orrdale; she'd see the reservoir below, she couldn't miss it.

At least the path was level, but dead boring; there was nothing to do but think. She was used to that, it was the only occupation when you were alone in a barn or a squat and you had to go to bed early because there was no one to talk to, and no light, no warmth either except in the sleeping-bag.

She didn't travel much at night, the cops were liable to pick you up and the end of that would be another foster home, another Uncle Bill. The world was full of Uncle Bills, even the cops had their share. She cultivated the hard look: the hair-style, the climber's rucksack, the Nikes (the last two spoils from a brief liaison with a ram-raider who specialised in outdoor equipment) and yet that bloke in the Mondeo had come on to her before she'd been in the car five minutes. Waited for the clincher till he'd got her in a lonely valley though. Scared of Aids but drooling. They all were. Safe sex was a blow job? You could have fooled Perry. His money was good though: twenty quid. She could live on that for a fortnight, throw in a few free meals. And she might meet more like the Mondeo driver, she could handle the type, she could run faster.

'What was he like?' one of the girl hikers had asked, fascinated by her story.

'Weird,' Perry responded glibly. With hindsight he'd been totally predictable but she was acting the injured party here – and she needed the protection of this group. She had to go on; he could be waiting for her if she turned back. 'I mean,' she said, 'what kind of guy is it that picks up a girl, as good as rapes her, and he'd said this was a short-cut to the motorway? Then he throws her out of the car.'

'Why should he send you over the pass?' one of the men asked. 'Why not tell you to go back down the dale?'

'He meant her to get lost,' a girl said.

'I can't believe that.'

'No?' Perry raised thin eyebrows. 'He had a new Mondeo. He was some kind of inspector, he wore a tie. I'm – vulnerable.' She'd been about to say she was under-age. 'He wouldn't want me alive to testify. He wanted me dead.'

'What did he do exactly?'

She could kill the suspicious sod, he wasn't believing a word of it. She made a move to lift the Ray Bans but remembered in time that the shiner was too black to be recent. She touched the side of her head and winced. 'Banged me skull against the window, didn't he? That's assault, apart from the rest.'

Actually she'd been lucky to escape unmarked this time; pick up a girl with a black eye and you guess she's used to violence, that's how his mind would have worked. Perry knew men. But she'd snatched his money, nicked his shades and scarpered. He'd had the last laugh though; brought her up the wrong valley, told her there was this short-cut over the top of the hill. Why did he tell her that before he came on heavy? Drifting across the pass, her eyes on her Nikes but not seeing them, visualising the well-fed sweaty face of him, the little eyes wet with lust, she knew that the bastard meant to dump her right from the start. Well, of course – he had to call on the locals; he wouldn't want her with him.

Alone on the pass she looked back but there was nothing to see, not even the path. She turned frantically, searching for it, but there was only the interminable frieze of grass, and the light, and silence. Even the sky looked hostile, bleached out by the sun like in those western movies where men stagger through the desert and the screen goes glaring white and you know those men are going to die of thirst.

She started to panic. This was England – the Lake District where pensioners came on coach trips, for God's sake – and here she was: Perry the loner, the tearaway, lost and so scared she felt like crying, and she was the one who never cried. Uncle Bill used to belt her till the blood came, shouting he'd make her cry, but she never did.

She tried to breathe deeply but the first breath was a sob. Bags licked her hand. She didn't even know which way was forward now; in turning around she'd lost all sense of direction. If she did find the path again she wouldn't know which way to go. The sun was glaring; thank God for the fat man's Ray Bans. A glimmer of amusement meant a lift of spirit, a spark of common sense. The sun was in her eyes. On the climb out of the valley and as she'd started across the pass, it had been behind her; she'd felt the heat on the back of her neck. What she had to do was keep walking away from the sun. Tentatively she started to move.

The ground was rougher now, tussocky with the odd bright green patch which Bags investigated, looking for water and not finding any. She felt terribly sorry for him, he wasn't a farm dog – too well-fed; he was a pet who had followed her when she had been walking through a village back in the spring. He'd lost weight since then but he was still plump and he would always be a bit stupid. 'We'll find some water soon,' she promised him, longing for a drink herself, treating him as if he were a kid brother, but she always did that. He was all she had; he was family.

An object broke the skyline but it was only a stone. As she approached she saw that it wasn't one stone but several set carefully on top of each other. Human hands had done that. She hurried forward, glanced sideways for more evidence that someone else had been here and gasped. There was a path: a wide earthy track with prints of trainers – boots, shoes, it didn't matter – prints that had been made when the earth was mud.

Now, which way to go, left or right? She looked left and saw what she'd missed as she searched for a second marker: that the ground was starting to break up. The path vanished round the base of a small knoll with stones on top, and beyond were more swells and dips. Through a gap the hazy bulk of a mountain showed and there, just visible in the gap, was the top of a tree. She turned left.

They came round the knoll, both walking better now, and below them, seemingly quite close, a little blue pool shone in a waste of heather. Perry started to run.

They stayed at the pool for an hour: drinking, lying in the shallows. After a while they shared the last of the granary loaf which was all the food left. No matter, there was the twenty pounds. 'You can buy a lot of bones with twenty pounds,' she told Bags. 'Hell, we could have steak tonight!'

Once she got down to the dale it was eight miles to town according to the hikers, but there was a road. She'd thumb a ride.

She dressed and pushed back through the heather to intercept the path at an angle. The pool lay in a depression and the ground was squelchy, the walking rough again with high clumps and holes. Once she stopped on some bright green moss and ahead of her the ground quivered like a water-bed. She inched back, horrified; she had the impression that the moss was no more than a thick crust over something liquid and bottomless. She retreated in a panic, casting about desperately for the path, for those piles of stones that marked its course. None showed but leftwards she could still see the big grey mountain, which was some comfort because by now she'd lost sight of the tree.

She made for the mountain. A big bird flew up and started to circle, calling like a lost soul. She drew a shaky breath, feeling not just a return of her terror when she was lost but an enhancement of it, as if, nearing the end of this fraught journey, something – her fate, the curses of the Mondeo driver – was going to catch up with her. To cap it all Bags was leaving, making for a long bank that looked man-made so the path could be that way. She followed, shouting at him to wait. Without him she'd be the last living being in a hostile world.

The dog drew away from her, not in a straight line but moving this way and that, checking, head raised, nose up. There was a breeze here: slight but blowing towards them. He'd smelled something.

She reached the bank: a kind of wall of crumbly black soil overhung by heather. She moved along the foot of it following the dog. They came to a maze of deep ditches below dikes. Sometimes there was a skim of water in the bottom with gravel and surprisingly pale sand. She didn't like it, felt hemmed in and, some six feet below the level of the moor, she couldn't see the beacon of the mountain. She found a break and scrambled out with relief. There was the mountain, and there – quite close – was a pile of stones.

Bags was barking. To hell with him. She staggered to the path, resolved not to leave it again until it came out on a tarred road.

She could see the dog as she walked down the track – *down*, she noted exultantly – and the top of that tree was in sight again and quite near. Bags was way behind her now, barking frenziedly at a black bank. She shouted. He heard and turned his head. She kept walking and he erupted again. Rabbit, she thought, he'd chased one down a hole. He'd come, eventually.

The tree marked the top of a steep wooded incline. More mountains were showing now, enclosing the head of a valley, and then suddenly the trees ended, there was a turfy shelf and a ruin. Far below was a stretch of water like a big brown puddle in an expanse of pale mud. Lines of walls ran down into what remained of the lake and on the far side cars glittered in the sunshine. She was back in the real world.

The path seemed to end at the ruin but, wiser now, she scouted about the tumbled walls until she picked up the trail which descended in wide zigzags. Half-way down Bags came galloping after her, a bone clenched in his jaws. So it was a dead sheep that had sent him crazy. She sniffed suspiciously. At least he hadn't rolled on it.

Rick Harlow composed his picture to his satisfaction and pressed the button just as the dog burst into view. He swore, then saw that the collie made some kind of statement: a sheepdog on ground that had been under water for forty-five years. He was a friendly animal, bouncing up to the stranger – he'd have been grinning if he hadn't had a bone in his mouth. Rick snapped him again, thinking that if the bone had been human, the animal might have picked it up in the old churchyard. They'd exhumed the bodies before the village was submerged but unmarked graves could have been overlooked. A story might be made out of it, although an item about a dog robbing graves wouldn't go down well with the local paper, and it wasn't strong enough for the nationals. However, the picture might find its niche one day, nothing was ever wasted.

'I could charge you for taking photos of my dog,' Perry said, coming up.

He studied her with interest. Bones too sharp, they gave her the look of an inquisitive rodent, what he could see of her face behind the big Ray Bans – which were obviously not her own, she'd had to pad the arms with sheep's wool. The bristling yellow haircut was striking, it would come out well in colour against the background of grey hills and beige ruins, but he was using black-and-white film.

'You can prove you own the dog?' he asked idly, and was surprised to see her jaw drop. 'I'm not a professional,' he added quickly, 'I'll not use it, I'm just practising. Come far?' Why should she be bothered about his photographing the dog?

Perry was assessing him but poised to walk on. Smart Levis and shirt, casual but clean, not a hiker. Designer glasses: an egghead. She'd taken fright at that cool question: proof she owned Bags? He sounded just like a pig, but he wasn't, he spoke too nicely and his eyes weren't hard. He would have a car and she needed a lift; the expensive camera meant cash and if she could cadge a meal she could save her own money. But he wouldn't be a walk-over, he was youngish, laid-back, and he was taking her measure – and probably getting it right. She sighed, feeling suddenly very tired; there'd been too much hassle today.

'We come over the top,' she said, gesturing limply. 'What is this place?'

They were standing on what might have been a cart track but the walls, the ground between them and a little humpy bridge ahead were uniformly brown: a light fawn without a blade of grass in sight.

'This is the original Orrdale,' he told her. 'Don't you carry a map?'

'What would I do with a map? I'm none the wiser; what's all this dirt? It looks like a desert.'

He shook his head helplessly and his eyes went to her trainers. Like her jeans they were splashed with the black peat mud. 'You must have had a rough trip. You came over the top on your own? Weren't you scared?'

Her eyes narrowed. It was the tone he'd use to a kid, but there was an odd comfort in it; he understood what it had been like up there in that empty world. 'It was a bit spooky,' she admitted. 'If I'd known what it was like I'd never have started out but then – ' She stopped.

'Then what?'

'Well, I had to, didn't I? There was this inspector bloke who give me a ride and – and he beat me up and threw me out in the middle of nowhere. I met some hikers and I come with them part-way. I couldn't go back because of that bastard. He was bad news.' She was explaining too much – and he didn't look as shocked as he should.

'What do you expect?' he said. 'Getting in a car with a strange man. How old are you?'

'Eighteen.'

He raised an eyebrow but he didn't dispute it. 'So,' he said, starting to move towards the bridge, 'where did you spend last night?'

That was a new one. Usually they asked where she proposed to spend this one. 'You with the Social?'

'Being nosy is my job. I write stories for the newspapers.'

She relaxed a little. She watched TV when she had the chance so she knew there was no limit to reporters' questions. 'We slept in a field last night, me and Bags here.'

'Put him on the lead. The farmer's coming and he's an awkward old devil. And take that bone away from him.'

A Land Rover was advancing past the parked cars. Perry slipped the baler twine through Bags' collar but he wouldn't give up his bone. The Ray Bans fell off and she cursed. Rick handed them to her, staring.

'Where did you get that shiner?'

Her face set, then cleared like magic. She sparkled and was suddenly captivating. 'You should have seen the other guy!'

He wasn't amused. 'That didn't happen today. Someone else did that, not the bloke you said threw you out of the car.'

She glared at him. She was like quicksilver: down, up, down. 'That was why. The second one, the old man today, he saw the shiner, thought I was used to it. It gave him a kick, you know?'

A born victim, he thought, but she had some pluck; she'd crossed the pass on her own, and she was obviously not a fellwalker, too young for starters. She couldn't be more than sixteen.

'You didn't tell me about this place,' she pointed out, watching his eyes, needing to change the subject.

He glanced round absently. 'It was a village, a hamlet really; you can see what's left of the houses, and the church; you must have come through the old graveyard.' He didn't look at Bags, didn't want to imply that the dog could be carrying a human bone. 'The dale was flooded in the fifties,' he added.

'They were all drowned?'

'No, no. A dam was built and a reservoir formed slowly. People moved out long before the water reached the houses.' He stopped and looked back, trying to relate the waste of mud and fallen stones with old photographs of whitewashed cottages under towering sycamores, the church, grazing cattle, families hay-making on a soft June day. 'They lived here for two thousand years,' he mused. He turned back to her. 'If you came over the Corpse Road you passed an old hill-fort.'

She shrugged. 'I didn't see no fort.' She was more interested in the present. They were coming to a gate in the road wall. 'Where are all the people from these cars?' There were a few brightly clad tourists exploring the village, fewer than you'd expect from the number of vehicles.

'Those will be looking for souvenirs, not that anything will be left. Under the stones perhaps. A lot of people will be fell-walking and – What's wrong?'

She'd gasped and clutched his arm. The Land Rover had stopped at the gate to the fell and an elderly fellow was releasing several collies from the back.

'You're all right,' Rick said. 'Your dog's on a lead.'

'No. The grey car, see? Is it a Mondeo? The driver's getting out. That's – I'm with you, right?' Her fingers dug into his flesh.

'OK, you're with me. You're not telling me that's the guy – '

'Yes, the one who tried – who raped me – sent me over the mountains – to get lost – to die – ' She'd lost all her poise.

Rick considered how to handle the situation. The driver was standing beside the Mondeo watching them intently. He didn't have the air of a man who'd raped a young girl a few hours ago; he was a middle-aged, middle-management type carrying too much weight and at this moment rigid with what could well be anger. Rick thought the girl was lying, or at the least exaggerating, but she was scared and she was only a kid. And then he thought that the guy could have tried something if he'd thought he could get away with it, the bastard. He felt a rush of adrenalin. He noticed that the farmer, old Isaac Dent, was quite near, not going about his business but watching. They wouldn't have much to brighten their existence in this part of the world.

'You can give me the shades for a start,' the Mondeo driver said as they approached. His voice shook a little. He was furious.

Rick's car was further down the road. He urged the girl forward, turning a bland face on the fat man as if someone else were being addressed.

'You!' It was a shout. The man stepped forward as Rick shouldered Perry away and, raising his camera, took a shot of the guy, head lowered, an angry bull. He stopped. 'What the hell d'you think you're doing? You stay out of this!'

Rick swung neatly and snapped the Mondeo's number plate.

'Hey! Give me that camera!'

'Don't make it worse for yourself,' Rick said, with the kind of cool arrogance designed to make the other do just that. 'There's a witness.' He nodded towards Isaac who had moved closer. 'I'm Harlow,' Rick said loudly. The fat guy looked as if he might be about to have a stroke. 'From *The Sun*,' he added. 'Crime. I'm taking the kid to hospital for a DNA test. You're not going to get away with it.'

The fellow hesitated and Rick saw his mistake. 'No,' the other said tightly. 'If she's saying I raped her a DNA test is just what I want.'

Rick started to follow the girl. 'Listen,' the man said, coming after him, glancing at Isaac, lowering his voice to a hiss. 'That little slag has got twenty quid of mine and a pair of shades that cost a hundred and thirty. And she says I raped her!' His voice rose.

'Tried, couldn't get it up, so what?' Rick shrugged. 'Save it for the police. And your wife – when she sees the front page of *The Sun*.'

The other came after him and Rick turned to face him, trying to look like a hard man, bothered about the camera which wasn't insured. However, there were witnesses. Evidently the fat man realised that too. Whatever he'd intended, he thought better of physical contact. 'She took my money,' he grated. 'Picked my pocket, must have slipped the notes out of my wallet, let her fucking dog out of the back – I thought she just meant to let it out for a run, but she grabbed her rucksack and took off: chasing after some hikers, screaming. I'm known in these parts, I'm a – it's as much as my job – I drove away. Then I found my shades had disappeared. She's wearing 'em. You think that little tart can afford Ray Bans?'

'You've got kids?' Rick asked.

'What's that got to do with it?'

'Kids her age?'

'Hell no! My girls are children.'

'Fourteen, thirteen? How would you feel if a rapist broke into your – '

'Mine are kids! She's a full-grown whore!'

'She's fifteen.'

'Oh Christ!'

She was waiting further up the line of cars. 'Come on,' he urged. 'Keep moving before he recovers.' He pushed her towards his Escort, unlocked it and opened the doors. Bags got in the back, dropped his bone and climbed on the seat. Rick reached in, picked up the bone and threw it over the wall, slamming the door before the dog could jump out and retrieve it.

'What did you say to him?' Perry asked as they drove down the road. 'He looked as if he'd been hit by a bullet.'

'I said you were fifteen.' She giggled. He threw her a sideways glance. 'That guy never raped you.'

'What makes you think that?'

'He's respectable.' The tone was ironic. 'A family man. What did he do?'

She looked sulky. 'You nicked his shades,' he persisted. 'They cost a fortune. You hurt his pride as much as anything. And there's that twenty quid.'

His tone stung her. 'That was for a blow job! He paid up front, so there!'

He gasped and drove for a moment in silence. After a while he said, 'How old *are* you? Yes, I know what you said, but no way are you eighteen.'

She sniffed. 'You don't think I'm experienced enough to be eighteen?'

'That's it. That's it exactly. It's girls like you get themselves murdered.'

'Oh, come on. I know how to look after myself.'

'So how did you get that shiner?'

'I got away, didn't I? I been with that fellow for three months. I told him if he hit me again I'd split. He did and I went.'

'Who was this?' Rick was aghast at the violence and repelled by the sordidness of it but then he remembered that it was all grist to the mill: how the other half lived. 'And where did it happen?' Enlightenment dawned. 'Oh, you were with the travellers on Low Kell Common.'

'It was just temporary. I'm not a traveller, I'm a loner.' The statement was automatic, her thoughts were elsewhere. 'That what you said about *The Sun*. You're not going to put me in the paper?'

'Of course not.' He thought better of that. 'You're a very interesting person,' he added gently, 'but newspapers like sensational stuff: sex and violent death, you know? And I'm not with *The Sun*; that was said to scare the inspector. Now what would he be inspecting?'

'I thought it was cows.'

'Never. He's not dressed for it. I'll find out. It's as well to know your enemy.'

The drama pleased her and she flashed him a gamine smile. 'You're on my side?'

'Isn't that obvious?'

'But – you're not a reporter at all?'

'I'm a free-lance. I sell items – that is, stories – to the highest – well, not exactly the highest bidder, but I get paid.'

'You going to write about the inspector – no, you said you wouldn't mention me.'

'Besides, there's a law of libel. At the moment we've got a stand-off: both sides know the other guy's been naughty but neither's going to the police, right?'

She grinned and wriggled like a six-year-old. He would have liked to know her background: young offenders' institution, foster homes? He wouldn't ask. She was like a little feral cat, to be treated with circumspection. One wrong question and she'd make him stop the car and she'd leave with her rucksack and her dog, even, he thought ruefully, with something of his, like the camera. And he didn't want her to go. But was it wise? Still, he didn't *know* she was under-age.

Isaac Dent marked where the bone fell and moved unhurriedly to retrieve it. A tourist stopped in front of him.

'What have you got there?'

Isaac was disconcerted. On his own ground he wasn't accustomed to being addressed with authority, and never so by a tourist.

'Old sheep's bone,' he growled. 'One o' my animals.' His glare said, And what's it to you?

The man held out his hand. 'Give it to me.'

Isaac's eyes widened in disbelief. 'What right you got – '

'Hand it over, man!'

Isaac did so. He was over seventy and his generation could still be intimidated by a classy accent.

'What is it, Charles?' Now the wife was in on the act, ignoring Isaac, studying the bone.

'You're a poor shepherd,' the man said. 'You don't know what a sheep's leg looks like?'

Isaac's mouth opened and closed.

'Why, it's – ' The wife looked from the bone to her husband, and then she did stare at Isaac. 'How did you come by this?'

He blinked at them uncertainly. 'Picked it up. Just this minute.' He waited tensely.

'You do know what it is,' the man said, and it wasn't a question.

The woman said sternly, as if Isaac were a small boy, 'My husband is a doctor. This is a femur – a human leg bone.'

Isaac nodded slowly. 'I thought you was just tourists. Wanted to spare you like.' He looked across the razed village to the knoll where the church had stood. 'The girl's dog were carrying it and they come through the old graveyard.' He looked to see if they followed his reasoning.

The doctor turned to his wife. 'The graves were exhumed before the water reached them.'

'It seems small, Charles.'

'Of course. It's a child's femur.'

2

'Why didn't you tell someone what this Uncle Bill was doing?' Rick asked, appalled. Everyone knew it happened, but coming direct from the victim it was brought home. 'If you couldn't tell his wife, there were your teachers.'

'You reckon they'd have believed me? They never believe kids. I wasn't the only one either; you don't know the half of it. Most of my mates, boys as well, got screwed in the centres. Or the foster homes.'

'Oh no, I can't believe – '

'You blind and deaf? Everyone sees the News. You can't have missed all those blokes being sent down: been abusing kids for years and years.'

She was right. Hardly a week went by without some revelation concerning paedophile rings and children's homes. Perry didn't seem heated about it, only scornful of his shock when it was laid out for him.

She lounged in an easy chair at the open window of his flat in Plumtree Yard, drinking Coke while casually filling him in on her background. Not recent developments (he guessed she'd been on the run when she joined the travellers) but her upbringing. It was the not unusual story of the mother who didn't want her and the stepfather who wanted her too much, of thieving and expulsion from school, of foster homes and Uncle Bill: the man who could thrash and fondle in the same day, the same hour. 'Plenty more where he come from,' was her comment, and his anguished concern for her overrode the horror. He wanted to hold her, to convey, by physical contact, security, comfort, and he knew the last thing he should do was to touch her. Initiative must come from her. What initiative? The only affection she knew was for an old fat collie. Rick suppressed his emotions and tried to observe her objectively, pleased that she should be relaxed, trusting one man at least although alone with him in a secluded flat.

Plumtree Yard was indeed secluded. Only a short distance

from the centre of Kelleth, it was approached by a tunnel between an estate agent's and an Oxfam shop: a roofed alley that widened to a well between the back of an old mill and this eighteenth-century house that was now two flats. On this fine evening swifts were hawking the air above the roof-tops, their screams louder than the murmur of traffic in Botchergate and the sound of television from Edith Bland's flat.

Perry hadn't turned a hair when she heard noises coming from his fellow tenant. In her short life noisy homes had been the norm. Fortunately Edith, who was slightly deaf, kept the TV in her bedroom, along with the telephone. Her bedroom was above Rick's, and since he worked in his living-room the noises from upstairs were no more intrusive than those of the distant traffic.

'I like it here,' Perry said suddenly. 'Can I crash on your floor?'

He gulped. 'Be my guest.' He started to say that she'd find the floor hard but saw that that could be construed as an invitation to share his bed. He had no guest room. Now he was tongue-tied.

He'd brought her home – what else could he do? He could have put her on the road to Scotland, which she said she wanted to visit, stopping first at the supermarket to buy food for her and the dog. But any idea of her pushing across the border this night died in the supermarket. How could she cook steaks on the road, cook anything? And she was so thin. He'd watched indulgently as she filled a trolley in Safeway, he'd paid and he brought her home. He fed the dog and cooked the steaks while she showered, emerging from the bathroom in clean slacks and a black T-shirt that made her look like a biker's moll.

At first she'd been disappointed by his home but it was only temporary, he told her, he had his own place in Manchester. His reason for being here puzzled her; he had come to the Lakes because it was reputed to be one of the few areas in the country that was relatively free of crime. 'Let's go for something upbeat,' a features editor had suggested. 'Try a series from the outback: remind our readers there are places where women can go out alone at night, where their kids come home from school unaccompanied, where people live normal lives – and all under a benign police dictatorship.' It was the dog days when journalists scraped the bottom of the barrel for items to fill the void.

Rick thought he could turn his hand to anything – including

fantasy – so he accepted the commission. He could turn a blind eye to the drugs and vandals, and thefts from cars at beauty spots, so he was looking for anything upbeat in this old sandstone town ('a rose-red city half as old as Time' – he'd have to work that in somewhere). In fact he'd been agreeably surprised by Kelleth's secret yards, unlittered in his book, in the rough but friendly inhabitants whom he could idealise.

Rick was a good writer and an inquisitive journalist; he knew his own worth. He made enough from papers and magazines to keep body and soul together and run an eight-year-old Escort, but the big time, the big story, eluded him. He followed every thread, seized every opportunity but something was lacking. Today was typical. Alert for old-fashioned values, for nostalgia, he'd paid a second visit to the site of the drowned village but, like the first time, he'd seen only mud: a landscape without human interest.

There had been figures, passion even; there was the fat man's rage, Perry's panic, even old Isaac's avid curiosity, but these had nothing to do with his series. What he needed – The telephone rang.

Startled, he saw Perry jerk awake. A fine host he was; how long had he been ruminating while she slept?

'Rick,' came Harald Fawcett's voice, 'did you forget us?'

'What?' He was disorientated. 'Forget you, Harald?'

'You should be here, dear boy. You were asked for drinks at eight.' Gently disapproving.

'Oh, my God!' Rick's eyes slewed to Perry, who was suddenly wary and sullen. He swallowed and said pleasantly, trying to reassure her with his tone, 'I'm so sorry, Harald; a guest turned up and I clean forgot – '

'Bring him with you. We're waiting. Melinda's eager to meet you.'

'I'm not sure she feels – There's a dog too.'

'A lady? Splendid. What kind of dog?'

When he replaced the receiver Perry was on her feet, wide-eyed. He knew she was about to leave. 'We're going to my landlady's for a drink,' he said wildly. 'I promised and I forgot. You'll like them.'

There was no alternative. If he left her in the flat she'd be gone by the time he returned, and he had to go to the Fawcetts' because they'd invited this Pink woman who Harald had said could open media doors for a young journalist. Ridiculous proposition; as Rick understood it Melinda Pink was an aged writer who probably still used a fountain pen. But Harald and Anne were his landlords and must be humoured, this apart from common courtesy. So he had to go, and Perry should go with him.

'I can't leave Bags,' she said. 'And I'm not taking him; he smells. He always farts if you feed him too much, and you did.'

'You were in the shower and he insisted. Put your sleeping-bag down beside him and he'll know you're coming back.'

In Nichol House Anne Fawcett emerged from the cellar with a bottle of Moselle and held it under the cold tap. 'That'll have to do,' she told her guest who was filling bowls with nuts. 'Really, Harald is too exasperating: asking total strangers along on the spur of the moment. People who don't know us go away from here thinking he's mad and I'm domineering, but he does need supervision. You can't have him talking about cutting up dead bodies at the table –'

'This is only drinks.'

'You know what I mean; half the time he's in a fantasy world. He talks about crime as if it were real.'

'It's real enough,' Miss Pink said.

'I meant the books he reads and, of course, his own novel.'

'It keeps him occupied.'

'Thank God. There's so much to do with the properties, and this house – shopping, the garden; I really can't find the time to take him for runs now he's given up driving. Of course he couldn't go on, concentration seemed to go at the same time as memory. It's so good of you to take him out with you.'

'But I enjoy his company,' Miss Pink protested. 'I can go along with the loss of memory – which isn't that bad, and if his brain misses a cog now and again, it's like switching channels: you can pick up the new subject if you listen.'

'Friends can. People who don't know him can be terrified, or they exploit him. Not if I'm around, of course. I only hope Rick had the sense to tell this woman that Harald's showing his age.'

Turned seventy herself but well-preserved in her neat jade

pants suit and Gucci spectacles, Miss Pink reflected that her hostess wasn't all that perceptive, and wondered about her background. A robust woman in her sixties, Anne was handsome but there was an air about her that suggested yeoman stock rather than landed gentry.

Miss Pink's friendship with Harald Fawcett had never been close. Although she'd known him for decades, they had met only occasionally and that by accident at climbing centres. They had climbed together once or twice but until now she hadn't visited him, had known little more of his home life than that he owned land in the Lake District. It was when she was asked to produce a new guidebook on the Border country that she had contacted him, thinking it possible he'd have a vacant cottage that she might rent for a short stay.

On the telephone Harald had been delighted, but curiously vague about accommodation, and she wasn't surprised when his wife came on the line to explain that it was she who looked after the properties. Anne was polite but forceful; there was one vacant flat in town, she said: looking out on the churchyard. Miss Pink demurred, having anticipated some secluded cottage in a sylvan setting, even with a lake in view. Anne was dismissive; this was high summer, everything was booked, the best places were reserved a year in advance. Miss Pink thought of work, of money and the maintenance of her own house in Cornwall, now itself let to summer visitors, and she agreed to take the flat for three weeks. It turned out better than she'd expected.

The churchyard at Kelleth was a lush oasis in the centre of town, bordered by a pedestrian walk and buildings ranging from eighteenth-century cottages to the Victorian pile of Barclay's Bank. The flat was above a bookshop and the outlook was green foliage and old tombstones. On the far side there was a glimpse of tall windows with white trim and the dull red walls of Nichol House, the Fawcetts' place.

The Fawcetts' family home was Orrdale House, familiarly referred to as the big house, and now occupied by their son, Bob, and his family who had opened it to the public. Harald had confided to Miss Pink that although he regretted leaving the house where he'd been born and brought up he was quite happy to have exchanged crowds of visitors for the peace of a smaller but private place and an overgrown garden. Manicured lawns and herbaceous borders weren't Harald's style, while running a large commercial enterprise would have been anathema.

Years ago he had published a novel on the spiritual aspects of mountaineering. It had some small success and then sank into obscurity. He had published nothing since but for some time he'd been working on a crime novel. He told Miss Pink that he found the research as exciting as the writing. She believed him, he was interested in everything. Unfortunately his grasshopper mind and the loss of memory meant that application was lacking. He saw plots and characters everywhere and could be distracted by a stone.

Miss Pink had been in Kelleth for three days and she'd taken Harald with her to the Roman Wall and a Bronze Age circle. Already she was familiar with the glazed eye, with the enthusiasm that would be appropriate to the moment but bore no relation to the exciting topic of a few minutes ago. Hadrian's Wall suggested third-century crime with Picts in the heather and nervous mercenaries on the Wall. Excavations at a mile turret would make a grand setting for murder on a modern dig, he maintained, and kept that up until mesmerised by the potentially lethal antics of a motorist leap-frogging along a line of slower moving vehicles.

'What should be done with that road-hog?' he asked.

'Nothing can be done before the event.'

'Say he meets a charabanc and it plunges off the road to avoid him and catches fire, killing all the occupants. Schoolchildren. It would make a powerful story.'

'Over the top. Let's say two or three victims. The coach doesn't catch fire, and the walking wounded escape through the emergency door.'

He wasn't listening. 'I could be the judge,' he mused. 'In the days before capital punishment was repealed.'

'Even then it wouldn't have been brought in as murder. No intent.'

'The families of the victims wouldn't see it like that. A novel would give more scope: written in the first person. I'd be a father. I'd stalk him.' Miss Pink shot him a sideways glance. He was seeing images inside his head. 'There *was* a fire,' he murmured. 'A slow death? Poor, poor mites. So' – harshly – 'fire for him too.'

'Suppose your road-hog were a woman.'

'Ah.' He returned to the present. 'Difficult, that. Do *you* have lady murderers?'

'I write romances, but yes, I've had the occasional murderess in a short story.'

'Needs research. I haven't met any bad women, d'you see. I can kill men with impunity but even there, when I come to think deeply, to concentrate, I cannot cope with a slow death. It would be the same as torture, wouldn't it? No, a quick clean bullet's best, or a stab straight to the heart with something long and fine. A stiletto or a poignard.'

No wonder he terrified strangers, the more so because his voice was so sweet and gentle most of the time. For all his good manners and his vivid imagination he had blind spots, seemingly incapable of assessing the effect he had on his listeners, or maybe – she had considered this – maybe he was playing games, employing shock tactics for amusement. He was eccentric, not mad. This imagery, this other world where he came and went so easily, was no more than the creative world of any writer. The difference between herself and Harald was that where she recorded her observations like a reporter and never confused one world with the other, Harald lived inside his characters and their crimes and, it would appear, was close to a point where they would be crossing the divide between the imaginary world and reality. At the moment she thought he was using her as a sounding board, trying out a plot: Harald, who wouldn't crush a beetle.

3

Harald wasn't shocked by Perry. On the contrary, and unfazed by the punk hair-style, he was delighted. Here was a strange species, and in his own drawing-room. He regretted the absence of the dog; his Jack Russell had died recently, he explained to her, he couldn't face the idea of a replacement as yet but it would have been nice to talk to a dog again. Perry was totally disarmed.

She had been shy, inclined to hostility when she saw the drawing-room with its crowded bookshelves and pictures, its parquet floor and old thin rugs. She found the room intimidating and she glowered as Harald stood up to greet her. The remark about the dog transformed the hard little face, intriguing Miss Pink who was struck by the contrast between the mannerly Rick Harlow and his urchin friend. He was watching the girl intently and Miss Pink found this a trifle disturbing. She guessed Perry was under-age. Anne could have had the same thought, observing the girl with a disapproval that bordered on antagonism.

'I'll bring Bags here tomorrow,' Perry was saying. 'I couldn't bring him this evening because he smells.'

'Put him in the bath,' Harald said. 'Bags?'

'After that panther in *The Jungle Book*.'

'Ah, Bagheera. How old is Bags?'

'I don't know. We only met in March. He followed me when I was walking through some village.'

Anne stared. 'You didn't try to find his owner?'

A shutter came down over Perry's face. 'How could I? I didn't know where he lived. Anyway he liked me better than where he came from. Why would he follow me otherwise? Obviously he'd been abused.'

Ears were pricked at the term. 'He's fat enough,' Rick said, smiling.

'Feeding a dog don't mean you're above thrashing him.'

This was received in stiff silence; it seemed likely that even Harald guessed that she had more than dogs in mind. Anne glanced at Miss Pink. 'Drink?' she asked, trying to establish normality.

Perry asked for Coke but there was none. Anne was at a loss. Harald was interested. 'You have to drink something,' he pointed out, meaning it literally.

'I'd love a cup of tea,' she admitted. 'I'm still thirsty.' Then, with a burst of bravado: 'I come over the mountains to that drowned village.'

Harald stroked his chin. His eyes went to Rick.

'We met at Orrdale,' he explained. 'At the old village, not the big house. She walked over from Birkdale without a map.'

'I didn't mean to,' Perry protested. 'Some bloke gave me a ride –' She stopped. This was not the kind of company that would be impressed by the episode with the Mondeo driver.

Rick rushed to the breach. 'Harald, who is it that drives a grey

Mondeo: some kind of civil servant or local government guy: fat, forty-ish, goes round Birkdale, probably all the dales?'

'That's Jonty Robson,' Anne said. 'He's the VAT man; you know: Value Added Tax. He lives up by the golf course, here in Kelleth. Why?'

'We had a confrontation at Orrdale – about parking. The fellow seems to be on a short fuse. Probably the heat. The water in the reservoir's shrinking by the day. All the houses must be visible now, what's left of them, just a foot or so of the old walls. I had the booklet with me today with that lovely photograph of the farm in high summer, shaded by huge trees, a walled track leading down to it. Now the trees are gone and all the rest is just piles of muddy stones.'

Anne nodded. 'That was my home.'

Rick gaped. Harald looked concerned. Anne addressed Miss Pink. 'Some of us didn't move far. I went only five miles: from the head of the dale to the bottom, a cottage first, then the big house when we married.' She regarded her husband fondly.

'You lived in that place?' Perry asked, awestruck. 'That drowned village?' She turned to Harald.

'Not me,' he said. 'I was born lower down the dale. The house is still there, you must go and see it. There are ponies – '

Rick left him enthusing about his old home and came over to Miss Pink, carrying his glass of whisky.

'What kind of books do you write?' he asked, sitting down.

She liked that, no apology about not having read any of her work. 'I write anything,' she said. 'Long or short, fiction or non-fiction, anything I'm asked to do, in fact. Popular stuff, you know, nothing technical. I'm lucky, I've carved out a niche for myself. It's hard for anyone starting out today, but then the young can cope; you have terrific energy. And enthusiasm,' she added as his face lit up.

'I can write about anything too,' he assured her. 'I could write a piece about this room.'

That wouldn't be difficult, it was full of character, not to speak of characters. 'Writer's block is another term for burn-out,' he went on earnestly. 'When I have nothing left to say I shall give up, do something else – like photography.'

The trouble with that was once he lost enthusiasm for writing he'd be burned out for anything else. She didn't tell him so, he wouldn't believe her. Instead she asked him about his present job and was wryly amused when he declared that his editor had been right, there was a different atmosphere in the far north. The only crime he'd discovered was drunken brawls outside the town's so-called night-club and thefts from garden sheds: lawn mowers, hedge trimmers, and really, you had to laugh, the thieves were probably unemployed chaps trying to keep their gardens neat. Miss Pink held her counsel, reflecting that lawn mowers and power tools (and mountain bikes and farm bikes, even the odd flock of sheep) would be sold on – and he had forgotten the cars that were broken into during the tourist season, but then she thought that he could be nurturing the theme to meet his editor's whim: the clean simple life of the Border country. She could go along with that.

She asked if his flat were congenial for work, thinking with pleasure of her own living-room on calm summer evenings with the swifts screaming round the church tower – and he was off again, enthusing on those quaint hidden yards, his eyes on fire: another Harald. Anne approached with the Glenlivet. He stopped in mid-flight and blinked uncertainly.

'You're not driving.' Anne was indulgent and relaxed. Evidently she had decided that Perry was harmless. Across the room the girl was gesturing excitedly. Harald appeared enthralled.

'I'm not used to single malts.' Rick blushed, embarrassed.

'You must let me see some of your work,' Miss Pink said comfortably. 'And I shall come and see your yard.'

'They tell me the yards were constructed that way to foil Scottish marauders,' Rick rushed in. 'Can't you see them?' His eyes shone. 'Dark winter nights, a moon, swords flashing.'

Anne shook her head, cradling the whisky bottle like a baby. 'Sorry, Rick, but the town plan is later than that. The Act of Union was – oh, I forget, but before the yards were built, or rather, the houses round the yards. Towns much further south have yards too.'

'All the same they are charming,' Miss Pink pointed out. 'There must be a great demand for the houses, I've seen no For Sale signs.'

'We-ll,' Anne drew it out, 'they're pretty primitive until they're done up, and that costs a fortune. Rick's place is a case in point. At some time it was one house, then Harald's father had it made into two units, but it's never been satisfactory. No soundproofing.'

'But you can scarcely hear the traffic,' Miss Pink exclaimed. 'The yards are like the churchyard: oases of peace in the centre of the town.' She beamed at her own wording.

'I was thinking of neighbours,' Anne said. 'Fortunately Edith Bland, above Rick, she has her television in the bedroom, and the telephone, so it won't bother him in his living-room?' She raised an eyebrow for confirmation and he nodded. 'Anyway, you're the last tenant.' She turned back to Miss Pink. 'I'm going to gut the interior and then refurbish it, make it into a comfortable house again.'

Rick, just a little under the weather, was amazed. 'Does Edith know that?'

Anne stiffened. He felt the drop in temperature and blundered on: 'She was telling me she's going to put up hanging baskets next summer. She was talking as if she'd be there for ever.'

Anne breathed deeply. 'My mistake,' she said tightly. 'Don't mention it, whatever you do.' She bit her lip and addressed Miss Pink. 'Edith's a farm widow and she whinges, you know? Everyone's hand is against her, particularly her landlady's. But she'll be far better off in a new bungalow than at Plumtree Yard. It's just that I have to be careful how I approach the subject. You won't say anything, Rick?'

'Of course not.' He took a gulp of his whisky.

Miss Pink said brightly, 'The only snag with the yards is that the houses all seem to face inwards; they must be very dark inside. Now my flat is full of sunshine for much of the day...' She rattled on and after a few moments Anne moved back to the others.

'She's going to have a problem there,' Rick muttered. 'Edith's an awkward old cuss and the way she tells it she reckons she has security of tenure. She's not going to take kindly to eviction, particularly from Anne?'

'Why particularly?'

'I'll tell you later. I'll bring some of my work over tomorrow morning. It's no trouble, my place is only the other side of the church.'

'I'll give you coffee. The grocer sells my favourite roast. Kelleth is quite sophisticated food-wise. It points to a high proportion of gourmets in the region.' But he was lost in contemplation. She studied him blandly. 'So you met Perry only today,' she continued smoothly. 'She's very young – to be alone on the fells. And without a map.' And now with a man twice her age.

'She's eighteen.' He'd read her thought and he was on the defensive. 'I rescued her,' he added, his face softening, and suddenly quite beautiful despite the aviator spectacles.

He'd met the child only a few hours ago – time enough for an episode of a carnal nature – yet there was a look of wonder about him that had nothing to do with lust. She was amused, realising that even in her seventies she hadn't forgotten what it was like to fall in love.

Isaac Dent saw them come into Plumtree Yard, walking like pale ghosts in the moonlight. He retreated, closed the door quietly and went back upstairs to the bedroom.

'He's brought her back with him,' he hissed.

Edith was getting into bed. She paused, one knee on the mattress, the lamplight glinting on her plastic curlers. 'What?'

He came closer. 'I said he's brought her here. She'll be staying. Didn't you know?' It was an accusation.

'I've got better things to do with my time than watch what he's about.'

'Then you better start watching. And keep your voice down. I reckon these two was with *them* this evening.'

'You said she never suspected.'

'I know she didna. Nor him. Likely, she'll go shortly. We got nothing to fear, any road. The opposite. You talk to un, find out what's toward. An' watch it on the phone; you got a screech on you like an old hen.' He stopped and listened. 'Them's quiet. But they didna see me, moon were in their eyes.'

'See tha turn light out when tha goes,' Edith said, easing down in the bed, pulling the sheet high, shutting him out.

There was a light in the ground-floor flat and the curtains were undrawn. Rick was on his feet looking down. Isaac halted in the shadow and watched. Suddenly the girl stood up. She'd been on the floor. Isaac remembered the dog then. They'd left it behind when they went to the pub, or to Nichol House. He waited a moment or two but Rick didn't make a grab at her, instead they moved away, into the kitchen at the back. The window was open but they talked softly, he couldn't make out the words. He went back to pick up his Land Rover in Doomgate.

'How old is Edith?' Perry asked as Rick handed her a saucepan.

'Around sixty, at a guess. Big heavy type, wears curlers in bed.' Perry gaped. 'I know,' he went on easily, 'because she still has them in her hair in the morning.'

'I can't imagine people that age – ' Perry stopped.

'The boy friend's turned seventy if he's a day. You saw him: the old shepherd who was so interested in the slanging match with the fat man.'

'You're kidding.' She stared at him, then shrugged. 'And this guy, this *pensioner* visits – ' She cast her eyes at the ceiling.

Rick took the milk out of the fridge and reached for a tin of cocoa. 'Life doesn't stop when you reach sixty,' he told her, meaning sex.

'Well, why aren't they married?'

He smiled indulgently. 'I seem to have missed something here. You're disapproving of two old folk having it off?'

She shook her head impatiently. 'Hell, who cares? What I mean is, why does he have to creep in on the sly like? For God's sake, in these days?'

'He's probably married. I don't know, I've never spoken to the old chap; all I know is he's got some sheep at the head of Orrdale. I've seen him there twice.' He grinned. 'Maybe he followed me today. I told Edith I was going up there to take some shots of the ruins. She didn't like it, said it showed a lack of respect.'

'Respect for what?'

'I assumed she meant the people who were turned out of their homes, although they'd have been a lot better off: moving to modern houses. I mean, the farms they left looked idyllic but they'd have had no electricity and no public transport. I suppose Edith's thinking that Orrdale was part of her childhood, of history; she'd sentimentalize it, forget the primitive lifestyle and remember the good times, you know how it is.' No, he thought, turning back to the stove, this kid didn't know much about good times, but, given the opportunity, he'd show them to her. This evening had been a good start. She'd met nice people.

4

The dragon was guarding her lair this morning. That was how Perry thought of Mrs Fawcett although Rick said she was just over-protective where Harald was concerned. Perry didn't think there was anything wrong with Harald, he was clever and happy (except for being sad about his Jack Russell) and he was very polite. And he liked her. When the dragon opened the door the look on her face meant she was about to be sent away but then Harald appeared and there was no question of her being dismissed. He could be stubborn.

They sat in the garden: like a bit of jungly wasteland but clean, with trees for shade and big white daisies in the tall grass. After Bags had explored he came and sat with his nose on Harald's knee and gazed into the old chap's eyes with that daft look of his. Harald scratched the dog's skull where he liked being scratched.

'We're going to take him along the river walk,' he told Anne when she came out with coffee.

'No.' She held Perry's eye and said firmly, 'We're not free until after lunch. Then we can take him on the common where he can run loose.'

Harald hesitated. Perry saw that he recognised some restrictions and that this was one of them. He wasn't to be allowed out with just herself for company, the dragon would come too. She said pleasantly to Perry, 'It's a beautiful day. What are you and Rick proposing to do this morning?'

'He's with Miss Pink.' Perry was sulking. 'I didn't have nothing in mind really.'

'Kelleth has some interesting shops, and there's a folk museum.'

'They don't let dogs in them places.' The street grammar was deliberate, a gesture of defiance.

'Leave him with me,' Harald said. 'Much nicer for him in the garden than going round the town. You go off and enjoy yourself and this afternoon we'll give him a good run, and we can come back here . . .' He shot a glance at his wife.

'We'll see you at one thirty then,' Anne said smoothly, and Perry knew it was an order. Anyway, who'd want to stay where they weren't wanted?

Miss Pink was filling a kettle at the sink when the girl drifted through the churchyard, the sunshine brilliant on her head. Rick had told her Perry was taking the dog to Nichol House and she guessed what had happened. There was such a forlorn air about the child that Anne must have turned her away. Really, there was no harm in her, and she amused Harald. What was wrong with Anne?

She returned to the living-room with the coffee tray. Rick was leafing through a copy of *Place Names of Cumberland*. 'What did you mean,' she asked, 'when you said the woman in the flat above you wouldn't take kindly to eviction, particularly from Anne?'

'They're both from Orrdale. They grew up together. Didn't you know?'

'I know nothing about her. I've known Harald for donkey's years but I hadn't visited him before this time, and even now he's said nothing about his wife's background.'

'He's her second husband. She was married to a farmer in Orrdale. But I didn't know until last night that the farm pictured in the book about the flooding was her home, and I don't know now if she means her married home or the place where she grew up.'

'What happened to her first husband?'

'He disappeared.'

Miss Pink stared. Rick grinned. 'Edith's words – my neighbour. I asked her what she meant, what was behind it, but she just looked at me and said very deliberately: "No one knows." Couldn't get another word out of her. Isn't that frustrating? People drop exciting hints and that's as far as it goes.'

'What you do then is go to someone else and quote the last piece of gossip, which will lead on to the next. It's a matter of continuity.'

'Oh, my! That's brilliant. You do know your stuff, don't you?

I'll try to strike up a conversation with the boy friend. There's this old shepherd who visits Edith. It's weird – ' He stopped, abashed. Miss Pink could be the same age as the shepherd.

She saw his embarrassment and reverted to the original subject. 'So Anne will have obtained a divorce eventually,' she mused. 'And then she married Harald. In the meantime she was running the farm on her own? But she's a powerful woman, she'd have had no trouble.'

'It wasn't like that. Edith wouldn't talk about why the husband went except that it was around the time that the water was rising and people moving to other farms. Anne never went to the one her husband had been allocated but went to live in a cottage on the Fawcetts' estate. She was pregnant at the time.'

'I see.' Miss Pink drew it out. 'So Bob Fawcett at Orrdale House isn't Harald's son; he changed his name by deed – '

'No, no. Bob is Harald's son, but the son by Anne's first marriage is in California.'

'Oh.' She absorbed this, staring sightlessly at the shimmering foliage outside the open window. Pigeons were crooning in the church tower. From the walk immediately below the window came the murmur of people pausing at the bookshop.

'So you see,' Rick was saying, 'Edith is going to dig her heels in when Anne tells her she has to leave her flat, even if it's to go to a modern bungalow. It's a matter of principle – and she hasn't got a good word to say... The fact is, I think she actually hates Anne. She can be venomous when she mentions her.'

'Well, if they have the same background... And Anne married the squire.'

'It goes deeper than that. Edith calls her a slut.'

'Really?' Miss Pink sighed. 'I suppose it's understandable: a remote dale, not many eligible young men. Land. The worst quarrels in the countryside are over land.'

'Love comes a close second; well, sex. Edith is plain and heavy and almost certainly short of money.'

'And Anne is a beautiful woman.'

'There's no comparison.'

'But what you're saying is that Edith draws comparisons.'

*

Perry wandered among the tombstones trying to read the names, but this was the town's old graveyard and the headstones were mostly of soft red sandstone, the lettering eroded and indecipherable. She made for the entrance to Plumtree Yard then, and was nearly run down by a young girl on a mountain bike. They swore at each other simultaneously.

Perry stared after the other as she skidded to a stop outside Nichol House, dropped her bike on the flags and rang the bell. Perry remembered Rick's saying that Harald had a son at Orrdale House, so this could be a granddaughter: another person to make a ridiculous fuss of Bags. Oh God, thought Perry, not another to swell the party exercising the dog this afternoon! She crossed the walk fuming, looking for trouble, for someone to vent her resentment on.

Edith Bland was shaking a mat at her front door, which was on the ground floor but at the side of the building. She eyed Perry maliciously.

'I'm Mrs Bland,' she announced. 'You here to stay?'

Perry hesitated, not sure how to respond to hostility in a strange country. 'What's it to you?' she countered, feeling her way.

'How old are you?' Edith's voice was even higher than usual. She didn't like strangers, least of all kids, and impertinence was something she would not tolerate.

'I'm eighteen,' Perry said. 'How about you?'

'If you're eighteen so'm I.' It wasn't often Edith found someone she could quarrel with openly; she had been raised in a village where bad blood festered in the dark places of the soul.

'Right, you're nearer eighty.' Perry was cheerful. 'So what's your problem? You fancy Rick?'

This was no neighbourly quarrel, this kid was evil. 'You're out for what you can get.' Edith's voice climbed. 'I know what you're up to. I heard you come in last night, I hear – '

'Bollocks. You don't hear nothing. It's *us* hear *you*.' Perry grinned, remembering what Rick had told her. 'You got the phone in your bedroom and you got a carrying voice; we can hear every word you say – why, we can hear you turn over in bed!' She was carried away, triumphant.

Edith was beyond rational thought. 'You stole off of Jonty Robson there: his sun-glasses, his money – now you're after what you can get from Mr Harlow. You're a trollop, that's what you are.'

Perry laughed. She was enjoying this; she always went up as an antagonist went down. 'I'm young,' she said calmly. 'And Rick's fun; he's not a dirty old man what comes creeping in here in the middle of the night. What is it with old folk? You think people will jeer at you if they know you still try to screw?'

The blood had drained from Edith's cheeks. She held to the door jamb for support. Christ, Perry thought, she's going to throw a fit on me.

'He's my *brother*!' Edith hissed. 'You – you – ' Her mouth opened and closed like a fish's, there were bubbles of spit at the corners.

'OK, OK.' Perry tried to soothe but she had to laugh all the same. 'It's not going to do any harm.'

'No harm?' It was weak, uncomprehending.

'You aren't going to get pregnant at your age,' Perry said. 'And I won't tell on you, honest. I promise.'

Edith turned blindly, closed the door and sat down on the stairs. She thought she could hear laughter. She swallowed, staring at the line of light round the letter box, waiting for the flap to lift and something else, something worse, called through it. They poured petrol through letter boxes and followed it with a match. She visualised a milk bottle being inserted – no, too big, a watering can then: one of those long-spouted sort like she was going to buy when she got the hanging baskets.

Something clicked in Edith's brain: the pieces of a picture shifting to reassemble themselves. Not *her* front door but Rick's, with that slut inside. A watering can filled with petrol from Isaac's Land Rover, a match. It would be like hell: the flames, the stench of roasting flesh, the agony ... She stood up shakily and started to climb the stairs.

She changed into her Crimplene trouser suit and was applying lipstick when someone called from below. Her hand shook and then she froze. The bitch had dared come back?

'Are you in, Edith? It's me: Anne.'

She descended slowly. Anne Fawcett stood on the step. She said carelessly, staring at Edith's smudged lipstick, 'I've been knocking for ever. When are you going to get that hearing aid?'

'I'm on my way out,' Edith said. 'Can't it wait?'

'No.' Anne moved impatiently, poised to enter. They had never liked each other, they had nothing in common except the old days. They eyed each other and the air crackled. After a moment Edith turned and went back up the stairs.

'I won't keep you long,' Anne said, entering the front room that was monopolised by a huge round table covered with brown chenille. 'We're worried about you,' she said bluntly, sitting down without being asked. Her lips stretched but her eyes stayed sharp. 'We're none of us getting any younger, and those stairs are a trial, aren't they?'

Edith sat on the other side of the table, the hostility no longer apparent, her face expressionless. 'And?'

'And what?' Anne was affronted. When Edith continued to stare, she went on, 'It's not as if you were a stranger – and you're a tenant in one of my – one of our properties. We feel responsible. This place is old and . . .' She glanced round disparagingly. 'It's tacky. Not your fault,' she added quickly: 'ours. It needs new doors fitted, draught-proofing, new windows – double-glazed, central heating. In fact,' she said brightly, into her stride now, 'we're considering making the two flats into one unit again; like it was before my father-in-law split it up.'

'I'd have to think about it,' Edith said slowly. 'I don't know as I'd want a house on two levels.'

'We're going to sell.' Anne was harsh, seeing how it was going. 'It'll make a nice little town house for a young couple. Have you seen those new flats being built at the back of Kwiksave? Be ideal for you.'

'I'm well suited here. I got glaucoma. You didn't know that, did you? I'm going blind.'

'Oh, I'm sorry.' Anne paused, deflated, then saw her opportunity. 'All the more reason to move into a modern flat: no stairs, all-electric – '

'I know where everything is here! I been here twelve years. You sprung this on me, why couldn't you give me warning?'

'Actually we've been considering it for some time – '

'We? Who's we?'

'The family.'

'The family,' Edith mimicked, and Anne's eyes widened. Edith said conversationally, 'So what did happen to little Joannie?'

Anne gasped. After a long pause in which she tried to control her breathing, she said coldly, 'I have no idea.'

'And Walter Thornthwaite?' Edith's plump face had softened. She was smiling, gently curious. 'No one wants to be put away when they're old,' she said. 'Least of all folk who can't look after theirselves; they just pine away and die like old dogs. They don't get treated too good neither, not always.' Anne hugged her breasts, mesmerised. 'You're thinking of Mr Fawcett there,' Edith said kindly, 'so imagine how I'd feel: blind, being forced to leave my own home . . .' She looked round the cluttered living-room. 'You see how it is?'

By the time Rick left Miss Pink knew it was too late to go on the hill. There would be a breeze on the summits but at her age and always, alas, more than a few pounds overweight, it was unwise to climb two thousand feet-plus on a cloudless July day. She decided instead on a visit to Orrdale House where rooms would be shaded and cool.

She kept her car in an old coach house in Doomgate, a narrow lane off Botchergate where the tar was softening in the sun. She wondered how you removed tar from dogs' feet, and had a sudden image of Perry in the churchyard, without the collie. So she'd left him with Harald. A nice gesture.

The roads shimmered as she drove out of town. The trees drooped heavily but the air wafting through open windows was sweetened with honeysuckle and she regretted the mountain tops, now soft dove shapes beyond the heat haze. It would be crazy to climb in the sun but maybe a short walk – just a mile or so – to a north-facing crag where she might doze in the shade?

She passed Orrdale House with its elegant Georgian façade, its lawns scorched by the heat, black ponies somnolent under sycamores this side of a ha-ha.

She passed the dam and now the lake was on her left, the ugly tide-line obtrusive on the far shore, glimpsed only occasionally below the road. Here there were trees with little crags, and set back from the verge was an old wall, not always continuous. Where trees had fallen in winter storms the gaps had been repaired with fencing.

After a few miles the road ran out on the flat and there was no more water, only dried mud and the remains of the village.

There were not many sightseers as yet, hardly enough to warrant the presence of a police car, Miss Pink thought, slipping into the last slot in the small car-park. The heat was oppressive as soon as the car stopped. She sighed and got out, looking south to find some shadow below a north face, but the sun was too high and the only shade would be under trees. She considered the hanging woods beyond the old Corpse Road and knew there would be flies.

She started to apply insect repellent, idly surveying the scene, noting that there were figures on the knoll where the church had stood and they had an air of purpose about them. Two could be in uniform and all were quartering the ground like dogs. She reached for the binoculars.

'We should have brought a dog,' the constable muttered to his sergeant. 'I mean, it's not here, is it? There's no disturbance.'

'It could have been lying on the top: been worked out of the ground by the water, then the heat. Something like frost heave.' The sergeant, drenched with sweat, was suffering. 'Wild-goose chase,' he growled, glowering at the two detectives who were conferring at the far corner of what had been the graveyard. 'If Dent was here he could tell us where he picked it up,' he continued.

'I thought it was his dogs found it.'

'Aye, that's more like. The doctor said something about a dog. Where *is* the fellow?'

'Here come the tourists,' the constable announced with relish: anything for a distraction. 'One any road. An old girl. Bird watcher.'

The detectives had noticed her too and observed her approach with resignation untinged by interest: a powerful figure with large binoculars and a white cotton sun hat, wearing jeans and dusty boots. They knew the type: unfazed by authority and bloody inquisitive. Predictably she climbed the knoll towards the men in plainclothes and stopped, panting.

'Too hot,' she breathed, looking past them to the uniformed

men in shirt-sleeves. 'What are the police doing here?' Evidently she had mistaken these two for fellow tourists.

The older detective hesitated. 'Making sure everything's secure,' he ventured, 'now the water level's dropped. This was the old graveyard.'

'The graves are giving up their dead?' She was going to be chatty. 'Have they found anything?'

The older man moved towards the others. The younger mumbled something. 'What was that?' she asked sharply.

'We're together.' The youngster was flustered. Miss Pink had that effect on some people. 'We're all police,' he blurted.

She accepted it as an introduction of sorts. 'Melinda Pink,' she stated. 'And you are?'

'DS Mounsey, ma'am.'

Her eyes shifted to his companion. 'And?'

'Detective Inspector Tyndale.'

'Why detectives?'

'I – really couldn't say.' He remembered the boss's words. 'It's to make sure everything's intact like.' He nodded and tried a smile – a ghost of the one with which he'd charm the girls – and walked away. Behind her dark glasses Miss Pink's eyes were shrewd, the heat forgotten. She looked back at the cars. More vehicles were arriving at the dale head, finding spaces along the verge, disgorging tourists.

'Were you here yesterday?' someone asked. It was the DI, who'd approached as quietly as a cat walking in dust.

'Yesterday. Let me think.' She could switch moods with ease and it didn't matter that she'd been authoritative before; that was with the other one. 'Yesterday,' she repeated, willing him to elaborate. 'Did something happen yesterday?'

He said nothing, stone-walling.

'Yes,' she said brightly, 'I was at Hadrian's Wall, so I wasn't here, no.' She beamed at him.

'Thank you, ma'am.' He moved away.

Keeping the inane smile in place she drifted down from the knoll, pondering who might have been here yesterday, what could have happened then to interest the police, suddenly remembering Rick and Perry. Her jaw dropped. Not Perry, surely they couldn't be looking for the child? No, they were looking on the ground, searching for something: a weapon, some smallish artefact, not a person. In any event Rick had seen nothing. He'd have said.

A man approached from the direction of the cars. He greeted her politely and she responded automatically, then looked after him. He was middle-aged but he moved like a youngster and with total assurance, as if he owned the land. Bare-headed and blond, he wore old faded jeans, a blue shirt dark with sweat, and mountain boots. He carried no pack. Not a tourist, hardly a policeman – too fit. She blinked, trying to place him. He swung up the knoll and walked deliberately to the police who were now grouped together. Miss Pink returned to her car and headed for Orrdale House.

'How nice to meet you,' Marina Fawcett exclaimed. 'We've heard so much about you from my father-in-law and I was reading one of your books only recently. I'm afraid I can't remember the title ... Look, why don't you come round the house with this party and then we'll have some tea? There's no one else about at the moment; my daughter's with her grandparents and goodness knows where James is. And my husband's with the – ' She threw a glance at the visitors who were waiting for the guided tour to start and pretending not to listen. 'Bob's away somewhere. You haven't been here before? You'll enjoy it, and the rooms are cool.'

Having guessed that the blond man could be Bob Fawcett Miss Pink had to restrain her curiosity and join the group, not listening so much as absorbing images. Marina Fawcett was a strapping figure of a woman; it appeared that Fawcett men chose their wives with deliberation: wide-hipped north country types, matronly women who would produce worthy heirs. Marina was fresh and pleasant, not a beauty like her mother-in-law but attractive and with a good speaking voice, no doubt in demand as president or chairman on local committees. To complete the picture she was accompanied by a yellow Labrador.

Miss Pink trailed the party past fine furniture, meticulously polished, past faded Chinese wallpaper below a fretwork ceiling. They trooped through rooms panelled in oiled oak to a medieval kitchen floored with stone flags. Like many Border mansions

Orrdale had evolved rather than been built all of a piece. It went back a long time although not as long as man had lived in the dale. In her casual digest of local history Marina told them that ancient Britons were here before the Romans invaded, that there was a hill-fort at the head of the dale. She caught Miss Pink's unfocused gaze. 'And now we head back to the main entrance,' she said, with a hint of relief. Everyone was dying for tea.

The visitors were despatched to the café and Miss Pink was carried off to the private wing of the house. She sat by a window where she could feel a current of air while Marina retreated to make the tea. In contrast to the splendour of the rest of the mansion this was a homely room, a trifle shabby. A fine gate-legged table carried a film of dust, pages from *The Times* were scattered on a sofa and a coffee mug with dregs in the bottom had been left on a walnut sideboard. A Burmese cat was stretched like a dog on a threadbare prayer rug.

'I realise now that I spoke to your husband in the old village,' Miss Pink said as Marina appeared with the tea tray.

'Oh, so you know all about it.'

'I'm not sure – we merely said good afternoon. We didn't know each other, you see, didn't identify, as it were. How intriguing. I saw him join the police. They'd been very cagey with me. Is something going on?'

'They found a bone.'

'A bone. Human? Of course.'

Marina nodded, passing shortbread. 'A child's femur.'

'So they're looking for the rest of the skeleton. In the grave-yard? That's where you'd expect to find bodies. But why detectives? Why an inspector? That's a high rank if a grave's been disturbed.'

'If it was natural disturbance. That's the point. A child disappeared – oh, ages ago, before the village was flooded. The bone's very old, the preliminary report suggests around fifty years, and it's been buried. Well, it would have to be, wouldn't it, it couldn't have been lying on top of the ground all these years.'

'In the woods perhaps, where no one goes?'

'Oh no. It was found in the old graveyard – ' Marina stopped suddenly.

'That's where they were searching,' Miss Pink prompted. When

Marina didn't resume, she tried again. 'That's where your husband joined them. I saw no sign of disturbed ground. Who found the bone?'

'A doctor.' Marina was abstracted. 'A tourist. No, I'm wrong; he took it from a farmer – probably Isaac Dent, one of our tenants; he has the grazing up there. He must have told the doctor he found it in the graveyard, otherwise why look there?'

'Obvious place. Unless – what is this about a missing child?'

'It was before my time. You'll have to ask Harald and Anne. It's not unusual in this part of the world; small children lose their way coming home from school in a snowstorm – ' Miss Pink was staring. 'It's happened,' Marina protested, 'I mean, in the old days, before school buses and cars. Why, we even have to be careful nowadays; we have a rule that the children never go out on a pony or a bike without saying where they're going. Old mountain rule: Harald insists on it.'

'You're saying the child was lost on the fells?' There was a pause. 'It's odd Harald never mentioned it, but then we haven't come this way. I've taken him driving but northwards, to the Roman Wall and the stone circle at Lazonby.'

Marina wasn't listening. 'I doubt he would tell you about it, after all; it's something they prefer to forget. You pick up the odd snippet here and there, and that's probably invention.'

'And they never found the body? One wonders where he was last seen.'

'She, actually. There's a rumour that she was last seen with a man.'

Miss Pink was still. Sparrows chirped outside the window. 'More tea?' Marina asked brightly. 'I must make a fresh pot' – there was the sound of wheels on gravel – 'that's my old man.'

Bob Fawcett was amazed to find the elderly tourist from the dale head ensconced in his drawing-room, and to realise who she was. He told her that there was a problem, a police problem. 'I was telling Miss Pink that we have the police at the old village,' he told his wife as she returned with more tea.

'She knows about the bone,' Marina said comfortably. 'It'll be on the News this evening, that is, if the police see fit to release it.'

'I don't know that they will.' He sat down and accepted a cup. 'If it's from an old grave they'd rather not broadcast it: dogs running around with human bones – nasty that, they'd prefer to keep it quiet.'

'Would the CID be there if it was a matter of an official grave?' Miss Pink asked. He blinked at her. Not a very astute fellow, she thought.

'They're concentrating on the graveyard,' he pointed out, puzzled.

'What better place for an illicit grave?'

'Illicit?'

Marina said, 'She means that the man who killed Joan Gardner could have buried her there.'

His jaw dropped. 'No one ever suggested – '

'Oh, come on, sweetie! You've heard that story – '

There was a scurry outside the room and the Labrador burst in, followed by a young girl in jeans and trainers: a pretty child in her early teens with taffy-coloured hair and green eyes. She paused at sight of the stranger and was introduced: the daughter, Deborah. She shook hands hurriedly, obviously brimming with news.

'They're going to start a dig at the old village,' she told her parents. 'You'll give permission, won't you, Dad? Can I go and help?'

'Dig – for what?' Bob was staring at her.

'An archaeological dig, of course. They're looking for artefacts.'

'No.' Marina was decisive. 'It's not possible. Anyway it's nearly fifty years since – ' She stopped, aware of her daughter's bewilderment.

Miss Pink guessed that there might well be a dig, but it would be the police doing the digging, not archaeologists.

5

'We had a splendid day,' Harald said. 'We walked Bags and came back here for tea. That's a fascinating child, Melinda, she's had an incredible life – and at that Anne reckons she isn't telling everything.'

'I suspect she's concerned not to shock you; youngsters think we're too old for the raw under-belly of life.'

'Dear me.' Harald took this seriously. 'You think it's been so hard for her? That's tragic.'

'She's weathered it pretty well.'

'But so naïve, Mel, so vulnerable.'

'Maybe, but we can't adopt solitary teenagers in the same way that they adopt dogs. And she has Rick.'

'Rick would be a broken reed,' Harald said. 'Oh, he'd fight for her' – seeing her surprise – 'but he's not a street kid, he doesn't know the rules.'

'What are you talking about, Harald?'

'Why, she's an urchin, a Dickensian character, you must see that. Of course you do, you're a writer. So if her past caught up with her, can you see Rick dealing with evil?'

Miss Pink suppressed a smile, thinking that the worst evil Harald would have come across would have been poachers among his deer.

They were in the garden of Nichol House, the evening air fragrant with stocks and spiced with the smell of roasting meat. Miss Pink sighed; it was the wrong weather for roasts.

'You're tired,' he said, immediately concerned. 'Did you have a strenuous afternoon?'

'Just Orrdale,' she murmured. 'I had tea with Bob's family. Deborah says there's a rumour about a dig, an archaeological dig at the old village now that the ruins are exposed.'

It was as if a fine mask was drawn over his face. The features were visible but the skin tightened; it was the mask of the embattled landowner: blank and aloof. 'It's our land,' he said coldly. 'They have to come to me for permission.'

'It's only gossip. Deborah had met some students. It could have been no more than casual speculation, wondering what might be uncovered – if they were allowed to dig.'

'There's nothing there.'

He was disturbed. She tried to reassure him. 'It's the same inquisitive urge that makes you feel above the lintel in an abandoned house to see if the last occupant left something there, like his pipe.'

'There's nothing more than a few stones at Orrdale. And

they've been under water for nearly half a century; it's impossible that anything could have survived.'

'There was – ' she began, but at that moment Anne called them indoors and any reference to the bone was postponed. Moreover it occurred to her, as they moved into the dining-room, that if Harald didn't know about the find already, it could be only because Anne hadn't told him. And she must know because one of the younger Fawcetts would surely have telephoned her. So she left the initiative to her hostess; it was Fawcett land, their business.

Seated at the table she regarded her starter with a semblance of interest. An avocado was piled with tiny shrimps in mayonnaise; this was not a gourmet household. They sipped an uninspiring hock and Anne waited overlong before addressing her guest.

'So you had a good day.' It sounded portentous and was superfluous, she'd already ascertained that when Miss Pink arrived.

Harald frowned at his shrimps. 'She says they want to dig at the village,' he said moodily.

Anne's spoon clattered against her plate. She stared at him, obviously bewildered.

'An archaeological dig,' Miss Pink explained. 'Deborah heard some gossip. I had tea at the big house.'

'I know.'

Harald looked up sharply. 'Bob called,' Anne told him. 'She says it's only gossip, dear. Why should they dig? There's nothing to find.'

'That's what I say!' The cool mask had gone and he looked wretched. Suddenly his face cleared. 'The fort! Debbie's confused: they want to excavate the British fort on the Corpse Road.' He turned to Miss Pink. 'That's how we come into it – because that's our land. Down below, where the old village stood: that's Water Authority land now. I forgot.'

Anne nodded. She said comfortably, 'I expect we could give them permission to dig at the fort – '

'Well, wait a minute,' Harald protested, 'it's an ancient monument – '

'Not officially, sweetie, not listed as such. Anyway, we can leave the negotiating to Bob.'

'The negotiating perhaps, but I'm not having helicopters bringing equipment in, landing there above the wood, disturbing the wildlife. There are two badgers' sets in there, Melinda . . .'

The evening wore on, a little stiffly, not quite naturally, and not helped by the food, which was well cooked, plain and most unsuitable for a summer's evening: saddle of lamb and bread-and-butter pudding. The conversation was concerned with Lakeland generally and its wildlife. No one mentioned Orrdale again and the omission was glaringly obvious. Miss Pink left early, pleading fatigue, and everyone was very polite.

Strolling home through the leaning tombstones, vaguely aware of bats flicking round the lamps, she was thinking that she had seldom been present at such a meal, where people talked competently on one level when their thoughts were on another. She guessed that the focal point was Orrdale but how did it figure?

It was not yet ten o'clock. In her flat she switched on the television to catch the News and fell asleep. Half an hour later the telephone rang. It was Anne, breathless and urgent, apologising. 'You must have known something was wrong, but I couldn't say anything in front of Harald. You do understand – he doesn't know; it would be too – he'd worry . . .'

The bone, thought Miss Pink, making conciliatory noises.

'I do appreciate your tact.' Anne was overdoing it now. 'You had to know, Bob said you actually talked to the police, and you never said a word to Harald . . . You didn't, did you, before dinner?'

'No, all I mentioned was the dig, and I made light of that.'

'How perceptive of you. And Marina told you about the child who disappeared: Joan Gardner.' It was a statement, not a question. 'If any digging's proposed, it'll be to find the skeleton.'

'The thought crossed my mind,' Miss Pink admitted. 'But are the police that concerned? They can't identify a leg bone; teeth, yes, but not a bone. It could be legitimate.'

'All the graves were opened and the contents reburied. If this bone can be dated to around the time of the flood, and no children died then, it could be – You see?'

Miss Pink opened her mouth to ask why Harald was worried, remembered that he didn't know, realised that Anne was concerned he shouldn't know, and felt a touch of fear.

Anne said, as if telepathic, 'He's sitting in the garden, enjoying the bats. He doesn't have to concern himself; he lived at the far end of the dale – but you'll hear gossip, if you haven't already.'

'Not about Harald.' Miss Pink put a smile in her voice but she waited for the response with interest.

'About my first husband,' Anne said calmly. 'Joan was supposed to have been seen with a man before she vanished – well, that's innocent enough, there were numbers of men and youths about, hay-time in a farming community. But my husband – as he was then – he went too.'

'He – left the area? At the same time?'

'We'd considered emigrating to Canada. He proposed to find work and send for me and the baby. I was pregnant at the time. Well, then, d'you see – ' Fluency deserted her. She paused and resumed in a hard voice: 'He went suddenly, without a word. I did have a postcard, from Liverpool. He said he'd be in touch but I never heard again.'

'Is this public knowledge?' Miss Pink asked.

'Not exactly, but the family knows, and the old people from Orrdale of course. And the police,' she added, as if it were an afterthought. 'They came and asked questions. I couldn't tell them anything.'

She would have shown them the postcard, thought Miss Pink, and she hadn't mentioned the fact that, according to Rick, a farm had been allocated them – which was curious in view of her assertion that the couple had been considering emigration ... Anne was apologising again, stressing that she didn't want Harald worried, that his father had had an almost feudal attitude towards the villagers, and that the disappearance of the little girl had rocked the community. 'It's still there,' she insisted, 'the old horror. Finding the bone brought it all back.'

If Harald didn't know, she could only be speaking for herself. Replacing the receiver Miss Pink subsided in an easy chair, her thoughts returning to the first husband, puzzled by that reference to Canada. They could have considered emigration and rejected the idea and then, when he left – or was forced to leave, he had reverted to the original plan. He could have meant to lose himself in the wilds of North America – and perhaps he had done exactly that. Alternatively he could have met with foul play *en route*, or when he disembarked. There would have been criminals at the ports who'd anticipate that immigrants might be carrying quantities of cash.

There were two scenarios: he had disappeared because he wanted to abandon his wife, or he'd fled because he was involved with the disappearance of the little girl. It would seem that Anne suspected him, perhaps had always suspected – but no, murder wasn't implied until the discovery of the bone – that is, if it were proved to be that of Joan Gardner. It was still possible that the child had been lost on the fells, but then the body would surely have been discovered by the searchers, or their dogs. It must have been hidden, and that meant murder.

'So what else did you say?' Isaac paused in the act of lighting a cigarette. 'Tha didn't by chance say as Harald Fawcett coulda had summat to do with little Joannie?' The tone was insinuating.

Edith wasn't listening. 'Throwing me out like a bag of old rubbish,' she muttered, staring through the windscreen at the sheen of water beyond the dry mud flats. The dale was deep in shadow but an airliner was dragging a sunlit trail across the sky.

'Tha brains is as addled as tha hearing,' Isaac growled. 'An' if tha'd only keep tha voice down us wouldna have to come way out here to say owt.'

'Little yellow-haired slut.'

'Aye, now you got two women gunning for you. Tha's been careful most of tha life, why can't tha go on being careful? Tha's got whip hand, even with the girl. Her could be feared of police but you'm going to lose it all if tha go threatening the Fawcetts – '

'I never – '

'Tha said tha sent her away wi' flea in her ear – '

'I never mentioned Joannie; I just said like folks could be put away when they got old, an' she knew I meant him – Harald – and then I said I were meaning meself.'

'You'm talking daft. What else did tha say to get rid of her? Musta been summat.'

Edith turned on him viciously. 'I asked were *Mister* Fawcett worried about the bone, and I said as how the police would be wanting to question all of us old uns what was living here when

Joannie went missing. I said I might be able to keep them away from Mr Fawcett, seeing as she wouldn't want him bothered, the state he's in.'

'Well now.' Isaac leaned back in the driving seat and considered this. 'Now we have everyone in some sort of trouble. There's yon Harlow taken up with a lassie half his age, and here's Jonty Robson who'd like fine to get his hands on her and have his glasses back and his twenty pound, and more, no doubt.' He chuckled richly. 'Now *there's* a way to be rid of her: an anonymous phone call to police saying she's under-age.'

'No! I don't want nowt to do wi' police. I never done nowt.'

'They don't have to come to you. 'Fact, tha's only got to mention 'em to the girl and you'd be rid of her for good.'

'S'pose she's told Harlow?'

'Find out. You found out with Anne Fawcett. Where's yer brains? Think on, tha silly cow.'

Miss Pink was wakened by the telephone. Blearily she pushed back the bedclothes and stumbled into her living-room. The graveyard below the window was cold and dewy in the shade – and here was Anne *again*, saying Harald had a yen to go to Liddesdale, Miss Pink had said she wanted to look at Hermitage Castle and he was an authority on Border history, so why didn't they drive up there today, take a picnic lunch or continue to Teviotdale, have a bar meal at –

'Wait a minute!' Miss Pink could take no more of this. 'It's eight o'clock, I'm still half asleep, I *was* asleep – '

'I'm sorry. Come and join us for breakfast.'

She couldn't believe this was happening, even the apology was offhand. 'I need my coffee – ' she began.

'Quickly then.' Anne paused, then went on, lowering her voice, talking fast, 'The police will surely be here today. They questioned me before. They'll be back.'

'It was forty-five years ago,' Miss Pink protested. 'What more can you tell them now than you could at the time?'

'They might think he'd been in touch. And before, we didn't know she'd been – I mean, now they've found the – part of the skeleton ... It's Harald: I can't have him harassed, you know what he's like. He's an old man, Melinda, he'll get confused, God knows what they might make him say. Please take him out of the way.'

She was distraught. Miss Pink gave in, it was all one to her whether she went to Hermitage Castle today or sometime in the future. She did insist that she have breakfast before she left but it couldn't be a leisurely meal, not with the knowledge of Anne stewing on the other side of the churchyard.

By ten o'clock they were over the Border and following a minor road above Liddel Water. Harald hadn't seemed in the least put out by the early start; he was back to his normal self, making appreciative comments on the Southern Uplands, regretting that he had never found time to explore these lonely glens, so undramatic in comparison with the Highlands and yet, said he, Liddesdale had been at the heart of the Debateable Land, for centuries savagely disputed by English and Scots, even more fiercely by the Scots among themselves. 'All gone,' he said sadly, 'every peel tower, every castle – destroyed after the Act of Union.'

Miss Pink let him talk, and he was more voluble than ever this morning; it crossed her mind that he was talking in order to stop her from asking questions. Did he know about the bone? How shrewd was he? Definitely not the helpless old fellow Anne implied. Her eyes on the road, with fleeting glimpses of water among dry boulders below, of scorched slopes above, she set herself to manipulate the conversation, suggesting that the image of moss troopers and cattle raiders riding through the heather was glamorous but the reality must have been bleak.

'No doubt about that,' he agreed. 'Atrocities were rife: retaliation. They did take prisoners but captives were left to starve in dungeons, someone was even boiled – in a pot. There was a family who existed for twenty-five years on the flesh of travellers they attacked – '

'No, Harald, you're thinking of the Bean family over in Galloway, not this neck of the woods.'

'It makes no odds, it's all Border country, beyond the pale if truth were told.'

'You relish it. You're a bloodthirsty soul.'

He shrugged. 'It's history.' He was silent. She glanced sideways and saw that he had slumped in his seat, his eyes dull.

'A very long time ago,' she prompted.

'We have long memories on the Border.'

She stiffened and her gaze returned to the road.

'Rape and pillage,' Harald intoned, and shuddered.

'What is pillage?' she asked idly. 'It's one of those words you always mean to look up and never get around to it.'

'It means plunder: from the French, *piller*.'

There was a further silence which he broke eventually but as if talking to himself. 'Rape, yes, but not followed by murder. No need: rape wasn't a crime. A sin maybe. What was the Church's view on that? Did they have ministers here?' He regarded the bare slopes. 'Doubtful. At all events the victims would be women: adults. Raping children has always been a crime, a sin, a horror. And to murder a child! Of course he had to, to silence her. He could be identified.'

Where were they? With the moss troopers or closer to home, to now? 'Quite.' She spoke through dry lips. 'The same motive: often with grown women, always with children.'

He nodded jerkily. 'That's why she wanted me out of the way.'

'I don't follow.'

'In case the police insisted on talking to me.'

'What harm could you have done?'

'None, actually. But there I let her take charge. Walter Thornthwaite was her husband; it's her territory, her responsibility. And she's more than competent, she won't let them rattle her. You know' – he shifted in his seat and turned towards her – 'despite what it looked like it could have been an accident: placing his hands on her throat and pressing too hard on the hyoid.' He touched his own throat delicately. 'If he did strangle her it'll be broken but they'll never find such a tiny bone now. The foxes and ravens will have been at work.'

'You've known all along?'

'Of course. Everyone knew. Joan disappeared; a few days later he followed. It was obvious – although Anne's always believed in his innocence. Ostensibly.'

Perry and Rick were coming home through the churchyard. They had been walking Bags by the river and the collie was still shedding water.

'Miss Pink has something of mine,' Rick announced vaguely,

not wanting to admit that he'd handed over some of his features for a constructive opinion. 'You wait here, I shan't be a minute. Keep Bags on the lead.' He'd bought one to replace the baler twine.

'No need,' Perry said. 'I'm training him. Stay, boy.' She sat down on a bench. Bags dropped at her feet. She leaned back and closed her eyes, listening to the hum of insects in the trees, her head like fool's gold in the sunshine. After a while she felt the dog move and opened her eyes. The Mondeo driver stood a few yards away, his mouth open, his eyes fixed. Seeing her flicker of panic his lips closed and stretched in the travesty of a smile.

Perry swallowed. On the next seat were two women with strollers, their kids playing on the dry grass. There was no sign of Rick. She stood up and approached the women.

'Have you got the time?'

They glanced at her, transfixed by the haircut. 'Twelve o'clock,' one said, and looked meaningly at the church tower but the clock couldn't be seen from here.

'Come on, boy, race you!' Perry cried and dashed away, round the church, along the walk past Nichol House, glancing back to make sure he wasn't coming after her. He'd be known locally: a tax inspector, he wouldn't dare attract attention whatever he might intend on the sly. She made for Doomgate – and beyond the bollards that blocked access to the church walk a police car was parked, the driver behind the wheel, the windows down, a radio squawking inside.

She stooped and clipped the lead to Bags' collar, straightened up, stared with her generation's contempt at the driver and walked past, her eyes searching for a clear run, some yard where the car couldn't follow, trying to remember if there was a back gate to Nichol House by way of its garden so that she could abandon the dog. But anyone with a back entrance would keep it locked these days.

She was frantic; if they caught her they'd put Bags in the pound, they'd put him down ... She kept walking along Doomgate. There was no shout from behind her, no revving of an engine. Crossing the road she looked back. The police car hadn't moved and that man, the Mondeo guy, would never follow her now, not with police about. She walked on, looking for somewhere to hole up until she could contact Rick.

Getting no reply when he rang Miss Pink's doorbell Rick had wandered into the bookshop. Emerging with a copy of *The Second Jungle Book*, smiling as he visualised Perry's reaction to it, he saw that the seat where he'd left her was vacant. Then he realised that the big fellow talking to two women on the next bench was the Mondeo chap, Jonty Robson. So she'd seen the guy coming and had scarpered – but had Robson seen her, or was his talking to the women merely a coincidence? At that moment the chap left them and strode down the flagged path towards Doomgate. Rick approached the women. 'I'm looking for a girl with a collie,' he said.

They regarded him knowingly. They'd have seen him leave Perry a few minutes ago. 'She's in demand,' one said, elaborately arch, 'he's after her too.' Nodding at Robson's back.

Their eyes anticipated excitement. 'Although he says,' put in the other woman, 'that it's the dog he's after: knows who it belongs to, says it went missing.'

'Like she were one of them travellers and she stole it,' the first woman suggested.

'Which way did she go?' Rick was harsh. 'Don't tell me: he's gone after her.'

'Right, and maybe the police too.'

He moved away, having no time to consider that last comment because there, to his astonishment, was Jonty Robson, strolling casually round the churchyard away from the exit for which he'd been making so precipitately. Their eyes met across the tombstones. Robson halted and stared at him. Puzzled, Rick looked from the fat man to the exit. A police car was parked on the other side of the bollards. He grinned, enlightened, and crossed the grass to Robson.

'Can I help you?' he asked pleasantly, as if he stood on his own property. 'Or would you care to ask a policeman?'

Robson's eyes flickered then his head tilted to one side so that he resembled an interested mastiff. 'She's still with you,' he breathed.

Rick saw the danger and played for time. 'Sorry?'

'Don't give me that. She's fifteen, you said so. And here she's shacked up with you.'

'Shacked up? Oh, you're talking about the kid you abducted, right?'

'Lies, all lies. And you're not on *The Sun* neither.'

'Wouldn't stoop to it,' Rick said airily. 'I'm a freelance. I sell my stuff wherever there's a market. Sex and violence fetch a good price, particularly where Authority is concerned, like big fish in little ponds, respected family men, you know the kind of thing: blow jobs in the backs of cars.'

'I know where you live,' Robson said, his eyes slits above his fleshy cheeks.

'But only temporarily. Your *home* is here, you have neighbours, your girls go to school in Kelleth' – a guess, but Robson didn't deny it – 'your wife will have status, married to the VAT man. *You* will have status.'

'It's her word against mine.'

'You see,' Rick said chattily, 'when an item like this is broadcast – '

'Try it! You just try it!'

' – or appears in print, and you deny it publicly, it usually happens that other girls – women, schoolgirls, they come forward to point out that this isn't the first time, it's happened before – to them.'

'Of course!' The scorn was overdone. Robson licked his lips. 'Every slag in town will see her chance to make a few quid from the media.'

'A few quid more? How much do you pay them?'

Robson bared his teeth. 'Watch your back,' he grated. 'I'm going to get you both.'

Rick raised an eyebrow and walked away; he couldn't counter that threat. Fortunately Robson didn't appear to have noticed the Kipling; he'd surely guess that Rick didn't intend to read it himself. But so what, the man knew Perry was staying in the flat, he'd been watching. Not a pleasant thought. Rick didn't think she'd be waiting for him outside the flat but just to be on the safe side he walked round the churchyard instead of heading straight across for Plumtree Yard. Robson didn't follow.

He started to consider what should be done. He didn't think Robson would go to the police, he thought he'd come pretty close to the truth there when he'd suggested that Perry wasn't the first youngster he'd propositioned, and if Robson tried an anonymous tip-off he'd know that Rick would guess the identity of the informant and retaliate. Robson had everything to lose. No, it wasn't a charge of consorting with a minor that bothered Rick, he was worried about Perry's safety. If Robson could hang around the churchyard in the daytime, he could do so in the dark. Perry ought to leave Kelleth, and at the thought his guts contracted. He'd known her for two days and already he'd lost sight of what life was like before he met her. He couldn't remember being depressed, unfulfilled, bored, but he knew without a doubt he'd feel like that tomorrow, if he set her on the road to Scotland tonight. So why not go with her? He stopped in his tracks, grinning like a maniac, and then he sobered and glanced back, but there was still no sign of Robson. He headed for Plumtree Yard.

Two men were at Edith's door. One was dressed conventionally: dark pants, shirt-sleeves and, of all things in this weather, a tie. The other was in baggy jeans and a shirt in blue plaid. Beyond them Edith stood in characteristic pose defending her castle, arms folded, alert, defiant, listening as if she were granting a favour. Her eyes slid past her callers to Rick and her lips tightened. She nodded curtly. Her visitors turned, glanced at Rick, and turned back.

Footsteps slapped softly as someone entered the yard behind him. It was a uniformed policeman. Rick kept walking to his own front door and took out his key.

As he let himself into the flat he realised that the police had nothing to do with Perry or himself. The bone had been mentioned on local radio this morning – and Edith was old Orrdale. They were questioning people who had lived there when that child disappeared. He sighed with relief, dismissed them from his mind and started to wonder where Perry was. She'd have seen the police car and would wait until the coast was clear before she came home. Home – God, he'd have to see Anne Fawcett to settle up – No, he'd paid in advance. But he must leave properly, say goodbye, particularly to Harald. He'd wait for Perry and go round to Nichol House this evening, see Miss Pink too; she had his clippings.

6

The churchyard was a mosaic of moonlight and shadow, the leaves hanging motionless. Miss Pink, opening her curtains before she went to bed, recalled a weird movie of her childhood with vampires hauling themselves out of graves. A B-picture, probably accompanying a more appropriate film; her parents would have walked out had they suspected how long she would be haunted by those images of the earth giving up its dreadful dead . . . She stiffened. Something low crept across a path of light, turned back, nosed a headstone and moved on: Bags, dragging his lead.

She looked for Perry but there was no sign of her, nor of anyone else. Puzzled, she watched the collie appear and vanish without apparent direction. She sighed, aware of her responsibility.

He was still there when she emerged from the door beside the bookshop and he came to her immediately. Obviously he disliked being on his own. So what had happened?

She went to Plumtree Yard but the only light was in Edith's flat and there was no answer when she rang Rick's bell. She returned to her own place, Bags trotting happily beside her, accepting her as a friend. Miss Pink was more of a cat-person but she had nothing against dogs and this one was so amenable and well mannered it was a pleasure to be in his company.

She wrote a note: 'Bags is with me. M. Pink', went back and stuck it on Rick's front door. 'So we go home and talk while we wait for him,' she told the collie, but as she walked across the churchyard again she was hailed by the man himself, hurrying across the grass.

'Hi,' he gasped. 'Where's Perry?'

'I've no idea. I saw Bags from my flat, trailing his lead, so I came down and took him in charge. I left a note – '

'Where *is* she?' He looked away, throwing the question into the night.

'With the Fawcetts?'

'No, I've just come from there, they haven't seen her today. You know the police were here?'

'They'll be making inquiries about the bone found at Orrdale.'

'I think she saw them and thought they were after her – but that was this afternoon! She hasn't left, all her stuff's in the flat, but Bags: how did he get loose?' He paused, scratching at moss on a headstone. Bags sat down and leaned against Miss Pink's legs. 'I saw her go,' Rick went on, 'well – virtually. I was here.' He looked around. 'She was on that seat there. I went to your flat but you were out so I went in the bookshop. Bags was all wet, he'd been in the river. I told her to wait. "Put him on the lead," I said, and she said she was teaching him to stay, you didn't need the lead, I remember her saying that. And I came out of the bookshop and she was gone, and there was that fellow: Jonty Robson.' Rick stared at the bench with wide eyes. 'If he's touched her I'll kill him.'

'This is the man you were asking the Fawcetts about: the one who gave Perry a lift up Birkdale?'

'And raped – ' He stopped short.

'He raped her?' She was appalled.

'No.' He looked away, mumbling. She waited. 'It's – a bit complicated,' he muttered. 'There wasn't a rape, he's not that stupid – surely? But he did – er – make suggestions.' He swallowed.

'Then it's he who should be scared of her now.'

'Ye-es, but you see, she reckoned he owed her: taking her out of the way, dumping her in the wilds . . . I'm afraid' – he was terribly embarrassed – 'she lifted his Ray Bans.'

'His – oh, those pricey sun-glasses. I see.'

'And twenty pounds. Apparently he was paying up-front, if you see what I mean.'

She did. She saw what he had been skirting round, saw the possibility that Perry was a teenage prostitute, but that was immaterial at this moment except that it heightened the risks the girl had run, was running. 'So he's after his Ray Bans and his cash,' she said thoughtfully. 'And he can't go to the police because he's a family man.'

'He threatened me – and her. We had a confrontation. He said he'd get us both.'

Miss Pink looked down at Bags. 'If she saw the police – '

'She must have done. There was a patrol car beyond the bollards. According to some women she went that way so she must have walked right by the car. She would have been scared stiff.'

'You think she's a runaway.'

'She's been horribly abused.'

'And you want to protect her. Unfortunately, since she's probably under-age' – she paused hopefully but in vain, and his expression was truculent – 'you're laying yourself open to a criminal charge.'

'You think I care?'

'Ssh! Keep your voice down.'

'I love her!' It was an angry hiss.

'When she comes back, bring her over to me. Now you go back to Plumtree, take Bags with you . . . I think that if she thought that the police were after her, or Jonty Robson, or both, Bags would be an encumbrance. She probably tied him to your front door, or close by, and he worked himself loose.'

'That would fit. She couldn't put him inside the flat because I have the key.'

'Go home, but bring her across whatever time she comes back. She'll be safe with me.'

She left the light burning in her living-room but otherwise she acted normally, undressing and going to bed. She wondered where Perry could be. She was less worried about the police than about Robson – although she couldn't visualise the VAT man, the local Customs and Excise officer, as anything other than ridiculous in the circumstances. No doubt he had made overtures but it was himself who'd been taken for a ride, and if he recovered his expensive sun-glasses he should feel the score was even. As for the twenty pounds, she preferred not to dwell on that, whether it had been a transaction or a couple of notes slipped out of a wallet – and it was only twenty pounds anyway, when Ray Bans ran to well over a hundred. Here something snagged in the course of her waking dream; the Ray Bans were theft but the cash related to sex. The man had been ridiculed by a child, and the fact that she'd run when he reappeared suggested that she looked on him as dangerous. But if she'd told her story to other people – and Robson would assume that she'd told Rick – silencing her wasn't the answer . . .

He would have to silence everyone she'd talked to ... Silence? It was so quiet outside she could hear the bats.

A thrush sang a few notes. In the night? A blackbird was suddenly shouting full throttle, another thrush, then a wren. There was a rustle in the room. She opened her eyes to the grey light before sunrise, and the net curtain stroking the window frame in the dawn breeze. She lay still for a moment orientating herself and then she realised that Perry hadn't come home, or that if she had then Rick had seen fit to keep her at Plumtree Yard.

He came across at eight o'clock, accompanied by the dog. He glared at her when she opened the front door; he was beside himself with some emotion.

'She phoned!'

'Ah, good. Where is she?'

'In Scotland. She wouldn't say where exactly.'

'Come up and have some breakfast.'

He wouldn't sit down but stalked to her kitchen window and stared out at the churchyard. 'Why won't she tell me where she is?' he blurted.

She stopped breaking eggs in a bowl. 'You dialled 1471?'

'Yes. Number Withheld. And she said she was in a call-box, had to hurry, had no change. But there wasn't that echo effect you get in a call-box. I started to tell her to give me the number and the line went dead as she was saying something about Bags and hound meal.' He laughed angrily. 'That was why she called, to make sure Bags was all right, didn't even say why she'd left him. She'd tied him to that knob on the front door like you thought. She did say she'd be back for him, just to make sure I wasn't going to have him put down, I suppose.' His anger had turned to bitterness.

'Did she say why she left?'

'She said she saw Robson and then the police so she assumed they were together and he'd reported her after all. I said the cops weren't after her, they were looking into that disappearance decades ago, and as I told her about the bone I remembered the craziest thing: that Bags was carrying a bone when I met them! So I said the police were searching the churchyard where he picked it up and she said he didn't find it there, and then she changed the subject and started on about the amount of hound meal he should have, and then she insisted I keep quiet about her phoning and the line went dead without her even saying goodbye. She sounded scared.'

'She would be,' Miss Pink said. 'Because she *is* involved. Wherever Bags found the bone, the skeleton could be close by. She's realised that. The police will want to talk to her.'

'Oh Christ. What do we do?'

'Let me think.'

'I know what we do,' she said as she stirred the scrambled eggs. 'We take Bags for a walk, reversing Perry's hike from Birkdale to Orrdale. If he's found one bone he can find the rest.'

'So it'll seem as if we come on it by accident? But the police will still want to speak to Perry. He's her dog.'

'We'll tell the truth – more or less. She gave the dog to you and moved on. You're in the clear, Rick; you don't know her age – '

'I don't know her name!'

'You mean she didn't tell you her surname?'

'I don't even know if Perry is her first name. She told me it was short for Peregrine but people don't call girl babies Peregrine. I think she chose the name when she – ' He checked.

' – ran away.'

'I don't know that she's on the run.'

'It's not important. At the moment anyway.'

Bags was in ecstasy to be on the fells again but he hated the lead. 'We should have bought one of those extending contraptions,' Miss Pink grumbled as she was jerked ungracefully up a rock step, the braid slimy in her sweaty hand. Behind her Rick had no rhythm either but that was because he had no experience of going steeply uphill.

They came to the lip of the escarpment and rested by the old ruin.

'Bags was running loose when I met them,' Rick said. 'And how can he find anything if you're on the end of the lead?'

'I thought of that.' She leaned against the wall of what had been the gable-end of the ruin. 'But I'm also thinking in terms of a burial. Where did you see any soil on this slope deep enough to cover a body?'

'In the wood?' He looked doubtfully at the tops of the trees.

'For my money it's steep and rocky everywhere – oh!' She moved forward smartly. 'That wall moved!'

They walked round the gable-end, studying the stones. Where there had been a fireplace boulders had fallen from the chimney breast leaving the mass of wall virtually unsupported.

'Someone should push that down,' she said grimly, 'but not us; you don't know which way the top stones will fall. Come along, let's set Bags to work. I'm going to risk letting him loose now we're on top.'

'If it rains won't that destroy the scent?'

'I'm not sure. Rain might bring out more smells to confuse him, but it's not going to rain.'

She unclipped the lead. Bags plunged away, zigzagging excitedly about the ruin, lifting his leg at a clump of nettles, sniffing at sheep droppings. They watched him intently but he had no interest in any one spot and after a few moments he paused and glanced at them expectantly. Miss Pink sucked her lip and started up the Corpse Road, moving easily now as the path rose gently to the open moor.

Rick glanced back. 'You could be wrong about rain.' He was uneasy in this bleak place. 'It looks very murky in the west.'

'Summer storm.' She sniffed. 'Wind's from that quarter but not to worry; the central fells will get it, not us.'

'I'd hate to be up here in bad weather. You'll be used to it of course, being a climber.'

'Not at all. Walking on peat is hell at any time. You have to keep to the tracks on this kind of ground; that's why the cairns are so close together.'

'So this is where they used to dig their peat.' She blinked at him. 'They burned peat in Orrdale,' he explained, 'It says so in the booklet.'

'Of course! These are the old peat hags.'

'What – that black bank over there?'

'No, that's too high but you can make out vague lines . . .' Her attention returned to Bags who was running ahead but keeping to the path, showing no desire to leave it. Even animals took the easiest way if there were nothing to divert them. She frowned but she didn't comment.

A curlew got up and flew south, uttering its lonely trill. When it faded nothing broke the bright silence but the plod of her boots on dried mud. Rick, in trainers, made no sound. A knoll showed ahead, the path creeping round its base.

'That has to be the British fort,' Miss Pink said. 'We should go and look.'

'Bags isn't interested.'

'Wind's blowing the wrong way – but he's not interested in anything other than the walk. I'm starting to wonder if he picked up that bone on the path. It could have been carried some distance by a fox, even . . .'

'Even what?'

She didn't answer until they were climbing the knoll. She stopped and drew breath. Looking back she said, 'There could have been a body in the wood all the time and the searchers missed it.'

'They'd have had dogs, wouldn't they?'

'You're right. I forgot the dogs.'

They reached the top and Rick collapsed on a boulder. 'It was nearly fifty years ago,' he said. 'Does any of this matter?' Plainly field-work on a hot day had changed his attitude to investigative journalism.

Miss Pink considered the question. 'There's the Law,' she said heavily. 'It's still an open case: the body never found, no indication as to what happened to her – or where or how. Or why,' she added softly. 'Mysteries are fascinating, and one is compelled to know the answer.'

'But even if we found the body – skeleton as it would be now – we'd be no nearer. Obviously the child died – the only alternative is that she was abducted, right? Could that be possible: carried off by – what? Travellers?'

'You mean if that femur is not Joan Gardner's. No, I don't think she was taken away, either by a group of travellers or a solitary person. The police would have considered the possibility and traced them. There'd be some record – and rumours.'

They were silent. Miss Pink regarded the surroundings. Nothing remained of the old fort but a circular raised dike and a few stones almost obscured by a rampant growth of bilberries. Bags, sprawled on a bare patch, caught her eye and pushed himself to his feet. She stepped up to the top of the dike and took the map from her rucksack.

The Corpse Road continued in an easterly direction, the line of it quickly lost in the heather. Southwards a dip in the skyline marked the head of Birkdale. To the west, behind them, a small tarn shone like a silver coin in a depression.

Bags pawed her leg. He'd settled now, he was no longer excited, just quietly happy but bored with the halt. 'Where on earth did you find that bone?' she mused.

'That must be the tarn she bathed in,' Rick said dreamily. 'She was dehydrated. She said it was like a western movie up here that day and she thought she would die of thirst until she found the water. She saw it from the path.'

Miss Pink's eyes traced the line. 'She would, going west. We missed it coming east, the lie of the land was wrong. Now that could be the answer. Right' – she was suddenly energetic – 'we'll go to the tarn and start again from there.'

They scrambled down the knoll and set off through the heather, Bags bounding ahead. They shouted at him but he refused to stop and by the time they reached the water he was nowhere in sight although he'd left his tracks on the sandy margin. There were old tracks too: a dog's and those of a small trainer.

'He's run home,' Rick said hopelessly. 'He remembered being here with her and he's gone to look for her.'

Miss Pink doubted it although it was a romantic thought, not unexpected from a young man in love. She thought the dog fickle. Letting him off the lead had been a mistake; he hadn't bonded to either of them. He was friendly with everyone but attached to no one. He'd stay for a while, would even hang around when off the lead, but then he'd leave, just like that. They'd seen the last of Bags – and how were they going to tell Perry when she came back for him? If she came back.

There was nothing they could do. A walk without a goal was pointless; she had no desire to follow the Corpse Road dragging the reluctant Rick who, she felt sure, was blaming her for suggesting this useless caper.

They trailed back the way they'd come. They could have taken a line further left to intercept the path but that would have brought them to the deep channels and the old peat cuttings, and rough as the heather was, it was better going than the peat.

They came to the Corpse Road again and turned left. Ahead of them a swathe of light showed above the fell called High Calva and below an umbrella of plum-coloured cloud. Very faint, so faint as to be imagination, came the murmur of thunder and then, sharp and unexpected, the barking of a dog.

'Bags!' they exclaimed, and started to hurry.

It took an age to reach the collie. There was the heather, the peat, the sphagnum bogs on the banks of the beck that was the outlet from the tarn; there was the difficulty of locating the dog, but he never stopped barking. They knew he'd found something if only because of that, and the fact that he didn't appear to be moving around.

He hadn't touched anything, except probably to sniff. The leg bone must have been lying apart, the rest of the skeleton was set in a bank of black peat. Rain had washed the side of the pelvis clear and the point of one shoulder blade. The body would have been lying on its back and a tracery of ribs had started to appear but legs and arm bones on the left side were absent.

'Foxes,' murmured Miss Pink, taking a Swiss Army knife from her pocket. Delicately she scratched at the crumbling peat above the shoulder bone to reveal the rounded arc of the skull. The man and dog watched her intently. She stood back.

'It's a *little* skeleton,' Rick ventured.

'Oh yes, it's a child.'

'I wonder if there's any evidence left of how she died.'

'It doesn't matter – much. She was murdered.'

'How can you be so sure? She could have been lost.'

'She was buried. Look, there's over a foot of soil above her. There's a running stream here in wet weather. She was buried some distance back from the edge and the bank eroded over the years. The drought did the rest.'

7

The return was an anti-climax. Miss Pink refused to speculate, Rick did nothing else. Like many people confronted for the first time with violent death, shock made him garrulous. Where would the police investigation go now? Would it involve only the men who were living in Orrdale forty-five years ago, or others further afield? How reliable were people's memories after nearly half a century?

Miss Pink refused to respond. 'The water level's dropping,' she observed, halting at the first elbow below the ruin. 'But of course it will shrink until we have some rain.' She focused her binoculars. 'The place is swarming with people. As the moor will be,' she added grimly, 'as soon as the word spreads.'

'Isaac's here.' Rick had good eyesight. 'That looks like his old Land Rover. He'll graze his sheep up here, you know. It could have been Isaac.'

She looked at him. 'It could have been anyone.' Hardly, but he needed damping down. She looked back at the village. 'There's only a handful of people in the churchyard.' She was wryly amused. 'If that's the police they have a strenuous afternoon ahead.'

'How are they going to find it? We didn't mark the spot.'

She closed her eyes and sighed. She guessed exactly how it would go, there was no alternative; Rick couldn't be expected to cope with this climb again.

The police watched their approach with a lack of interest that sharpened as Miss Pink made for the one she remembered as an inspector: DI Tyndale. Rick lagged behind, his attention divided between their reception and the behaviour of Bags who was pushing against his legs, intimidated by Isaac's dogs. Isaac made a group with the uniformed police, two of them resting on their spades, turned earth at their feet. Everyone was watching Miss Pink, edging closer as they strained to hear what she had to say.

She told Tyndale. He didn't believe her. He looked beyond her to Rick. Miss Pink's eyes strayed past Isaac to the Corpse Road.

'What did it look like?' Tyndale asked.

She described it succinctly – after all, there was little horror about old bones. Pathos would come later when there was time to reflect on how they had got there. The others were now close, glancing from her to the inspector, waiting for his verdict: a crazy old woman who mistook sheep's bones for human, or the genuine article?

'How far is it?' Tyndale asked.

She shrugged. 'A couple of miles?' In the mountains you measured by altitude and time, not length. Two miles sounded innocuous to the uninitiated.

'You'll need to show us.' He sounded doubtful, glancing from Rick to Isaac.

Rick was appalled. Isaac said with finality, 'I don't know that place. My sheep graze this side' – pointing to the fell above the road. 'And it's high time I were at me shepherding an' all,' he added, and stumped away, his dogs slinking round his heels.

Rick left for Kelleth, taking Bags. Miss Pink and the police started back towards the moor.

'How did you know where to look?' Tyndale asked – before they reached the steep part and while he could still walk at her side.

'We didn't.' She opened innocent eyes. 'The dog was loose and he ran off, then we heard him barking.'

'Where's the dog's owner?'

She glanced back at the road, affecting to misunderstand. 'Why, didn't he say he was going back to Kelleth?'

'He's not the owner. Where's the blonde girl?'

Who had told him? Edith? Not important at this moment. 'You mean Perry.' She wasn't rattled. 'She's gone to Scotland and she left the dog with young Harlow.'

The path narrowed and started to rise. Miss Pink drew ahead and Tyndale was forced to fall behind. The two plainclothes men managed to keep up, breathing hard, but, looking down from the zigzags, she saw that the uniformed men were lagging. She didn't pause at the ruin but kept going steadily until the long black bank appeared. She left the path then and struck across the heather, suppressing a smile. Tyndale was wearing light town shoes.

'I still can't understand how you came to be here,' he gasped, unable to believe anyone would walk on this kind of ground from choice.

'I told you: the dog was barking.' She stopped. Mounsey, the DS, was a hundred yards behind, the uniforms still struggling on the Corpse Road. 'Mr Tyndale,' she said firmly, 'forty-five years ago I didn't know this place existed. Do you really think that my finding the body is suspicious?'

He glowered at her, more put out by the heat and the rough ground than her attitude. He said tightly, 'I think you know something we don't. You knew the body wasn't in the churchyard, not even near the village?'

It was a question, and he was guessing. She saw a way to protect Perry, to avoid having to confess that the girl had been here, in a sense had been instrumental in guiding them to the remains.

'There *is* a story,' she admitted. 'I hadn't given it much credit because there are always rumours in a case like this, but I heard that the child was seen with a man before she disappeared, that they were entering the wood – but the woods were searched. However, the book about Orrdale mentions the peat cuttings – ' Did it? Rick had said they burned peat, not where they obtained it. She plunged on, 'I thought: peat cuttings, the ideal place for burial, and perhaps she wasn't seen entering the wood but climbing the Corpse Road, going up beside the trees.'

'You didn't mention any of this to us.'

'You haven't interviewed me! We exchanged a few words two days ago but not since. You must have talked to Edith Bland,' she added. 'Now she'll have information; she was living here when the child disappeared.'

The sergeant was approaching. They started to move again.

'They were friends,' Tyndale said. 'Her and Joan Gardner.'

'I'm not surprised. Presumably they were close in age.'

They reached the black bank and moved along it until the pale bones appeared, reminiscent of dinosaur fossils in rock. He gauged the distance between the remains and the top of the bank.

'How long would it take for that much peat to accumulate?'

She stared at him. Could he be joking? 'Several hundred years?' she hazarded. 'But if she died by accident on top of the ground the foxes would have seen to the dispersal of the body, and ravens and so on.'

'Quite. It was a silly question.'

The man was human – no, crafty. That hadn't been a silly question but a trap. He couldn't rid himself of the suspicion that in some way, despite the lapse in time, she was involved. When he came to realise that, had it been so, she would never have led them to the skeleton, he'd abandon the suspicion. And by that time other features would be absorbing his attention and everyone could forget that Perry was here first, and that Perry was on the run from the police – or from someone.

Leaving Mounsey and the uniforms on the moor, Tyndale started back with Miss Pink. They were quiet until they reached the track, having drifted apart, each concentrating on the difficulties of the ground. They reached the Corpse Road and looked back to where the three policemen were visible, sitting on the bank.

'Who was the man she was with?' Tyndale asked, as if voicing a thought.

'I have no idea.' She thought that if a man had been mentioned in the original statements none of the villagers would have named him.

'She'd be a light load for a farmer to carry,' he mused. 'She'd weigh less than a sheep.'

'It was summer time. There'd be strangers about: ramblers, itinerants come in to help with the hay.'

'Of course' – turning bland eyes on her, speaking with apparent carelessness – 'you're friendly with the local people.'

Only the Fawcetts, she thought, and sketched a shrug and resumed walking.

He fell in beside her. 'Not many left now,' he said. 'Harald Fawcett, old Isaac . . . anyone else?'

'The obvious one.' She allowed her discomfort to show. It would be unnatural not to mention the name. 'Was Walter Thornthwaite's death ever registered?'

'Not to my knowledge. But we mustn't jump to conclusions.' There was a hint of amusement in his tone.

'Only you were mentioning who was alive,' she said tartly. When he didn't rise to this she went on, 'There will be a number of people who were young at the time and they've moved away. Some went to Canada.' As Walter Thornthwaite may have done, but that was Tyndale's department.

'We'll trace them,' he said, and then, alarmingly: 'How senile is Harald Fawcett?'

About to protest strongly, she hesitated and said slowly, 'Senility is like virginity. Either you have it or you don't. You can't be part-senile.'

'How much credit can we put on his statements?'

'None. He confuses events, and crimes: historical and current, fact and fiction. He probably includes his dreams. His wife will be able to fill you in better than me.'

'She wouldn't be objective.'

He thought she was? No, another trap, he was fishing.

'What do you know about Edith Bland?' he asked, disconcerting her again when she thought they were considering rapists and murderers. 'Isaac's sister,' he said, as if reminding her.

'They're siblings?' She giggled. 'Rick told me he visits her. I imagine Rick thought it a – romantic liaison. I don't know anything about Mrs Bland. I've never spoken to her. Are you telling me the fact that they're brother and sister is significant?'

She was teasing him but he responded seriously. 'Possibly. Who knows? Anything may be significant in a murder case.'

They came to the ruin. 'Don't go under that gable-end,' she warned as he made to cross the tumbled stones. 'It's ready to fall.'

He turned away and they regarded the remains of the village several hundred feet below. 'At the risk of sounding critical,' she ventured, 'aren't there more important calls on your time than an ancient murder?'

'Not at the moment, but I doubt that it'll be pursued with the kind of enthusiasm we'd give a murder that happened yesterday. It's a matter of resources. We're not going to be able to trace all the possible suspects – unless something happened that would point us to one person.'

She tried to think of a clue concealed among those fragile bones that might point them to the murderer, but even if the hyoid were found and it was broken, indicating strangling, that would only tell them how she was killed.

'The identity of the man may never be known,' came his voice, 'not without a witness coming forward – and who's to say that wouldn't be from spite? Either that or a confession.'

She wouldn't let him see that this last had struck home,

wouldn't say heatedly that confessions were often made by people who were mentally disturbed. She thought of Harald uneasily.

Surprises continued without remission, each one delivering a jolt that sent adrenalin surging through Miss Pink's ageing system. This must be how vulnerable people suffered strokes, she thought, stepping into the hall at Nichol House at the invitation of a total stranger, a large tanned man with the suggestion of fine features discernible in the plump moon-face. He beamed at her.

'I'm Clive Thornthwaite,' he announced, closing the door, extending a hand.

She tried not to gape, realising tardily that there was no reason why the son from the first marriage shouldn't be visiting. He ushered her into the kitchen – the *kitchen*? Bemusedly she was wondering why he hadn't changed his name, and then wondering why he should. 'I'm holding the fort,' he was saying. 'They're visiting with Bob and Marina and I'm cooking dinner. You'll stay, of course; you came to see them.'

'I've come straight down off the hill – '

'You look splendid: like a Valkyrie.'

He threw a handful of almonds in a pan. Miss Pink was fascinated. On one side sultanas and onion rings drained on kitchen paper. A wooden chopping board was heaped with cubes of meat.

'I'm doing a *biryani*,' he told her. A timer pinged. 'Would you mind seeing to the eggs?'

She removed a pan of boiled eggs from the stove and placed it in the sink.

'Cold water,' he ordered, tossing the almonds. 'Run the tap on them before they go black.'

She did as she was told and leaned against the sink. She counted eleven little pots of spices beside the chopping board.

'My mother can't cook,' he said. 'As you'll know if you've eaten here. I grew up with that, of course, which probably explains me. Backlash.'

'I don't follow.'

'I'm a chef. Didn't she tell you?'

'All I know is that you live in California.' And I didn't get that from your mother. 'Do you have a restaurant?'

'Not at the moment. I work for a movie director. We commute between Bel Air and his place on the coast near Pebble Beach. Where are my manners? What will you have to drink?'

'Is there any lager?'

He produced Budweiser and she realised he must have spent some considerable time shopping. Foreign beers and spices didn't go with the Fawcett image. He sautéed the meat expertly, one hand cradling a large whisky, but his attention was flatteringly on herself – until she asked how long it was since he last came home.

'Quite a while.' He peered at the meat, glanced at the clock, then doubtfully at the window which was open wide to the garden. 'This smell is going to fill the house,' he muttered. 'Ah well, they won't notice. You would, I'm sure. Tell me, how do you live when you're home?'

He didn't want to know where she lived, but how; this man was more interested in people than in geography. She studied him: a few remaining wisps of hair, neither blond nor grey but something between. She'd put his age in the mid-forties, which would be correct, Anne had been pregnant when the reservoir was filling. A pleasant fellow, overweight but light on his small feet. He was wearing leather sandals and khaki slacks, a red T-shirt under his striped apron. She told him about Chrissie Clarke who was a fair cook, and who looked after herself and the house in Cornwall – and the cats. 'Ah, cats,' he said, and they were away. In California they had two Siamese and a Burmese who went everywhere with them. He talked as if the movie director were a friend rather than an employer.

Several drinks later, the *biryani* in the oven and themselves ensconced in the drawing-room, the french windows wide to the air, Clive still in his apron, there was a bustle in the hall. Anne and Harald were back and Miss Pink hadn't even washed her face. Embarrassed, she struggled to her feet.

Anne stopped on the threshold, alert and uncertain. Harald pushed past her smiling, first at Clive, then at Miss Pink. 'He's made you welcome, I see. Where have you been? You've caught the sun. Let me get you – ah, you have a drink.' He went to the sideboard.

Miss Pink saw the query in Anne's eyes. Suddenly she realised that where Clive was concerned, her news could be terribly distressing. 'I would love a wash,' she said, staring hard at her hostess.

'Come upstairs,' Anne said.

In a big cool bedroom, blinds slatted against the sun, Miss Pink said, 'We found the body.' Anne was silent. 'Not a body,' Miss Pink amended. 'A skeleton, what remains of it: buried in the peat half a mile or so from the Corpse Road. Bags – the collie – found it; Rick and I were walking up there this morning. The police know.' Still Anne didn't react. Miss Pink said, 'Are you that shocked? Didn't you think she was dead?'

Anne recovered with a gasp. 'I'm shocked – yes. However much you anticipate it, it's a shock when it comes.'

Really, after forty-five years? 'I thought I should warn you,' Miss Pink went on evenly. 'Tyndale – the inspector – implies all the men who were living in Orrdale at the time are suspect, but he only knows of three.'

'Harald, Isaac Dent – who else?' It was too cool.

'Your first husband.'

'Ah yes, Walter. And since no one knows if he's dead, it's assumed that he could be alive.'

Miss Pink dismissed that with a shrug. 'Tyndale was asking whether Harald's statements – his word – could be relied on.'

'Harald had nothing to do with her. He wasn't interested in little girls.'

'Of course not. What bothers me is that he might get real events confused with fictitious plots. He doesn't think about what he's saying. I mean, why did you ask me to take him to Liddesdale yesterday?'

Anne didn't answer. She was thinking. 'It would be impossible to find any evidence against him.'

'You're not saying – not that there *was* evidence!'

'No. What I'm saying is that, with the weird things he comes out with, they could misinterpret: could think he was referring to Joan's murder, or at least *a* murder, and then put pressure on, trick him into a confession. But a confession from Harald would be invalid, wouldn't it?'

'But you're worried.' It was Miss Pink's turn to be thoughtful. 'If it wasn't Harald – and of course it wasn't,' she added quickly, 'then who was it? You see, if we could fasten – no, I don't mean that, but if the blame lies elsewhere, then Harald's in the clear. D'you see what I'm getting at? If someone knows who did kill Joan and tells the police, you have nothing to worry about.'

Anne stood at the window gnawing her thumb. It would be a difficult decision: to clear one husband by condemning the other. Miss Pink said comfortably, 'No hurry. Incidentally, I said nothing to Clive about any of this. How much does he know?'

'Nothing.' Anne seemed miles away. 'He knows nothing.'

'Do we – do you tell them?'

'Of course. They have to be warned' – she read Miss Pink's expression correctly – 'about a visit from the police. Let's fill them in, shall we?' Her tone was light, too light.

'I must go back to the flat.' Anne regarded her doubtfully. 'It's a family matter,' Miss Pink said firmly, at the same time realising exactly how much of a family matter it was.

'Come down and finish your drink.' Now the tone was hard. 'It would look odd if you dashed off after a wash.'

'There's just one thing,' she said, when Miss Pink emerged from the bathroom. 'It's going to be tricky with Clive. I mean, Walter is – was his father.'

'Needs delicate handling.'

'Exactly. So if I could ask you not to mention anything. *Anything?*'

'I'll go as soon as I've made my excuses.'

She reckoned without etiquette. 'No way!' Clive protested as she downed her lager and refused another, citing the need for a bath. 'You were invited to eat with us. You're going to sample a genuine Indian dish.'

'Of course she's staying,' Harald echoed. 'No question. Another of these alien beers, Melinda?'

'Darlings!' It was Anne. 'Melinda's been on the hill all day, she's dying to change.'

'So why did you wash?' blurted Clive, and grimaced as he realised that washing could no doubt have been a euphemism. He was about to rush on when the doorbell rang.

Miss Pink caught Anne's eye and mouthed 'Police.' Why hadn't she anticipated it so soon? Tyndale had brought her down from Orrdale, dropped her outside the churchyard and driven away. Guessing that he'd be occupied with the murder scene – no, interment site – and the skeleton, the thought that he might find time to visit people this evening hadn't crossed her mind.

The others were irresolute. Harald said doubtfully, 'Shall I answer the door, my dear?' Anne made a flustered flapping gesture and hurried out of the room.

Clive moved to Miss Pink, glancing at Harald. 'What's going on?' he hissed. 'Is there something I should know?'

Harald had heard him. 'They found a human bone,' he said quietly. 'Almost certainly from the child that went missing in the fifties.'

There were voices in the hall. 'We found the skeleton this afternoon,' Miss Pink whispered. 'Act ignorant. I haven't told you.'

Anne appeared with Tyndale. He focused on Miss Pink, stayed expressionless for a moment, then he smiled, but not with his eyes. He turned to acknowledge the introduction to Clive. Anne didn't mention her son's surname.

Harald came forward, the courteous host, pressing the inspector to be seated, bringing whisky, nodding affably when Tyndale explained that this was a social call, just to give them the latest news. He hadn't expected Miss Pink to be here before him.

'They've only just come in,' she told him. 'I haven't had time to tell them.'

'Is that so?' He looked at their expectant faces. 'You haven't heard that we've found the remains, presumably those of Joan Gardner.'

Harald cocked his head like a terrier. 'Where?'

Clive was massaging his mouth. He stared at his mother. Anne was frowning.

'On the Corpse Road?' Tyndale glanced at Miss Pink as if uncertain of the topography.

'In the old peat cuttings,' she supplied.

Harald's jaw dropped. 'She fell – fell in a hole, broke a leg maybe?'

'She was buried,' Tyndale said.

'Oh. Well. Obvious, of course. I've done it myself: burial. Dogs aren't going to smell it in the peat. It was either that or drop it in a crevice in the wood, but too accessible there – to the dogs. I thought about it a lot. Disposal is always a problem.' His eyes glazed. The others hung on his words. 'Killing is easy,' he assured them, 'too easy when it's spontaneous, but even when it's premeditated, when you have it all worked out: the weapon, opportunity, alibis – planned meticulously ... I enjoy the planning – but then you have the body to dispose of. Because however careful you are about blood and washing, and plastic sheeting, you must leave some trace of yourself on the body. So above ground is out of the question, and water's only marginally better ... Concrete? Bridge foundations?' His eyes lit up. 'The dam? Even that's not foolproof; there was a case recently where a body was found in concrete foundations – and they weren't looking for it! No, there's nothing, no perfect method of disposal, same as there's no perfect murder.' He was morose. 'Eventually they're going to catch up with you. Peat preserves tissues.'

'It doesn't. Only the bones are left.' Tyndale could have been enjoying an academic discussion. 'The hyoid bone will be there. If it's broken, she'll have been strangled.'

'Could have been broken with the weight of the soil. Or an animal could have damaged it, or made off with it.'

'No. The remains are set in the peat. Like concrete.'

There was a heavy silence. Clive stood up. 'If you'll excuse me: I have to check the oven.'

'Grand smell,' Tyndale said. 'Your son's a cook?'

'Chef,' Harald corrected proudly, 'for a cinema tycoon in Hollywood. We've got pictures.' He hurried out of the room.

'Well, that's distracted him,' Anne said, with relief. 'He does love a good murder.'

'Is this a good one, ma'am?'

'It was so long ago,' Miss Pink put in. 'One views it objectively, like a report in a newspaper. Did you know the girl, Anne?'

'I did.' She stared at the glass in her hand. 'We all knew her. Silly child.' She sighed.

'You think she went willingly?' Tyndale asked, almost casual.

'That girl was nine years old.' Anne was bitter. 'She behaved as if she were twenty. She always went willingly.'

'Like that, was it?' Tyndale said. 'Couldn't her mother cope?'

'She died when Joan was born. The father died years after the flood. He should have been put down at birth. We were a very isolated community, inspector.' Her tone was loaded.

'Edith Bland was friendly with her.'

Anne's lips thinned. 'Edith could tell you a great deal, but not necessarily the truth. People block out those times, others genuinely forget, some create fantasies.'

Harald drifted back shuffling a stack of colour prints. He sat beside Tyndale on the sofa. 'This is the house on the coast,' he began eagerly. 'And this is a telephoto of the sea lions on the beach below...' Tyndale was all attention.

Anne exchanged glances with Miss Pink, both struggling to find an innocuous topic of conversation.

'We're going over in the autumn,' Anne announced, rather wildly. 'Have you been to California, Melinda?'

Miss Pink forced her face to relax. 'One of my favourite states,' she enthused, her eyes on Tyndale's bent head. He was starting to go thin on top, she saw. 'And so varied,' she went on: 'deserts, forests, that glorious coast; you'll love it.'

Clive came back. 'Is the inspector dining with us?' he asked politely. 'I'll need to set an extra place.'

'Oh, no thank you.' Tyndale was startled. 'I have things to do.' He stood up, returning photographs to Harald. 'We have to recover the skeleton before the rain.'

'Rain!' Anne glanced out of the window. 'It's going to *rain*?'

'There was a storm over towards Scafell today,' Miss Pink pointed out.

'We've been getting long-range weather forecasts,' Tyndale said. 'It was essential when we were working in the old village; if the water had risen we'd have been forced to abandon the digging. It doesn't matter now of course, not there, but it could hinder the recovery on top.'

'What is the long-range weather forecast?' Anne asked. 'We haven't been able to water the garden for weeks.'

'We use the bath water,' Harald said, smiling.

'It's going to rain,' Miss Pink said. 'It's too hot. The weather has to break soon.'

Tyndale took his leave bemoaning the heat wave.

'Now tell us about this body,' Harald ordered as they settled with fresh drinks.

There wasn't much left to tell, only the peripheral details of how Bags had broken away, nothing more. Tyndale had covered the rest. Odd that he should have asked so few pertinent questions.

'Why did he come?' Clive asked.

'To give you the news,' Miss Pink said.

'And to see how we reacted.' Anne smiled at her husband. 'You ran true to form, darling. I loved the bit about the dam.'

'Pity I didn't suggest it sooner. They'd have been tearing it down with jackhammers.'

'Not on your say-so. He knew you were teasing him.'

'I was deadly serious. Haven't I always maintained that disposal was the biggest obstacle for a murderer?'

'Yes dear, repeatedly.'

'Are we ready to eat?' Clive asked, evidently accustomed to his stepfather's flights of fantasy but not prepared to indulge them, at least tonight.

'What happened to Rick?' Anne asked as Clive seated them bossily at the table with instructions not to move, except for Harald who was serving wine from a dumpy bottle. Miss Pink took an experimental sip and rolled it round her tongue. Spicy wine for spicy food; Clive had good judgement. 'Rick came back to town with the dog,' she said, and fell silent, thinking about that.

'Was Perry with you?' Harald asked. 'We haven't seen her for days.'

She stared at him. Anne said, 'She did come back? Rick called last evening, looking for her. He was panicking, wouldn't come inside.'

'She didn't come home,' Miss Pink said slowly. 'She phoned him from Scotland.'

'She left Bags behind?' Harald sank into his chair, appalled. 'She'd never do that!'

'She'll be back,' Miss Pink soothed. 'I imagine she's a runaway and the police scared her off. She'll lie low for a while.'

'Who'll lie low?' Clive asked, entering the dining-room with a casserole. 'Who're you talking about now? I miss all the best bits in the kitchen.' The room had darkened and he switched a light on.

They told him about Perry as he served the *biryani*. He didn't seem much interested. Miss Pink explained that the girl had been introduced to them by Rick Harlow.

'Who's her knight in shining armour.' Harald chuckled and

related how Jonty Robson had the tables turned on him by this yellow-haired waif who'd escaped with the fellow's sun-glasses and twenty pounds.

'I never knew that!' Anne cried. Harald pursed his lips and there was an impish gleam in his eye. 'She stole his wallet?' She was furious.

'Not at all.' He was enjoying himself. 'It was payment up-front. He took her for a loose woman.' His tone changed. 'So she's gone to Scotland,' he murmured, and then, brightening: 'We were in Liddesdale yesterday, Clive. Do you remember Liddesdale?'

There was a flash, the light flickered, and eyes glazed as they counted. The thunder was muffled. 'A few miles away yet,' Harald said. 'I wouldn't like to be on Helvellyn at this moment.'

'Tell me about Liddesdale,' Clive said.

Thunder crashed above the town and the bats were going frantic among the moths. As yet there were only a few spots of rain. A body was stretched on a flat tomb, spectacles gleaming in the lamplight. The trees drooped listlessly. Miss Pink stared at the prone form; now she saw that it was Rick.

'Are you asleep?' she asked, advancing. 'Or merely drunk?'

His hand moved and he sat up. 'Oh, it's you. I was waiting for you.'

'It's been a long day,' she said heavily. 'How about coming over for breakfast tomorrow?'

'I feel quite fresh.' And indeed he sounded jaunty.

'You've been sleeping. I've been socialising and the drink has suddenly hit me. I need my bed. Are you implying that you've discovered something that can't wait until morning? Is it Perry?'

'Perry's all right. She knows the cops aren't interested in her. No, I've been learning things about Orrdale and – you know what? This is going to be my breakthrough: the story of Joan Gardner. The rural idyll shattered by a dreadful crime. Forget modern horrors: child killers, serial murderers and so on; it's the background that makes this story: the fells, the drowned village, the body in the peat – '

' – your landlady's first husband,' Miss Pink added coldly. 'You can't do it, Rick. I've been at Nichol House all evening. Walter Thornthwaite's son is there, from California: a nice man who's made a success of his life despite everything. He's very fond of his stepfather. You can't destroy that family. I won't allow it.'

'But Walter's way in the past! Anyway, you can't stop me.'

She gasped. 'How – ' She was about to ask how he dared defy her, and realised that this was histrionic. She sat down beside him. 'Tell me what you've discovered,' she ordered.

'Thank you.' It was ironic. She caught a stale smell of beer. 'I went to the newspaper office first,' he began chattily, 'and with hindsight it's not surprising that I didn't learn much there: local paper, conservative editor in those days, I gathered – well, prudent might be a better term. There was no speculation in the accounts of the Joan Gardner case; even reading between the lines there wasn't a hint of foul play. A parallel was drawn with a boy of nine who went missing on the fells in 1907. Four days lost in the mists and he survived; the difference being it was assumed that Joan Gardner had died out there: hypothermia, whatever.'

'It was summer time,' Miss Pink murmured.

'The man wasn't mentioned,' he went on as if she hadn't spoken. 'There was the usual guff about her being a happy child – '

'For happy read friendly.'

'What? I suppose so. Are you implying something? Yes, you are – '

'Go on: a happy child . . .'

He glanced at her suspiciously. 'Motherless,' he said slowly. 'A masculine household: brothers, a father, all dead now . . . this is significant, isn't it?'

'Editors of local papers are wise old birds. They have to be, they live among their readers. So you came away from the newspaper office empty-handed?'

'No.' He was resentful, staring at her. 'I learned that the guy who wrote the booklet *The Drowned Village* is the chap who runs the bookshop.'

'Yes?'

'So I went to him.'

'You have been busy.'

He ignored the sarcasm. 'I wanted to know what he knew about Orrdale that he hadn't put in the book. He said he didn't put the rumours in, particularly the one about Joan being seen with a man, and Walter Thornthwaite disappearing shortly after she did.'

'Incidentally, how long after?'

'What? I don't know. Does it matter?'

'Probably not. What else did he tell you?'

'That Edith Bland was Joan's friend and that her tipple is cherry brandy. Dave Murray knows everything. That's him: the fellow at the bookshop. He's gay, not that that's of any significance except it makes him a good informant. Gossipy, you know? So I talked to Edith.'

'I see how you came to fall asleep on a tombstone. And what did Edith tell you after you'd got her drunk on cherry brandy?'

'Hell, I had to work my guts out even to get inside her flat but once I'd convinced her that I was lonely because my girl had walked out on me – '

'Yes, what did happen – '

'Let me tell it my way.'

She inhaled sharply but she was too tired to push it. 'Once I was in,' he went on, regardless, 'she revealed everything. Actually it wasn't much really, only confirmation. Come to think of it, she did point out that Joan lived with men – oh hell, that sounds so gross! What I mean is that the girl had lost her mother and was brought up in an all-male household. Brothers, no sisters. Oh yes, and she said Walter Thornthwaite was a sly lusty fellow, and she for one was never surprised how it turned out. Now what do you make of that?'

'Interesting.'

Walter Thornthwaite being sly and lusty was an unexpected slant on Anne's first husband and food for thought. Miss Pink was also intrigued by what she was learning about Joan Gardner – but, she reminded herself, she wasn't necessarily learning about the child, only hearing people's opinions. Gossip was valuable less for what it told you about the subject than for what it revealed about the gossips.

8

'Mr Tyndale!' Anne was losing patience. 'How can you expect anyone to remember a sequence of events that happened nearly half a century ago?'

'I have to ask the questions, ma'am.' Tyndale was sticking to his guns. He glanced round his bright little office that overlooked the bus station. 'Try it this way: there had to be a moment when you realised your husband – your first husband – wasn't only absent but missing.'

Anne frowned, doing her best to remember. 'They were searching for Joan,' she said slowly, 'so he was out every day. It could have been the third evening that he didn't come home.'

'What did he take with him?'

'You mean, on the search or when he left for good?'

There was a pause. 'On the search,' Tyndale said.

She sighed. 'This is too difficult.' All the same she tried. 'He'd have taken something to eat . . .' She trailed off.

'And his dog.'

'They'd all have taken their dogs, all the men who were out searching.'

'And on the last day, the day he didn't come back: he took his dog then?'

She hesitated. 'He must have done.'

'So did the dog come home alone or did it disappear with him?'

'It didn't disappear, but for the life of me I can't remember when it returned. Dogs come and go; you don't notice.'

'But he took no clothes, no personal items?'

'No.' It was morning but she looked exhausted. 'It's all there in my original statement.'

'Would it be correct to say that the last time you saw your husband was that morning, when he left to search for the child?'

'He could have come in for his tea.' She shifted in her chair. It was hot in the room; the night's rain had freshened the air but the sun was shining through a window closed against the bus fumes. The door was open but the room was stifling. 'At this distance I could have the days confused,' she said. 'He might have come home to eat and then gone out again. There's always something to do on a farm. The police asked me at the time,' she added pointedly. She nodded. 'I remember now, all this was happening as we were packing up to leave. I'd been thinking I couldn't remember because our days were so monotonous. Just the reverse: everyone was at sixes and sevens; the water was rising and we had to get out.'

'How long after he left did Mr Thornthwaite send the postcard?'

She stared at his tie: green with a motif of tiny golden retrievers. Was there a ruling that senior ranks must wear ties? 'Some days later,' she said.

'Did he send it to the village or to your new address?'

'I have no – I can't remember. It would have made no difference. The postman would know where we'd moved to. Look, inspector: I was asked at the time, there has to be a record – '

'You didn't produce the postcard.'

'Of course not. He'd walked out without telling me he was going. Why would I keep his card? He'd left me all alone with a baby on the way – I was angry.' She'd lost her poise and now she had the look of a farm wife rather than the lady of Nichol House.

'Do you think he killed Joan Gardner?' Tyndale asked.

She held his eye. 'All these years I've refused to speculate. She could still be alive, they could both be alive' – she made an expansive gesture – 'in Canada, America. Anything could have happened; he could have abducted her, maybe she persuaded him to take her away. I told you she was much older than her years – and she'd do anything to get away from home – presumably. I refused to consider – violence.'

'Now you have to.'

She gave the slightest shrug. When she remained silent he continued, 'There can't be many people left alive from those days. We have to trace the survivors. I've seen the statements made at the time but I don't remember any suspect being named in them. Mr Thornthwaite was mentioned but only because he was missing too. People were careful not to make connections. What do you think now, since the body was found – buried?'

She said calmly, 'I shall continue to think he's innocent.'

He nodded, noting the tense, accepting her attitude; Walter was her son's father. He was depressed at the thought of trying to trace the man through the police on another continent. It wasn't the distance so much as the ramifications of an information network going back to the days of filing cabinets and paper rather than computers. Resources would never stretch. And there was no guarantee that he went to Canada; he could have gone to South Africa, Australia, anywhere ...

At midday Jackson and Carla Hoggarth were dropped by their cab at the bottom of Whelp Yard to stagger up the passage carrying their cases and duty-free spirits, and a pair of rugs, souvenirs from Guatemala. They were conker-brown from the tropical sun, exhausted from the flight, and bad-tempered, Carla insisting – as she always did – that if Jackson would only tip handsomely, drivers would carry luggage to their door. Jackson pointed out that they'd spent all their sterling at the airport. Carla said he couldn't have done – 'And will you look at my petunias!' she shrilled. 'That's kids pushed that pot over. You can't leave the place for a couple of weeks without – '

'Here, hold these.' Jackson thrust the rugs at her and fumbled for his keys.

The yellow front door opened to a smell of cooked food. Carla gasped. 'This place stinks! Let me open some windows. You'd never believe a smell could last that long.' She sniffed angrily. 'That's curry! When did we ever have curry?'

Luggage was dropped in the passage. She rushed to the kitchen at the back. Jackson moved into the front room, glad to be home, thinking about the local pub, the wives, his tan, golf, English TV again ... He snatched at the curtains and twitched open the blinds. He turned round and stared.

The room looked like a dump. She'd never left it like this. And then he heard her: a small sound at first, more of a whimper, then a high moan, a silence – ominous as a baby drawing breath – and then the full-throated screams.

He knocked over a coffee table as he plunged for the passage. She had raised the blinds at the kitchen window – her adored new kitchen in blond pine and apple-green counters, the floor of eau-de-nil tiles, the breakfast nook with its crystal cruet – and now the table listing under a chaos of smashed crockery and cans. The stench was nauseating: curry and butcher's shop. Blood had splashed the ivory walls and the Swedish settle, dripping down its back to pool among the delicate flowers of Carla's Liberty cushions.

Miss Pink was enjoying a gossip with Dave Murray when Rick stumbled down the step into the bookshop.

'Thank God I found you!' he blurted, addressing Miss Pink. 'I've been ringing and ringing. The police have got the yard sealed off. Those plastic tapes. Go and see what's wrong, will you?'

'They've sealed off Plumtree Yard?' She was astonished. Murray – a handsome man running to seed – looked utterly bewildered.

'Not Plumtree. Whelp!' It sounded familiar.

'Whelp Yard?' Murray asked.

'Of course.' Rick swallowed. 'Perry's there. No one else, that's why she's there: no other occupants in the yard. The house was empty. She holed up in it. You have to go!' He clutched Miss Pink's arm.

She stood her ground. 'Why didn't you ask – There's a man on duty, I take it?'

'Yes, and cars, lots of cars. Something terrible's happened. I can't take this – I'm going back there – ' He turned to rush away.

'Wait!' She moved to the doorway. Murray came after her and the three of them stared across the churchyard. 'There's no hurry,' she said. 'If the police are there – '

'I have to know what's happened. The reason I didn't ask was because it doesn't have to be connected with her, see? It could be that someone's shot up – injected – in the yard, an overdose; could have been just a drunken brawl, a stabbing. I mean, in the open, nothing to do with the house.'

'Perhaps you should stay clear.' Murray was diffident. He glanced at Miss Pink.

'It might be prudent,' she said carefully, knowing it was definitely so. 'Have you known all along that she was there?'

'Only since yesterday. I really did think she was in Scotland before, but yesterday she called me again and wanted to talk.'

'You went there?'

'Of course. After dark. There's a way in at the back, a door in the garden wall. She unbolted it for me. She climbed in over the wall herself.' He grinned, then sobered and was frantic again.

'Did you go inside the house?' Miss Pink asked.

He nodded. So his fingerprints would be everywhere. If anything had happened to Perry – and suddenly she thought of Jonty Robson.

'I'm going across,' Rick said.

'No. I'll go.'

'What's your excuse?' Murray asked, and she wondered if he knew more than was apparent.

'I've learned she was there, from Rick, and I've gone to see if she's all right – in view of the activity. I'll bluff my way in somehow.' She didn't know how but if this was the only way to stop Rick incriminating himself, she had to make an effort. Now why should he be incriminated?

'As if we didn't have enough on our plate!' Tyndale stared gloomily at an overturned garden pot spilling compost and wilted petunias. There was no shade in Whelp Yard and the Scenes of Crime people were taking their time getting here.

'We could stand just inside the front door,' Mounsey pointed out. 'Kitchen window's open, there'd be a through-draught.'

'Dream on, lad. This isn't a domestic. He's taken the body away, not to mention the weapon; no one else goes in that house till SOCO arrives. Now what?'

A uniformed man had entered the yard from Doomgate. 'There's a Miss Pink, sir, says she'd like a word. She's a bit – firm.'

She was waiting in the sunshine on the other side of the tapes, looking cool in a pale blue safari suit and a straw hat.

'I'm looking for Perry,' she said. 'Is she all right?'

Tyndale studied her face then motioned to an unmarked car, all its windows down. They sat in the back.

'You said she was in Scotland.' he said. 'What makes you think she's in that yard?'

'I thought she was in Scotland. She's a runaway; she saw the police activity some days ago, thought you were after her, and bolted. Apparently this is where she holed up.'

'Where exactly?'

'In a house.' She couldn't conceal her anxiety. 'Please tell me, Mr Tyndale, has something happened to her?'

'She's not there.'

'Then why are you here?'

'There's been an accident in a house, and it's the place where she – where someone was living. Squatting, rather. The owners came back from holiday today and discovered it.'

'What did they discover? An accident? To whom?'

'We don't know. There's evidence of foul play.'

'But no body?'

'No body, ma'am.'

She looked out at the brilliant Street. Small children with bicycles had collected in front of the garages on the other side of Doomgate. Behind her, had she looked over her shoulder, she would have seen the rear of Nichol House. Her thoughts were on Robson however. She wondered when Rick would remember him.

'When did you see her last?' came Tyndale's voice.

'Who?'

'Perry – What's her last name?'

'I don't know.' She saw his disbelief. 'She didn't say. She didn't trust anyone.'

'And you saw her last . . .?'

She had to concentrate. 'I haven't seen her for three days.'

'How long was she living here?'

'It can't be more than three days.'

'You came here, visiting her?'

'No.'

'Why not?'

'I didn't know she was here.'

'Until when?'

'This afternoon. Just now; I was in the bookshop . . .'

'And?'

She was making matters worse with her enigmatic responses, and not protecting Rick at all. Tyndale was going to discover his involvement in no time.

'Rick Harlow – the man who was with me when we found the skeleton – he told me she was here, in Whelp Yard.'

'Why didn't he come himself?'

'Because if the girl is on the run he didn't want to attract attention to her. You could be here for some reason quite unconnected with her.'

He didn't believe her. What was worse, she wasn't sure whether she believed Rick herself. She felt frustrated and depressed; she shouldn't have come, but she hated to think how Rick would have acquitted himself, sitting in the hot shade of this car, staring at the entrance to the yard, tormenting himself with the thought of Perry injured or even dead, answering questions with wild abandon.

'Can't you tell me anything of what's happened?' she pleaded. '"Evidence of foul play"? What's that? Blood?' He frowned.

'Blood,' she said. 'How much of it?'

But more vehicles were drawing up and men emerging from them with bulky equipment. This looked like a murder investigation.

'I have to leave you now,' Tyndale said. 'Where can I find you later?'

'I have a flat above the bookshop in the churchyard. I shall be there – ' She cut it short, having been about to say, 'or at Nichol House,' but remembering in time that if it were murder anyone could be suspect, but particularly men who had known Perry.

She started to get out of the car and, glancing towards the churchyard, saw Rick approaching. Tyndale, coming round the back of the vehicle, looked to see what had alerted her, and smiled thinly. 'Saves me a journey,' he said.

She thought of putting on a garrulous act, but if she did he could well dismiss her, and momentarily she was forgotten. He was focused on Rick.

'What's happening?' The man was breathless, addressing Tyndale, flicking an eye at Miss Pink who stared and said nothing.

'There's been an accident,' Tyndale said.

'Who? Who to?'

'Inside the house.'

'Perry?'

'Why?' Tyndale asked.

'Why? She was there: squatting.' Rick glowered, no longer bothered about misdemeanours.

'I meant, why kill her?'

'No . . .' It was a sigh more than an exclamation. He turned to Miss Pink, shaking his head in denial, pleading.

She took pity on him, cursing Tyndale. 'There's no body,' she said firmly. 'Merely evidence of an accident – '

'Thank you, ma'am,' Tyndale grated, furious. 'I know where I can find you.'

'So where's Perry?' Rick demanded of him.

'Tell me about her.'

The fellow was a chameleon. Having dismissed Miss Pink in a temper, he was suddenly man-to-man, oily. She started to retreat.

'Wait!' Rick cried, scrabbling in his pocket. He produced a key and tossed it to her. 'Look after Bags,' he ordered, and turned back to the inspector with a grin like a snarl. She didn't like that direction about Bags; he was anticipating a protracted session with the police.

She crossed Doomgate and entered the churchyard, casting a speculative glance at the closed front door of Nichol House but continuing to the bookshop. Dave Murray was alone but he'd seen her coming through the tombstones and was eager for information.

She told him what she'd learned, adding that she'd left Rick with Tyndale. 'What's your interest?' she asked bluntly.

'A mystery a few yards away? Isn't that reason enough, without me knowing the chap who's keen on the girl – well, in love with her, judging by the state he's in.'

'Yes, he wears his heart on his sleeve.'

'What? How quaint, but true, yes.'

'Do you know her?' Miss Pink asked.

'No. I saw her. He came in here – when was it? A couple of days ago, bought *The Second Jungle Book*. Said it was for his lady, would you believe! Looked like a dreamy poet. So I had to see this paragon. She was sitting on that seat under the maple there. That yellow hair! What is it, a crew-cut growing out? And thin as a rake, face like something peeping out of a hedge bottom. What's she like?'

'A street kid, but adaptable.' She thought about that while

Dave studied her face. 'She can take care of herself – although this time she seems to have been caught out.'

'You said there's no body.'

'That's what Tyndale said. But he wouldn't lie about a body.'

'He could be keeping a lot back all the same. Cops aren't exactly the soul of honesty – or virtue, come to that. They're going to give Rick a hard time.'

'Why?' She thought he was right but she wanted to know why he thought so.

'Why? He's been there – that's the Hoggarths' house she was living in: a couple of ageing yuppies who were in Guatemala. Rick will have left his fingerprints.' He paused. 'What's happened to her? I mean – how much blood is there? Enough to warrant –'

The shop darkened as Clive Thornthwaite stepped inside. He nodded to Miss Pink and raised his eyebrows at Dave. 'What's going on? Doomgate's full of police cars.'

'You tell him,' Dave said. 'You were there.'

Clive listened with a kind of wry astonishment. He wouldn't know any of the people involved of course – at least, those *known* to be involved: Perry and Rick. There had to be at least one other.

'I'll need to get back and warn the others,' he said.

'Warn them?' Miss Pink repeated.

'Some of our back windows overlook Doomgate. The cops will want to know if we saw anything.' He pondered. 'He'd have to carry the body down the passage to Doomgate.'

Miss Pink gasped. 'There's an entrance into the garden at the back,' she said weakly.

'It's kept bolted,' Dave said. She turned to him, speechless. 'All back entrances are bolted or locked even in this town,' he assured her.

'Rick said he went into the house that way.'

'She'd bolt it after he left.'

'Possibly she didn't. She could have forgotten.'

'He could have taken the body out that way then,' Clive said. 'He'd have had a car in Chapel Street.'

Miss Pink said desperately, 'We don't know there was a body.'

'I was asking,' Dave said, 'how much blood there was. Enough to assume a death?'

She shook her head. 'I didn't go inside. I suppose we'll know soon enough,' she added miserably. 'And before the police find me I must go and rescue Perry's dog.'

Bags was overjoyed to see her, although she suspected he would have welcomed anyone who would deliver him from an empty house. His lead was hanging on a hook in the tiny vestibule, half of which had been blocked by a rough wooden partition. Momentarily diverted she tried to guess its purpose and, moving to the side, fending off the excited dog, she discovered a cupboard door. Of course, this had been one house and the stairs had been blocked off. Edith Bland had her own entrance at the side of the building.

In the yard, where Bags was forced to relieve himself immediately, she glanced up and saw movement in the fold of a net curtain. Edith was keeping an eye on visitors.

They went down to the river where Bags paddled after the ducks and Miss Pink strolled from one end of the paved walk to the other, pondering Perry's circle of contacts, recalled to her surroundings only when the dog emerged from the water. She put him on the lead and started back.

Rick had not come home. She would no more leave the collie alone for an indeterminate period than she would leave a child. She found some cans of dog food and a bag of hound meal in the kitchen and retreated, locking the front door. A heavy woman in Crimplene slacks and scarlet mules was shaking a mat at the side entrance. She paused and eyed Miss Pink's load.

'Where's Mr Harlow?' she asked suspiciously. 'You were in his house.'

'He lent me the key.' Miss Pink would say no more than was necessary at this moment. 'You must be Mrs Bland. I'm Miss Pink.'

'I hope he's not been took sick.'

'He was quite well last time I saw him.'

Edith stared at Bags with dislike. 'That dog come with the girl. Where's she gone then?'

Miss Pink hesitated. 'I understand she left.'

'Why didn't she take the dog?'

'They're a nuisance when you're hitch-hiking.' Miss Pink smiled vacantly.

After a moment the woman said – blurted rather: 'When's he

coming back? It's not nice to be living upstairs and not know who's moving about underneath.'

'I've got the key, so anyone in the flat has to be him or me.'

'Yes, but I don't know you, do I?'

Miss Pink opened wide eyes. 'Do I look that suspicious?'

'I don't know I'm sure. You could be anybody.'

Miss Pink studied the woman. Recent events might account for this streak of paranoia. 'Of course!' she breathed. 'You were Joan Gardner's friend.'

'That's got nowt to do with it!' Edith threw a frantic glance sideways towards Nichol House. 'You want to be asking *her* about Joannie Gardner: her and her grand house forbye her man's – ' She stopped and glared.

'You'll have known Walter Thornthwaite,' Miss Pink said pleasantly.

'Aye.' Edith paused. 'Everyone did. Who told you about him?' She studied the older woman: her age and clothes, the load of dog food. 'You're a reporter,' she ventured. Miss Pink raised an eyebrow. 'I don't see why I should tell you.' Edith was truculent. 'It's none o' your business. Besides, I didna know the man.'

'Really? It was a tiny village; a lot of people were related. One way or another.'

'He were a neighbour, but not close.'

'A sly lusty fellow.'

'What's that supposed to mean?'

'It's what you told Mr Harlow.'

There was a longer pause. 'Maybe,' Edith said grudgingly.

Miss Pink nodded and walked away, thinking that the difference between herself and Rick – his success, her failure – was that he brought a bottle of cherry brandy to the interview.

Dave Murray stopped her before she could reach her front door. 'Message for you,' he called. She waited for him to disengage himself from an elderly couple.

'From Anne Fawcett,' he said, coming to the door. 'Will you go over to the house?'

She deposited her load inside her door and went back through the churchyard to Nichol House. Clive broke into a smile as he opened the door. 'Ah, good! It's her!' he called over his shoulder. 'Mum's concerned,' he whispered. 'Come and reassure her. So who's this guy?'

Bags wagged his tail and grinned. Miss Pink was about to ask what kind of reassurance was needed when Harald appeared. Bags rushed at him in a frenzy of greeting.

'You've been in the river!' Harald announced, all his attention on the collie. Clive chivvied Miss Pink past him and along the passage to the kitchen. Anne turned from the sink where she was washing lettuce.

'I'm so glad you've come. Clive, take Harald into the garden – oh, darling' – flustered as he appeared in the doorway – 'the dog – a bit damp, sweetie; he can dry off in the sun. Clive!' It was an order.

'Come on.' Clive looked resigned but he turned to his stepfather. 'Woman-talk here; we're in the way.'

'Not on your life.' Harald beamed at Miss Pink. 'I've been on surveillance at a bedroom window all afternoon without being able to make head nor tail of it. Police HQ are mum, the chief constable's unavailable, so what's Tyndale up to, eh?'

'I don't know anything really,' Miss Pink said, looking to Anne for guidance.

'You were sitting in the car with him for long enough,' Harald persisted. 'What did he have to say?'

'Darling! That's between Tyndale and her. It could be personal.'

'Rubbish. She'd gone over there to find out what was happening. As I would have done – ' He bit his lip. If you'd let me, trembled on the air. He raised his chin. 'Admittedly I'm a trifle indiscreet on occasions but I was watching up there for hours. Now I need to know.'

Miss Pink glanced at Clive who shrugged. 'We don't know any more than what you told me: an accident, signs of foul play.'

'And Perry had gone to ground over there,' Harald added, watching her. 'And Tyndale's taken Rick in.'

'I didn't know that,' she said. 'I anticipated it. He asked me to look after Bags, gave me the key to his flat.'

'Good. We'll share the dog. Of course they'll have to release Rick.'

'How do you know that?'

'He's not a killer.'

'There's no body.'

Harald sat down, put his elbows on the table, his chin on his hands. He stared at her. Bags pawed his knee. 'Where's the body?' he asked, scratching the dog's skull.

Clive shook his head helplessly. Anne said, 'That sounds awfully callous, sweetie; you liked the girl.'

'So did Rick.'

Miss Pink nodded. 'I see what you mean but it would have to be a sudden rage: impulsive. He's not impulsive.'

'Passionate,' Harald murmured.

'Let's go out in the garden and dry Bags in the sun.'

Bizarre events, unconventional behaviour. Ignoring Anne's obvious disapproval Miss Pink led her host out to a seat under a tulip tree.

'What's your theory?' he asked as they sat down.

'Jonty Robson has an evil temper and he threatened Perry.'

'How would he know she was at the Hoggarths' place?'

'How do *you* know?'

'There's only one house in Whelp Yard, and anyway you told Clive. You're slipping, Melinda.'

'Not so much slipping as suspicious, suspecting everyone.'

'Quite right too.' He wasn't in the least put out. 'But how would Jonty know?' he repeated.

'He saw her in the churchyard two days ago, he told Rick he knew where he lived; he could have followed Rick to Whelp Yard. He's married, isn't he?'

'Married with two daughters. He'd have an alibi.'

'Would his wife give him an alibi for murder?'

'Wives do that.'

Their eyes met. 'Not completely mad,' he said gravely. 'I know a hawk from a handsaw.'

9

The day's heat built up to another storm, its fringe sweeping Kelleth and disrupting outdoor activities. The Robson girls, Charlotte and Becky, soaked to the skin on their ride, had to be brought home early by their father because it was their mother's night with the Operatic Society. The girls didn't have their own ponies but rode regularly at the local school. When Christine Robson arrived home she found them in their bathrobes and fiercely accusing each other of spilling her Chanel talc.

'What were you doing in my bathroom anyway?' she shouted. 'You've got your own.'

'It's Dad's bathroom as much as yours,' Charlotte retaliated. 'And no way was I going to get in a bath with her.' Glaring at Becky.

'I told her to use ours,' Jonty protested wearily. He found his daughters, aged twelve and ten, disturbing and uncontrollable. They knew it and took full advantage.

'Do you know how much that talc cost?' Christine began ominously, but the doorbell chimes saved the girls from answering. Christine wiped the snarl from her face and went down to the front door. Two strange men stood on the steps. 'Yes?' she asked coldly. Acceptable callers telephoned in advance. The tie marked the first as a Mormon, but he was too old, and the retrievers were wrong. Salesmen then, and you only had to look at the house to see that the Robsons had everything.

'If you're selling – ' she began.

The older man produced some form of identification. 'Mrs Robson?' At her fierce nod he pronounced ranks and names and looked past her. The girls had rushed downstairs and were blocking his view of the father.

'What is it?' Christine snapped, catching his drift but knowing this family was in the clear, and no way could it be a neighbour causing trouble, not in this neck of the woods. It had to be a mistake.

Jonty pushed the girls aside and put a hand on her shoulder . 'Mr Robson?' Tyndale asked brightly.

Jonty peered to the side where his wife's Fiesta stood in front of the garage. 'We still have the cars,' he said. 'You had me worried there for a moment. Thought you'd picked up one of 'em: joy-riders. What did you do, chuck?' – to Christine. 'Run a red light?'

Tyndale considered the wife and girls and his eyes came back to Jonty. 'Perhaps we could have a word, sir?'

'Of course,' Christine put in coolly. One co-operated with the police: attended their functions, mixed with senior ranks at the golf club; the Robsons were on speaking terms with the assistant chief constable. 'Come in!' She stepped back, bumping into the girls, turning to hustle them towards the stairs. Jonty stood aside and eyed the visitors doubtfully. He'd had more than one large whisky since bringing the girls home and he was suddenly alert to Tyndale's rank. A warning bell rang distantly.

'We'll go to my study,' he said, meaning to be casual but sounding a trifle aggressive.

'What an idea!' Christine was amused. 'We'll talk here, in comfort. Now girls, off to bed with you. Daddy and I have business.'

'It's Friday,' Charlotte said, dropping on the sofa, her bathrobe falling apart. 'We stay up on Friday.' Eyeing her mother, daring her to countermand the privilege. Her sister settled beside her, grinning.

'Upstairs,' Jonty ordered. 'Take a video and be quick about it. What are you drinking?' Turning to the visitors: 'Glenlivet? Highland Park?'

'Nothing for us, thank you,' Tyndale said, not even suggesting that a cup of tea would be welcome. Behind his back Christine glared at the girls, her eyes directing them to the staircase.

'I shan't say it again,' Jonty told them tightly.

Charlotte's lips thinned, the bathrobe now revealing that she was wearing purple briefs. 'We're staying,' she said. 'It's Friday.'

'You get to your room this minute or I'll tan your hide so you won't be able to sit down for a week, let alone ride a horse.'

The girls gaped. Christine stared at him. Charlotte pulled her robe together and followed her younger sister who'd made a dash for the stairs.

Jonty released a deep sigh. 'Girls!' He glowered at his wife. 'Spoiled rotten.'

'Tea?' Christine asked on a high note, and went out without waiting for a reply.

'Perhaps you'd prefer to come down to the station,' Tyndale said quietly.

'What the hell for?' Jonty hesitated. 'You're CID,' he went on, more reasonably. 'Has something serious happened?' There was no sound from outside the room.

'You know a girl called Perry, sir?'

Jonty pursed his lips. 'Perry what?'

'We thought you might be able to tell us that.'

'No. I don't know anyone called Perry. Is that the surname or first name?'

'What was the name of the girl you gave a lift to in Birkdale on Monday?'

His eyes flickered. Christine was standing in the doorway. 'Yes, that's right,' he said, 'I did pick up a hitch-hiker that day. I didn't ask her name.'

'You've seen her since.'

'No.'

Christine took a step forward, her eyes fixed on her husband.

'At Orrdale,' Tyndale said. 'The drowned village. You spoke to her when she came down off the fell.'

'No. I never saw her again.' Jonty took a gulp of his whisky and stared rigidly at the inspector. Christine was expressionless, she could have been watching a rather dull play.

'And two days ago,' Tyndale went on, 'you were in the churchyard at the same time as her.'

'If I was I didn't know it. Someone's got it in for me, inspector. Can I ask what all this is about?'

'We have reason to believe she's met with an accident. Or worse.'

'I don't see what it has to do – '

'Rick Harlow.'

'Excuse me?'

'Rick Harlow: the man she was – staying with. You threatened him – and her.'

'Oh, come on! This is a load of bull. Who is this Harlow character? D'you know what I am, who I'm with? Customs and Excise.'

'He means he makes enemies.' Christine's tone was icy. 'Someone's getting their own back. Tax men, VAT men: they're sitting ducks for the wildest accusations.'

'Perhaps you'd come down to the station, sir.'

'You – you don't believe – you can't believe – ' Jonty was spluttering.

'Oh, no question.' Tyndale spread his hands. 'It's just a matter of identification – '

'Identify – who?' He looked terrified.

'What,' Tyndale corrected. 'Not whom. Some sun-glasses: Ray Bans.'

'Ah.' Jonty shot a glance at Christine. Her hand was at her throat. There was a long pause. 'That's right.' He nodded solemnly. 'I missed a pair of Ray Bans some time ago, left the car unlocked one morning in Botchergate, looked for them that afternoon – gone. Too easy, lying on the dash; my own fault, cost the earth. Where'd you find them?'

'Perhaps you'd come and see if they are yours, sir.'

'Why, of course. Of course.' He didn't ask again where they'd been found.

The rain had stopped. They let him drive his own car and he followed them down the hill into town, driving very slowly and carefully, not because he was over the limit but because he wanted to make no mistakes, even the most trivial, like not stopping at a Stop sign, anything that would weigh against him. Oh God, he thought, if only he could turn the clock back, if only this could be last Friday evening before he'd ever heard of Perry – and he'd never even known her surname. A sob burst from him. He was finished: job, house, family, everything thrown away for one moment's satisfaction – which he hadn't had anyway. But need it be the end? She wasn't the first (although she'd certainly be the last); there'd been plenty of others: glad of the money, even glad of a lift for Christ's sake. He'd never been caught before. He checked. His eyes widened. He wasn't caught now. It wasn't illegal, was it? Oh Jesus, she was under-age! Fifteen, Harlow had said. But he wasn't to know that. He could get away with it; there'd be Christine to placate but if he could cope with the police he could deal with her. She had everything to lose, after all he was the breadwinner, and at her age she had no hope of finding another man with a steady job. No, Christine knew which side her bread was buttered; he could brazen it out: his word against a slag's. He steeled himself as he entered the station yard to park beside Tyndale's beat-up Cavalier.

Dusk had come early with the low cloud ceiling, and lights burned in the building. There was a nip in the air and he felt chilly in his thin shirt. There was no one about and Tyndale spoke quietly, ushering him into a building which at this hour of the evening had the air of a fortress occupied by secret police in the Third World. He thought of bright lights and sleep deprivation.

'Hang on a minute,' Tyndale said casually. 'Take a pew.'

Jonty blinked. There was a passage, seats, the younger detective nudging him towards them.

'I'll be glad to have those shades back,' he said chattily, only just stopping himself in time from adding that they were worth six times the twenty quid Perry had filched from him.

He sat down with a sigh, wondering at what point he should come clean – which he had to do. There were witnesses; that old farmer at Orrdale had seen – and heard – the confrontation with Harlow. Of course the police would understand; he had to deny everything in front of his wife and the girls. No way was he having his young daughters –

A door opened. Rick Harlow came through, glanced at him, stared, eyes widening. 'You fucking bastard!' he shouted, lunging forward, arms outstretched, reaching for the throat. Jonty threw himself sideways as the passage seemed to fill with men grabbing at his assailant, interposing themselves, shouting – but Rick's voice rising above them: 'What have you done with her? Where is she? Is she still alive? You sod, you bleeding murderer!' He was in a frenzy of rage.

'No!' Jonty cried. 'No, it wasn't me! I never touched her, she ran off – '

Rick was hustled away. Jonty appealed to Tyndale who was standing there, regarding him with interest. The other one, Tyndale's side-kick, was dabbing at his mouth with a handkerchief.

Tyndale nodded. 'We'll have a chat, shall we?' He was affable but there was no apology for the fracas and Jonty was too shattered to protest. 'Who was that?' he asked weakly.

No one answered. Too late he remembered what he'd said, and what had occasioned it, and that he was going to have to come clean.

'He confessed,' Tyndale said.

'He killed her!' Miss Pink's hand shook as she refilled his coffee cup.

'No, no. He admitted he knew the girl: confessed to a – commercial transaction. In the end he admitted threatening Harlow – he blustered, of course, terrified when he learned it could be a case of murder. There's too much blood, you know – but there, you didn't see it. On the other hand he was relieved when we asked to search his car. Agreed immediately, so I knew he hadn't carried her in it, not after she was badly injured – or dead. And he didn't, the car's clean as a whistle – no, I don't mean that, there's dust and stuff. It hasn't been vacuumed since before last Monday when he met her.'

'Where did you find the Ray Bans?'

'In the Hoggarths' house. Harlow told us it was the girl's stealing those that had made Robson so angry. But if he killed her in that house, he missed the glasses. Not surprising, the place was in a mess. And if he was there, he wore gloves; he wasn't concerned about giving us his prints.'

'Were they his Ray Bans?'

'He's playing safe: they look like his but he couldn't be sure.'

She took the coffee pot back to the kitchen, moving slowly, thinking that Rick was still in the frame. She was under no illusions concerning this visit. The inspector had arrived at her flat at nine o'clock, looking drawn but still functioning, even after hours of interviewing, and more time spent chasing people up on computers. She wasn't surprised to learn that he'd uncovered enough of her own background to guess that she might prove useful to him. That she had a police dossier she'd known since the sixties when she was actively opposed to the Concorde project ('cramped, noisy and hideously expensive') and had said so in print, incurring the wrath of both her MP and the unions. No doubt her dossier had been expanded over successive decades not least because on a number of occasions, when violent death was involved, she could have been suspected of knowing more than she'd seen fit to divulge. But if Tyndale, this canny Northerner, had discovered that at least one police authority labelled her subversive, he recognised her potential value and this morning he was ostensibly frank and respectful. He needed help.

He had begun with confidences: his suspicion of Rick (a partner always being the first suspect), Rick's enraged accusation of Jonty Robson – predictable in the circumstances, and subsequently Jonty's coming clean once he was out of hearing of his family. He'd been surprised at the passion behind Rick's attack, but that might be explained by the girl's being so young. Of course both men swore that they didn't know she was under-age – 'How do *you* know that?' Miss Pink asked. 'Have you traced her?'

'Her name was Sharon Ashworth,' he said. 'She was on the run from a foster home in Essex. She would have been sixteen in a couple of days' time.'

'You don't know she's dead!'

He shook his head. 'There's a trail of blood through the garden, even on the tarmac where he left his car ... Neither man has an alibi, not Harlow nor Robson – only the wife – and what's that worth? But she wasn't carried in the boot of either one's car – nor in Mrs Robson's Fiesta, incidentally. She gave us permission to look.'

'So she knows what happened.'

He shrugged. 'That's Robson's problem.'

'He's paying a high price.'

'It could have been higher, could still be, he's not off the hook. That body was carried in a vehicle, dead or alive.'

'But not by Jonty Robson,' she murmured, 'nor Rick.'

'Not in cars belonging to them.' He nodded, seeing she'd understood. 'Cars can be borrowed, stolen, hired – but this one wasn't hired; there'd be a record.'

She thought for a while. 'Why couldn't it have been a burglar?'

'If she'd been struck down merely because she was in the way, the body would have been left.'

'There must have been cases where thieves tried to conceal a body.' She racked her brains but couldn't remember any. She was concerned to get him away from the subject of Rick. It was far more likely that Jonty, with his foul temper – but then Rick hadn't shown much control at the police station either ... Of course, if he thought that Jonty had killed Perry ... Sharon Ashworth? She'd always be Perry to Miss Pink: short for peregrine, the swift predator. But this one had become prey.

'Have you known the Fawcetts long?' came Tyndale's voice out of the blue.

'For ever,' she responded inanely, then recovered with an effort. 'Forty years perhaps. Only Harald. I hadn't met his wife until now.'

'Has he always been so eccentric?'

She smiled fondly. 'People become absent-minded in old age. And playful,' she added quickly. 'Harald amuses himself teasing people. He's a great romancer.'

'He has an eye for the ladies?'

'He's always most courteous – ah, you mean romance as in sex. Dear me, no. I meant adventure, history, epics: that kind of romance.' Actually she'd meant Harald embroidered his tales.

'He knew the girl. He'll be worried.'

'Naturally. We all are.' She kept her voice steady. So this was the kind of help he was after: pumping her about her neighbours. 'Particularly as no one can be sure what's happened,' she added. 'Do you have a theory?'

'We have to find the body.' His eyes glazed and he looked very tired. 'Another empty house – or barn? Buried, thrown in the river, even taken back in the hills; lots of places to conceal a body in this county, but it's high summer and a lot of people wandering around to find it.'

'Not to speak of dogs.' They regarded the collie stretched out in a patch of sunshine. 'An odd coincidence,' she went on. 'There won't be much serious crime on your patch and here you have two murders – well, one and, at the least, a severe wounding – and both within days of each other.'

'The other was nearer fifty years ago but certainly they surfaced at the same time, roughly.'

'And Rick is doing a series on the crime-free North! I take it he's still in custody.'

'We have a few loose ends to tie up, ma'am.'

So communication – in this respect – was to be one-sided. She tried again. 'I gather you've put the old case on the back burner.'

'Of course. It's a matter of resources. Besides, it's irrelevant.'

10

The Land Rover skidded to a halt in the narrow lane. Most drivers would have sworn at the bullocks blocking the way but at close on eighty Albert Bainbridge was philosophical. He regarded the animals thoughtfully; they were Isaac Dent's beasts. Should he run up to Blondel now or on the way home from Kelleth? He'd need to help Isaac get the beasts back, and the shopping would be sitting there in the back of the truck in the midday heat. Better tell him now, get it over.

Driving the bullocks before him – there was no room to pass – he was pleased when the leader turned up Isaac's track. It was a long way to the house and he went slowly, casting a critical eye at the fields on either side. A fine crop of thistles and ragwort: no wonder the beasts went looking for a bit of decent grazing. And the house wasn't in much better shape: mottled grey patches where the whitewash had scaled off, the roof missing slates. He wondered how long it would be before Isaac gave up, or was eased out, more like.

His Land Rover wasn't at the back of the house but he hadn't taken the dogs. They were penned and barking. Albert cut the engine and stared at the dirty windows, all closed. He frowned; there was an odd note to that barking.

The back door was locked. He didn't go round the front; no one used his front door except on special occasions. Isaac had no special occasions. And he didn't look in the barns, the 'Rover wouldn't be there. He was puzzled. Isaac wasn't out with the sheep because he didn't have the dogs with him, but if he'd gone anywhere else he'd have seen the bullocks and put them back. He had to see them; the lane was a dead-end: turn left and it led only to Albert's farm and a couple of holiday cottages.

The dogs were housed in a row of pens. They weren't as noisy as they should have been and the two who were barking stopped as he approached. One whimpered. A third was lying down, another sprawled, flat out, eyes closed. All were without water.

'What's it got to do with us?' Tyndale asked. 'He had a skinful, stayed out all night; he'll be sleeping it off at the back of a pub car-park somewhere.'

'This farmer, Bainbridge, says the dogs have been without food and water for days,' Mounsey said. 'Well, more'n a day anyway.'

'So he's had an accident on the fell. That's a job for Mountain Rescue and uniforms.'

'He's not shepherding. He didn't take the dogs.'

'Then he's had an accident on the road! For God's sake, man, get your priorities straight! We've got a murder case on our hands here – '

'That's what I'm thinking of – '

'Eh?' Tyndale stared, blinked, considered. 'How do you make the connection?' He was interested.

'I don't.' Mounsey relaxed now that he had the other's attention. 'But it's a funny coincidence otherwise: a girl missing, lots of blood, an old guy missing who – incidentally – knew the girl.'

Tyndale fingered his lip, looking at his sergeant but not seeing him. He gave a sudden snort of laughter. 'That old lady, Miss Pink: she was talking about coincidences this morning and I've just realised there's yet another. Forty-five years since a girl and a man went missing at the same time and we know there was foul play. Now another girl and another man disappear, and there's all that blood ... How many more coincidences are we going to have?' There was dead silence. Tyndale said slowly, '*Are* they coincidences?'

'What can we do?' Rick pleaded. 'Where can we look?'

'Tyndale's searching,' Miss Pink said. 'You can't do a better job than his men, they're trained for it.'

Rick had arrived after Tyndale left, having spent the night cooling his heels in a police cell with an assault charge hanging over his head. To his surprise he'd been released this morning but with a warning not to go near Jonty Robson. Which he'd done immediately, only to find the man's house deserted. The whole family had left. He returned to the centre of town and Miss Pink.

'What do *you* think happened?' he asked. 'If it wasn't Robson, then who? Because if we could answer that, we'd have an idea where he'd taken her. She's still alive – isn't she?' His eyes were frantic. 'I mean, there is a chance? I can't sit at home and do nothing.'

In her mind Miss Pink agreed. She looked out at the graveyard and thought of driving – but where? Of empty cottages (getting the keys from estate agents), of unused garages and, further afield, of barns and abandoned farms. But the police would have thought of all those, and they would have contacted doctors and hospitals, because Tyndale maintained that with the amount of blood there had been in the Hoggarths' kitchen, treatment would have had to be urgent or she'd have died.

'Who?' Rick broke in on her thoughts. 'Or did Robson take someone else's car, or has he got another car besides his Mondeo? How can we find out? You know, he can't have gone far. He's a suspect, same as me, and Tyndale told me not to leave Kelleth.'

'Perhaps he did use another car,' she said slowly, 'and he didn't bring it back. Where would you hide a car?'

'An isolated barn?'

'Nowhere's isolated in high summer in the Lake District.'

'He could run it into a bog.'

'No bogs in England are that deep; you're thinking of swamps – ah! Water!'

'The river?'

'Again I don't think there are pools in it deep enough to submerge a vehicle. Quarries? I don't know the area that well. Let's go and talk to the Fawcetts.'

Going through the churchyard, Bags cavorting between them, they met DS Mounsey coming from the direction of Plumtree Yard. 'Looking for me?' Rick asked, deliberately casual.

'No, I was with Mrs Bland.' The sergeant addressed Miss Pink. 'We're trying to trace her brother's movements. Would you have seen him the last day or two, ma'am?'

She shook her head. 'Not since we came down to the dale after finding the skeleton. He was going on the fell then. Was it a stormy night?' She tried to remember. 'There was thunder about. Didn't he come down again?'

'He had to. His dogs are at the farm but they haven't been fed or watered for a while. He's missing, and his Land Rover.'

'Couldn't Mrs Bland help?'

'No, ma'am; she's got no idea.'

'Has she been out to his farm? Where is that, by the way?'

'Blondel. It's north of town. She doesn't drive so I need to find the inspector – ' He stopped short, wondering why he was blethering on to this old girl, and that in front of a suspect in what must be a murder case.

Rick was regarding him intently. 'Why are you chasing Isaac?' he asked. 'A young girl's missing; why aren't you looking for her?'

'They are,' Miss Pink said comfortably, urging him forward. 'Mr Mounsey is just one chap chasing up another disappearance. The others are looking for Perry, isn't that so, sergeant? Tell me, has Mr Tyndale considered that the vehicle used to carry Perry away could have been dumped in deep water?'

Mounsey swallowed and his head went up defensively. 'I'll tell him, ma'am.'

They moved on. 'An ingenuous young man,' she murmured.

'Thick.' Rick was savage. 'The police attitude leaves me cold. I don't believe they're looking for her at all.'

'Isaac Dent missing!' Anne repeated, leading the way to the empty drawing-room. 'First Perry, now this. Is there a connection?'

Rick and Miss Pink exchanged glances. They hadn't thought of that. 'How could there be?' Miss Pink asked.

'It's just you mentioning Isaac when I was expecting you to come out with the latest news of Perry.'

'There isn't any,' Rick said tightly. 'What we came for was to ask if you could think of anywhere Robson might have dumped the vehicle that he used to carry her away.'

'He's jumping the gun,' Miss Pink said sternly. 'We don't know it was Robson, but Perry must have been – transported from Whelp Yard in something, and there's no trace in the Robson cars so we wondered if whoever was responsible for that attack got rid of the vehicle that he used.'

Anne went to speak, and stopped. Miss Pink guessed that she had been about to suggest that if the car had been dumped the body could well be inside. 'Quarries,' Miss Pink said quickly. 'We were wondering if there's a deep quarry in the area.'

'Oh yes!' Harald was standing in the doorway. He looked interested and eager. 'But that means two villains,' he went on. 'Another car and another driver, d'you see: to carry the first driver away from the quarry.' They stared at him. 'But I can't think of any,' he confessed. 'Oh, there are quarries, but not with deep water in the bottom. What you're looking for is a pool beside the road, below the road.' Eyes glazed, but not his. 'Like the reservoir,' he said.

The crags started not far upstream of the dam. The four of them had squeezed into Miss Pink's little Renault, Clive having taken the family Volvo to visit the younger Fawcetts at the big house. Miss Pink slowed down after the dam but she was urged on by Harald.

'You can keep moving,' he said. 'The obvious place is that right-hand bend before the waterfall: nasty at night with the gleam of the lake and the fall. Confusing. It's about half a mile ahead.'

The road widened on the bend, giving room for two cars to pass comfortably. It was one of those places where irresponsible drivers would park in order to photograph the mountains that formed the headwall of the dale. The slope below the road was so steep that they looked over the crowns of a few oaks to the water below. The mud flats were too far away to be visible.

There was no wall on this stretch but a fairly new fence. One post was broken about ten inches from the ground and wire trailed down the incline. Twin lines that must be wheel tracks ran through the bracken and there was a bright yellow gash on a tree trunk that was horribly reminiscent of Perry's hair.

'Do you have a rope?' Harald asked, his tone as level as if he were thirty again.

'An old one,' Miss Pink said. 'I use it for towing. It's good enough for this.'

'I think, sweetie – ' Anne checked and glanced at Miss Pink who nodded reassuringly. Harald wouldn't have forgotten how it was done. In any event there was no one else, neither Anne nor Rick had climbed. She looked at Rick and saw he was so forlorn she knew the sight of those wheel tracks had destroyed any hope he had. They had been there too long. Drowning takes four minutes.

Her trainers wouldn't grip on lush vegetation but she had the security of the rope. She tied a bowline with the old expertise and Harald, equally deft, belayed himself to a tree. He nodded to her and, forsaking dignity, she lowered herself on her rump and started to work her way downwards from trunk to trunk.

Her groping hand encountered barbed wire and she swore; flies whined about her head suggesting only too graphically what the vehicle could contain. Because there was no doubt that there was a vehicle below – and suddenly she stopped.

Watching from fifty feet above Harald called, 'All right, Mel?'

She raised a thumb in response but she didn't move. When

had her thinking changed? When she and Rick had gone across to Nichol House less than an hour ago, they'd been thinking in terms of Jonty Robson – or someone – dumping a car in which he'd carried Perry, alive or dead. But just now, inching down this slope, following the twin ruts, she'd been visualising a Land Rover – Isaac's truck. Could it be – his vehicle, her body?

'What d'you see?' Harald called; it was a hint to her to get moving. She waved and continued, pulling against the rope which was too tight. Harald wasn't taking any chances.

She came to the last tree. It was rooted right on the edge of a crag which plunged for twenty feet straight into the water. She embraced the trunk and leaned out.

A few inches below the surface was the square outline of a Land Rover's roof.

The return wasn't strenuous. When she realised that there were now several people hauling on the rope, she gripped it with both hands and virtually walked up the slope. Before she reached them she recognised Tyndale among a number of uniforms.

'How did you guess?' she gasped as she stepped out on the tarmac.

'You spoke to Mounsey,' Tyndale said, 'and you were seen leaving Doomgate. And this is the nearest deep water.'

'You're on the wrong track; this isn't the vehicle Perry was taken away in. It's a Land Rover; there's no mistaking the outline. It's submerged. How on earth are you going to get it out?'

'The divers can break a window if the doors are jammed.'

She was startled. She had been referring to the difficulty of recovering the truck, she had forgotten that Isaac could be inside. There was no doubt in her mind that it was his Land Rover.

'He ran out of road,' someone said as Tyndale turned away, moving to one of the cars parked behind her Renault.

Harald said, 'What was he doing up here at night?'

'Coming back from shepherding?' she hazarded. 'What's wrong with Rick?' He was pacing back and forth in front of Anne, gesticulating, grinning maniacally.

'What's right with him?' Harald corrected, amused. 'That wasn't Perry's blood in the Hoggarth house. Tyndale checked with the Essex authorities. It's not her group; she isn't hurt at all, let alone murdered.'

She stared at him. 'Then whose blood was it?'

He shrugged. 'A burglar? We don't have to worry anyway; we're all present and correct: family and friends. No one's missing.'

'Perry is.'

'Ah, but unhurt. That's why Rick's acting like a lunatic. His lady's safe.'

Miss Pink moved to join the others. Behind her the police were lowering one of their number. She hoped her tow-rope could withstand a second load. 'I'm so glad about Perry,' she told Rick.

'It had to be someone who broke in!' he blurted. 'And she came along afterwards, saw the blood, panicked and ran again. This time I reckon she really has gone to Scotland.'

Miss Pink caught Anne's eye; was she too wondering where all that blood had come from if not from Perry?

Like a dog rounding up sheep, Tyndale collected Miss Pink's party and indicated that they should leave, but he had to know where they were going. 'I'll need a statement from you,' he told Miss Pink. His eyes rested on Rick and he hesitated.

'We shall be at Orrdale House,' Anne put in. 'As soon as the divers have been down perhaps you'll let us know the result.' It was her tone as much as the words that shook Tyndale. She saw he was affronted. 'Isaac is our tenant,' she said.

'I didn't know that.'

She turned away. Harald regarded the inspector. 'He drank,' he said gravely, shaking his head. 'Bound to happen: old age, poor judgement. I never liked this bend. The Water Authority should have built a stout wall along here instead of this flimsy fence.'

They piled into the Renault. 'A good thing we didn't bring Bags,' Rick chuckled, his equilibrium quite restored. They had left the collie in the garden at Nichol House.

'Edith has to be told,' Miss Pink murmured as she started back towards the dam.

'We don't know that Isaac's in the 'Rover.' Rick was assertive, concerned that no one should leap to conclusions this time. 'He may have jumped clear.'

'The police will inform Edith,' Harald said. Evidently he had no faith in Isaac's agility.

'She could know already,' Miss Pink said. 'She's with Mounsey.'

'Why?' Rick asked, amused.

'Why? Oh, she can't drive so he was going to take her to Isaac's farm – to see if there was any clue as to his whereabouts, presumably. You were with me when he told us, Rick!'

'So I was. I wasn't paying attention – '

'She drives,' Anne said.

There was a pause. 'I mean,' she went on, 'she can drive. I suppose she had to give it up. Certainly she doesn't own a car.'

'Why should she give it up?' Harald asked. 'She's not that old.'

'She has glaucoma.'

'Oh.' He was stricken. After a moment he said quietly, 'We must get her into a modern flat as quickly as possible. Plumtree's a death trap. Those stairs!'

'I don't think that's such a good idea, sweetie. She knows where everything is in Plumtree; she'd have to learn all over again in a new place. Much better to leave her where she's happy.'

They came to the entrance to Orrdale House, the drive flanked by pillars supporting the heads of stone horses. The Renault rattled across the cattle grid.

'So you've shelved the plan to turn the flats into one house,' Harald said.

'In the circumstances.' Anne was pleasant but firm. 'As soon as she told me, there was no question. Time enough to think about it when she's blind. Then she'll be forced to go into a home.'

'Glaucoma doesn't have to mean blindness,' Miss Pink pointed out. 'It can be arrested and contained with drugs.'

'Her condition's gone too far. Ah, there's Debbie,' as her granddaughter came cantering across the parkland on a stocky black pony. 'Hello, darling; you see we've all come to visit. Is everyone at home?'

'Hi!' Deborah bent low on her pony's neck so that she could see who was in the car. 'You didn't bring that nice collie. Uncle Clive's here; he's making something called Submarines for lunch. James is up at the dig.'

'What's that?' Harald asked.

'He won't say, just that we should be more adventurous with

our food, but whatever Clive produces is yummy, you know that, Grandad.'

'I meant, what dig are you talking about? Are they excavating the fort after all?'

'No.' The pony turned and took off nimbly. 'At the village,' Deborah shouted.

Miss Pink shifted into gear. 'Does Bob breed the fell ponies?' she asked, glimpsing a group of mares and foals in the shade of a horse chestnut. No one responded until Rick asked politely if she rode.

'When I can find a mount,' she said, glancing in the rear view mirror. It was wrongly angled to see Harald but Anne was staring after the galloping pony and her face was quite blank. Aware of Miss Pink's eyes on her she said, 'Marina breeds them. You're welcome to ride; they can carry any weight.' Which was the first time Miss Pink had known her be so casually rude.

She took the Renault to the front door of the big house. They got out and stood for a moment admiring the vista of woods and gentle hills at the foot of the dale. Anne said, 'You have to see the gardens; they're magnificent at this time of year. Why don't you and Rick take a turn in the rose garden before lunch? We'll call you in.'

Harald followed the flight of a crow and said nothing. Miss Pink, thinking that few gardens could be termed magnificent in July, said that sounded nice, and she and Rick strolled in the direction Anne had indicated.

'Wants to get rid of us.' Rick stated the obvious. 'Family business.' His companion was deep in her own thoughts. He didn't like the silence. 'Isn't it great about Perry?' he persisted.

'Great.' There was no enthusiasm. 'I wonder if she'll phone.'

'I'm sure she will. She needs to keep in contact with a friend. She's always running. That's no life for a girl.'

'Tyndale says she's about to have a birthday. It's not illegal to live with her once she's sixteen.'

'If you mean what I think you mean, I hadn't intended a sexual relationship.' He was stiff and disapproving. In any event, she thought with amusement, it wouldn't depend on him, but on Perry.

'I'm just pointing out you could no longer be charged with – what would it be? Corrupting a minor?'

He made a dismissive gesture. 'So she'll be sixteen,' he murmured, surprised and pleased, then his face fell. 'I wonder where she is at this moment, what she's doing?'

They halted and stared at the hills beyond the gardens. Both were uneasy. She wondered if he were remembering the blood in the Hoggarths' kitchen. Seeking to distract him and trying to avoid the subject of the submerged Land Rover, by association she arrived at Edith, and said rather wildly, 'So you can stay as long as you like in Plumtree now that Anne's decided not to turn the flats into one unit.'

'No. I shall join Perry as soon as I know where she is.'

'Finish your job here first. You're going to need money.'

'Besides, I hate Plumtree.' He wasn't listening. 'I'm on my own now.' He was before; he meant he missed Perry too much in the empty flat. 'Edith screeches,' he went on. 'D'you know, if you listened, I reckon you could actually hear what she's saying on the phone.'

'What does she say?'

'I don't know. I never listen.'

'I suppose, if she had some idea about Isaac's intentions, she'd have told Mounsey.'

'So that's what's bothering you: you think she knows what happened. You think Isaac's in the Land Rover, don't you?'

'We'll know soon enough.'

They did. Tyndale arrived when they were finishing lunch. Anne had taken a surprisingly long time before calling them indoors, indeed, etiquette had gone by the board today. Their stomachs were complaining loudly by the time they were summoned to join the party. In the shabby drawing-room Clive, beaming hospitality, welcomed them to a feast of baguettes stuffed with ham and salami and what he called salad fixings.

Both Bob and Marina were present, blandly avoiding any reference to missing persons, explaining that although they had most visitors at weekends, it was then that the local historical society waded in to supply guides. In fact, Marina told Miss Pink, the weekend was their most relaxing time, when all the family could be together. Referring to the absence of her son, she said casually, 'James will be in for tea. Actually we don't see much of the children during the daytime in the summer holidays. We're lucky to get Debbie off a pony. They say you'd like a ride. We can fix you up.'

They were still talking horses when Tyndale arrived to tell them that the body of Isaac Dent had been recovered from the submerged Land Rover, and his shotgun, both barrels discharged.

'Empty,' Harald corrected, without turning a hair. 'You don't carry a gun loaded.'

Marina was shaking her head. 'We never saw him the worse for drink, did we, Bob?'

'He was getting on. Like Dad said, old people lack judgement, and he'd been up and down that road so many times he'd have thought he knew it backwards.'

'He was shot,' Tyndale said.

'Who was shot?' Deborah, who had excused herself as soon as she'd eaten a sandwich, was in the doorway, her eyes on Tyndale, avidly curious.

Anne held out her hand. 'Old Isaac, love; he's shot himself.'

'I didn't say that.' Tyndale looked meaningly from Anne to her granddaughter.

She accepted the hint. 'What was it, Deb?'

The girl turned to her mother. 'That new foal, Mum; she's cut herself. It's not bad, but you ought to look at it.'

'I'll be down in a minute. You get the mare in, will you?'

Deborah hesitated, eyeing them hopefully. Her grandmother nodded, confirming the dismissal. Knowing they wouldn't talk about Isaac until she was out of earshot, she went, dragging her feet.

Harald broke the silence. 'Isaac would favour the gun,' he said. 'It's either that or hanging in these parts.'

'It wasn't suicide,' Tyndale said.

'I'd like to believe that' – Harald was unfazed – 'but a gun's not going to go off by accident as a chap's driving, is it?'

'Hardly.' Tyndale's tone was dry. 'Not to shoot him in two different places anyway.'

Even Clive gaped at that. He had been following the exchange with what looked like resignation, as if the suicide of one of the family's tenants was a kind of occupational hazard of living in the sticks. Now he was intrigued. 'How do you figure that?' he asked.

'There's a wound to the left shoulder,' Tyndale said: 'a cluster of pellets spreading out, but the main wound is under the right ear. The exit wound is – large.' In fact the other side of the skull had been blasted outwards.

'That's odd.' Harald was visualising it without a qualm. 'He fired twice?'

Anne was dumbfounded, as was Rick. Harald and Clive were fascinated, Miss Pink wary, watching Tyndale. How many suicides shot themselves twice?

'He was seated on the passenger side,' Tyndale told them.

'But he couldn't be!' Anne came to life. 'He must have moved over – floated there as the truck sank.'

The inspector regarded her thoughtfully, then shifted his gaze to Rick. 'There were shot pellets and a cartridge case in the Hoggarths' kitchen,' he said, and waited. Everyone looked at Rick.

'What are you saying?' His colour ebbed. 'No!'

'I'm not saying anything.' Tyndale was smooth as cream. 'But I'm wondering where Sharon Ashworth is now.'

Rick was blank. 'He means Perry,' Miss Pink said.

He said angrily, 'So he took a gun with him – he went there to – well, what? Rape her? Anyway, he was there – that's what you're saying, isn't it? And the gun went off – I ask you: why take a gun when you go to see a young girl? He meant worse than rape, the old bastard! So they struggled and the gun went off and he was scared stiff – so was she, of course. She ran one way, he staggered out to the Land Rover and drove up to the lake there and – and pointed the truck down the slope and shot himself deliberately. He couldn't face the music after Perry reported him.' He collapsed, exhausted after the outburst.

'He didn't drive four miles after losing all that blood,' Tyndale said, 'and – '

'You're suggesting a kid who weighs less than a hundred pounds carried him out to the Land Rover?'

'Or she had help. And he was found in the passenger seat. Like someone else said, you'd need another driver and another car to get the first driver back to town.'

'Oh God,' Rick sighed. 'Not again.'

*

'He didn't kill Isaac,' Harald said, but the statement lacked conviction. 'You look fierce, Mel. What is it?'

'Why would Isaac go to Whelp Yard with a loaded shotgun? It's out of character. He's not – he wasn't a psychopath.' She'd had only the briefest glimpse of him, hadn't actually spoken to him, but she couldn't see a septuagenarian farmer as a homicidal rapist. Of course, it happened, but brains didn't snap without some kind of warning.

Harald said dully, 'He was normal – within the limits of an ingrown community.'

She looked at him sharply, then at Anne who spread her hands and sighed as if it had all become too much for her.

Tyndale had taken Rick away for the second time to help the police with their inquiries – that loaded expression – leaving the Fawcetts and Miss Pink stunned and silent until Harald voiced his assertion of Rick's innocence.

'Did anyone know Isaac well?' Clive asked. 'I guess Mum grew up with him but you wouldn't have socialised?'

'Of course not.' Anne was dismissive. 'They were neighbours – once; nothing more. Besides, we were a different age group.' She caught Miss Pink's calculating eye. 'Edith was much younger than I,' she said firmly, 'Isaac was older. A few years means a great deal when you're young. And I was married; I had my own interests.'

It took one to know one; Miss Pink was another person who became voluble when she was trying to distract people. She looked round the room: Anne, Harald, Clive; she would like to talk to each individually. She had the feeling that Bob and Marina were innocently puzzled, and so disturbed by the bizarre event in Whelp Yard that they were blocking it out. As if to confirm this Marina stood up. 'I must go and look at that foal,' she said breathlessly.

Bob murmured an apology and followed. Now Miss Pink had the impression that the remaining three were presenting a united front towards her. After all, she and Rick had been excluded from what she was sure had been a pre-lunch conference – probably Bob and Marina as well; she sensed that her absence now would be a relief.

'I'm worried about Rick,' she said, rising in her turn. 'I'd like to go back to town and see if there's anything I can do. And there's the dog . . .'

Anne picked up the cue neatly. 'The dog will be all right in our garden, but if there's anything you can do to help Rick ... We'll go home with Clive. What kind of help did you have in mind?'

'I'd like to speak to him, ask if he needs a solicitor – and clothes, of course, if they're going to keep him at the police station overnight.' She was lying. Rick could take care of himself for the time being. She was heading for Isaac's farm.

11

Miss Pink couldn't put her finger on her motive for keeping quiet about her destination except that she had the feeling Anne would try to obstruct her. And Anne rather than Harald because she seemed to have more to do with the Fawcetts' tenants.

She didn't know the location of the farm. Mounsey had mentioned Blondel. Was that Norman French? The Cumbrian names were a miscellany of ancient Europe: Norse, British, Gaelic, French, and the inhabitants bore all the traces of their ancestry. Harald, for instance, so obviously of Norse extraction with his pale hair and eyes, not to mention the spelling of his name. His son: even more of a Scandinavian type. And Clive was handsome under the flesh although his looks could be derived from his mother since he didn't share his father with Bob. Of course Thornthwaite could have been a Norse type.

So – where was Blondel? North of Kelleth, Mounsey had said. She stopped in a gateway and studied the large-scale map. She found the place by working outwards from Orrdale House; Blondel was marked on a dead-end lane that was itself a turning off a minor road. 'Cloughfoot' said the hand-painted sign at the second fork. It didn't bother her; Isaac hadn't seemed the kind of man to advertise his presence. Sure enough, when she came to the first farm track, the lane ran on and at least two cottages showed ahead. She turned up the unmarked track.

'Mounsey got the news on his mobile,' Albert Bainbridge said. 'He'll have taken her home now so that's where you'll find her.'

He hammered another staple into a post. Beyond the fence the bullocks watched with mild interest.

Miss Pink had experienced a moment of fright when she came on an old Land Rover at the back of the dilapidated farmhouse, but when she'd cut her engine, and had found and quietened the dogs, she'd heard the prosaic sounds of hammering and had discovered this old fellow repairing the broken fence.

She'd hardly needed to say that she was looking for Edith, had come from the scene of the 'accident', before he was demanding details. Mounsey had been close-mouthed. She told him that the body had been recovered but she didn't mention the gun or the wounds, allowing Albert to assume that Isaac had run out of road. 'Although Lord knows what he were doing up there at night,' he said. 'But maybe it wasn't night?'

She said she didn't know but it would be all one if a person had had rather too much to drink.

'Isaac didn't drink,' Albert said, 'leastways not so he couldn't drive, but then maybe he did this time.'

'So you're looking after the animals,' she observed chattily. 'What's going to happen to the farm? I assume Edith will inherit.'

'No!' He stared at her, then gave a gap-toothed grin. 'She let you think that? Isaac were only a tenant. Farm belongs to the Fawcetts, don't it?'

'My mistake. She never actually told me Isaac owned it; that was what I assumed. So this was the place that was allocated him when the dale was flooded.'

'Wrong again! This were to be the Thornthwaites' farm – that's Mrs Fawcett, as is now; she married Mr Harald at the big house.' He checked and squinted at her. 'You don't know Mrs Fawcett?'

'What does she have to do with Blondel? Oh, I see: she owns it.'

'Well, in a sense; her married into the family so her got it back. This is how it was: Mrs Fawcett were Mrs Thornthwaite. Walter Thornthwaite were her first husband, and when t'old village were flooded, folk was given new farms, and Blondel were to come to Thornthwaites – as tenants, see? But then Walter – he left, and his missus let Isaac take over.'

Miss Pink looked around. 'It wasn't much loss to her.'

'It were a nice little farm at one time,' he protested. 'The best around. And look at t'place now! It's a mystery to me how Fawcetts never booted him out. Why, if I ran my farm like this un, Anne Fawcett woulda given me my marching orders years since! Now Walter' – his tone softened – 'he'd have made a fine job o' Blondel. He loved the land, did Walter; whatever come over 'im –' He stopped. 'But you know that story.' It was an accusation. 'You know yon skeleton were found in the peat.'

She looked him in the eye. 'There's no evidence to tie the child to Walter Thornthwaite,' she said earnestly, coming clean and not bothered by it. 'Just because they disappeared around the same time is no proof that he was responsible for her death.'

He returned her gaze. 'Aye, you been talking to folk. Did no one say as it coulda been an accident? Those girls were wee devils, always teasing – 'least Joannie was, and her the younger too! But a pretty little thing.' He shook his head. 'I mind the wife saying when she went missing as she'd always said Joannie Gardner would come to a bad end.'

'Teasing?' she repeated. 'Teasing the boys?'

'No! Men. Them weren't interested in boys as such.'

'Who's "them"?'

'Why, her and Edith, o'course. Only Edith, she weren't so much interested in – you know – bad things; her was just into general mischief.'

'What do you mean by that?'

'I dunno.' He was embarrassed. 'Maybe she egged Joannie on like. Oh, she were naughty all right but you wouldn't see young Edith going in a barn –' Again he stopped.

'Joannie did that? You knew?' Miss Pink was shocked.

'Not then: afterwards. We talked about it afterwards.'

There was a pause while she assimilated this. 'And Walter,' she prompted. 'But you liked Walter. He wouldn't –'

'No! Never. He were more of a – well, a stern fellow and – I don't know how to say this but he wasn't much of a lady's man, you know? For all he was married.'

Miss Pink abandoned all caution. 'You're saying he was gay?' Anyone who watched TV had to be familiar with current terminology.

Albert regarded the bullocks thoughtfully. 'I used to wonder,' he murmured.

She said quietly, so as not to disturb his mood, 'I did hear a suggestion that they might have gone off together: that Joannie persuaded him to take her to Canada.'

Astonishment was replaced by amusement. He grinned at her. She wondered how often he shaved; if he'd been younger the bristles might have passed for designer stubble. 'Who you been talking to?' he asked. 'That's the wildest tale I heard yet.'

'She was much older than her years.'

'True enough, but Walter Thornthwaite carrying off a girl to Canada? Never. He'd be scared stiff of her.'

Miss Pink frowned. 'So if someone said he was a lusty fellow it would be a lie?' He regarded her shrewdly. 'Perhaps it was Isaac who was meant?' She appeared to be asking herself that question.

'If Walter were, he hid it well. He were different from the rest. Afore us married, us all ran after t'lassies; lads is human, all said and done' – his eyes slid sideways and he smirked – 'even Mr Harald there at one time.'

Her guts gave a lurch. 'People would have known,' she said weakly. He shrugged and was suddenly a travesty of innocence. 'The big house was too far away,' she added, trying to draw him out again.

'Not on a horse.'

'You're saying he took her up there on a horse and buried her in the peat? *Harald*?'

'*Mister* Harald. Don't talk daft.' Suddenly he was hostile. 'I got work to attend to.' He picked up his box of staples.

'What's all this got to do with Isaac's death?' she asked desperately.

He stared ahead, his face set. 'Nowt. Who said it did? Isaac ran off t'road.' But she had seen his eyes flicker.

'And his sister was Joannie's friend.'

He glared at her. 'I don't know who you are nor what you're up to, but I'll tell you this: you know too much and if you take my advice you'll leave it there. Forget it. Joannie were killed nigh on fifty year since and whoever done it, it were just the once, never again. No one else been murdered in Orrdale. I'm warning you, folks don't like incomers what accuse the innocent: folks as had been minding their own business all these years.'

She regarded him with interest. 'Who frightened you, Mr

Bainbridge?' She didn't expect an answer and she didn't get one. He set off as if he'd been kicked, lumbering across the pasture as fast as he could go without actually running.

She became aware of the sound of water and now she noticed rock among trees lining a beck at the far side of the pasture. She strolled over and found the remains of a fence that would once have kept animals from plunging into a gorge. She wondered how many sheep Isaac had lost there since he took over the farm.

Above the gorge was a waterfall and a pool, then the rock walls closed in to form a chasm with black water in the bottom that looked very deep, and fast and powerful even now. When the beck was in spate an animal wouldn't stand much chance if it fell in. She walked downstream to find more falls – cascades, rather – but it was still a nasty place, a drowning place. She was astonished that Anne hadn't forced Isaac to repair the fence.

Albert wasn't in the yard when she reached it but his Land Rover was still there so he'd be keeping out of sight in the buildings. She drove off thinking that she'd come a long way from Rick Harlow who, along with Perry, hadn't been mentioned, but then Albert knew neither – presumably – and his sole reference to current events was that Isaac had run off the road. What would he have said had he known that there were two shotgun wounds in the body? That it was suicide? He might have said that but what would he have thought?

She reached the lane and drove at a snail's pace. A baby rabbit ran out from the bank and crouched, immobile, the sun in its shell-pink ears. Second brood, she thought, braking and easing to a halt. The rabbit didn't stir. She thought of Perry, 'like something peeping out of a hedge bottom', as Dave in the bookshop had said. Perry, the hunted animal tracked down to her hole in Whelp Yard by Isaac: cornered and fighting, the gun going off, once, twice – and Rick called in to take over and set up the 'accident'. She might go along with the basic scenario but that second wound didn't fit. It was a close contact wound: like an execution, and cold-blooded. She couldn't reconcile it with a desperate Perry or with Rick, raging and beside himself. She thought, most unhappily, of Harald who was unpredictable, of Anne who was concerned to protect him. But what could have taken Harald or Anne, or both, to Whelp Yard at the same time as Isaac? And what did the attack on Isaac have to do with Joan Gardner? 'Ah!'

She spoke aloud and her eyes focused as she let in the clutch, forgetting why she'd stopped. The tarmac was clear except for the strip of grass in the centre. She drove back to Kelleth.

'The point is, both Rick and Perry are suspects, and yet I don't see either of them killing Isaac deliberately. There's a lot going on behind the scenes that appears to have no direct link with them, and yet there are tenuous links. People are hiding secrets; they're cagey and very, very prickly. One question from me and I'll be out on my ear. I'm desperate so I've come to you to see if you can help. I think Rick is innocent; Tyndale thinks he's obsessed with Perry, and mad enough to kill. Not so: not to *execute*.'

She had persuaded Dave Murray to put a 'Back in 20 Mins' notice on the bookshop door and bullied him into coming upstairs to her living-room. Over mugs of tea she had given him the gist of the morning's events. He had listened intelligently but then he was a writer too. At the end he said, 'So you came to me because I'm the only person who can't be involved.'

She blinked at him. 'Ye-es, but how do you arrive at that?' He was involved; he knew the Fawcetts and Rick, Edith, everyone.

'I'm too young,' he said. 'I wasn't born forty-five years ago.'

Strange, he'd fastened immediately on that ancient crime rather than current events. Her mind adjusted. 'Neither were Rick and Perry,' she murmured.

He hesitated, eyeing her, his face expressionless. 'You're right,' he admitted. 'But then why did you think of me as uninvolved?' She looked away, aware of an ebbing of energy. 'I see,' he said gently. 'By imparting information, you're expecting to gain some: a quid pro quo?'

'And you're a friend of Clive's.' His eyebrows rose. 'I'm not thick,' she said.

'Oh no, although I've no doubt you can play the part like a pro when necessary. Yes, Clive and I are old friends, and we keep in touch even though we've run our course, as it were. I wouldn't want to see the guy hurt – and he's very attached to Harald.'

'And to Anne.'

'Naturally, she's his mother; it's less natural to be fond of your stepfather. However, Harald is a dear, don't you think? And another thing: he accepts gays without reservations.'

That reminded her of a similar comment. 'Did I say that Bainbridge implied Anne's first husband was gay?'

'I missed that. You're suggesting it's genetic?' He was surprised. 'I could understand it if Walter had lived – nurture, you know, not nature – but he died before Clive was born. What am I saying? I mean, he disappeared; he never knew his son. Genetic? Now there's a thought. I wonder if Anne...' He trailed off, following the thought.

'Bainbridge suggested Harald was something of a lad when he was young,' she mused.

'Oh really! Eliminate Walter as a child killer because he's gay, and you substitute Harald because he's a Don Juan!'

'Not me. Bainbridge.'

'Harald's a pussycat. Same as Rick – and Clive.'

'But passionate pussycats.'

'Not Harald.'

He was right. If Harald did feel things deeply he had himself on a tight rein. Eccentric, yes, but not mad. Well, not to show it. She shuddered, thinking of psychopaths.

He was watching her. She swallowed, casting about, needing to divert that intense scrutiny. 'You said you keep in touch with Clive,' she blurted. 'He came home very suddenly –' She broke off; what was she thinking of?

'As soon as the bone was found,' he supplied, and she sighed, deflated. 'That's right; I called him in California. Anne had been in contact with him already and yes, the reason he came was that finding the bone suggested that the skeleton was about to come to light. But he didn't come back because Harald was about to be unmasked as Joan's killer. Think about it. Walter was the suspect: Clive's father, but Anne's husband – once. Clive came home to support his mum.'

'Of course.' She nodded earnest agreement. 'Poor Clive.'

'He'll survive. Think how many children there must be who have carved out decent lives for themselves despite having a parent who was a murderer.'

'It must be hard when the parent is still alive.'

'Most of them are nowadays.' But he pondered this. 'One had always assumed Walter was dead,' he said slowly. 'He'd be very old, you know; I have the impression – maybe Clive told me – that he was quite a bit older than Anne, like – ten years or so. She's in her mid-sixties.' Blithely disregarding the fact that his host might well be in her mid-seventies.

'He could still be alive then. And now that there's proof that Joan was murdered, the police will trace him. That's going to be hard on all the Fawcetts.'

A breeze lifted the net curtain, floating it inwards like a daytime ghost. Dave looked past it to the tops of the tombstones. 'He'll have changed his name,' he mused, 'that is, if he's guilty. He'll have covered his tracks so they'll never find him, dead or alive. On the other hand, if he was innocent, if it was just that he was walking out on Anne and the baby, they'll find him soon enough.'

'Not necessarily. He could still want to cover his tracks in order not to have to pay maintenance. She needn't have married again. But he did send a postcard.'

'He could have changed his mind,' Dave pointed out. 'Or maybe there never was a postcard. Anne could have felt humiliated because he deserted her, so she told everyone the intention was that she should follow once the baby was born and he'd found work, and here was the postcard to prove there was no rift ... Don't you think?'

'If they'd intended to go to Canada why were they allocated a farm here? They were to have taken Blondel.'

'Who told you that?'

'Bainbridge.'

'But Blondel is – was Isaac's place.'

'Evidently Anne transferred it to him.'

'I don't believe it. There's no love lost between those two: well, three; Edith hasn't a good word to say for Anne. If Anne allowed someone to take over the farm it would have to be a friend of hers.'

'All the same, it was Isaac who got the tenancy.'

'You ask Anne. She never transferred willingly, I can tell you that.'

'And there's Plumtree – ' The telephone rang. Miss Pink reached wearily over the back of her chair.

'Oh, hi!' came a voice so breathless that for a moment she didn't recognise it as Rick's. 'Do me a favour, will you, love?'

'Of course.' Rick calling her 'love'?

'Bags. He's with you.' Without giving her time to respond he rushed on: 'His anaemia. Yeast tablets. By the telephone: two in the morning, two at night – '

'Wait a minute. I haven't got a key – '

'Anne has a spare. I'm fine but I have to stay down here for a bit – ' He broke off as if ordered to do so. 'Now, you got that straight?' he went on, breathlessly again, as if it were of dire importance. 'A blue tin by the *telephone*, right, love? Ciao!'

'What was all that?' Dave asked. 'You look gobsmacked.'

'Rick. Trying to tell me something. Something to do with the telephone? Can it be Perry? Expecting her to ring and I'm to tell her to keep her head down? Poor Rick, he's desperate. It's not going to work. I can't go and stay there, Tyndale would guess the reason. It was obvious that call was being listened to.'

'He's making you an accessory.'

'Nonsense. I can't be an accessory if he's done nothing wrong. I shall do what he asks: go and find the dog's yeast tablets.'

'And borrow the key from Nichol House.'

He was sharp as a knife. It was just what she was thinking: now she had a genuine excuse to talk to Anne again.

12

Anne was as suspicious as anticipated: polite enough but, as she pointed out, the yeast tablets were only a ploy; what did Rick really intend Miss Pink to do?

'Of course it was a ploy.' Miss Pink smiled and nodded as Clive paused on his way through the hall. 'Rick's desperate to know where Perry is, and he expects her to phone.'

Clive took a step forward. 'Why should he expect her to phone at the moment you're in the flat?'

'Unlikely,' she agreed. 'Unless they had an arrangement: that she should ring, say, every hour, on the hour. But he gave me no hint as to timing. I think he wants me to stay there.'

Anne inhaled sharply. Clive said, 'He can't expect you to give up your nice flat for that poky hole in Plumtree.' He grimaced and glanced at his mother. 'Well, it is, Mum,' he protested, although she hadn't reacted.

'I've no intention of staying there,' Miss Pink said. 'I'll pick up the tablets, see if by any chance he's left a message by the phone – although how he could have known he'd be taken to the police station again –' She stopped, stared at them for a second, and looked away.

'He'd have a contingency plan,' Clive said calmly. 'Particularly if he knew that your trip up the dale could lead to the discovery of Isaac's body.'

'In that case,' came Harald's voice, 'he wouldn't have come with us this morning. He'd have stayed in, waiting for Perry to telephone.' He must have been listening on the landing. Now he descended the stairs.

Miss Pink studied him in silence. Evidently the others were thinking too. Only Harald voiced his thoughts. 'But if they were co-conspirators,' he said, 'he'd know where Perry is. And if he killed Isaac, he wouldn't have hung around; he'd have fled with Perry. He's not a nincompoop; he knows he couldn't simulate innocence, could never hope to stand up to Tyndale's inquisition. No, Rick didn't know the body was in the reservoir. So he isn't the murderer.' He beamed at them.

'Of course he isn't.' Anne's tone was indulgent. 'However, there might be something else to find beside yeast tablets?' Her smile at Miss Pink was artificial. 'I'll come with you.'

'No,' Harald said. 'You stay here.'

They turned astonished faces to him. 'The police could be watching,' he explained. 'It's better for Mel to be seen to obey the letter of the message, not to take you with her, my dear. Tyndale would smell a rat.'

'Rubbish!' Clive was incredulous. He moved to the window beside the front door and peered out at the churchyard. 'Where could they be watching from?'

'The church tower,' Harald said promptly.

'Harald! However' – Clive relented – 'someone might tell Tyndale. It doesn't need two people to pick up the dog's yeast tablets.'

Harald said, 'When you return the key, Mel, we'll take Bags down to the river. Don't be long.'

Miss Pink saw that if the family couldn't keep her under surveillance they were going to make sure she wasn't out of their sight for long. She wondered what secrets Plumtree Yard might be hiding that they didn't want her to hang around there.

She looked for Edith as she entered the yard but the woman's door was closed and there was no sign of life at the upper windows. She let herself into Rick's flat, glanced at the flimsy partition and pursed her lips. She walked into the living-room and crossed to the telephone on the cheap sideboard. Besides the phone there were files and books, a torch, a hideous vase that looked as if it had been won at a fair, and two rather nice brass candlesticks. There was no tin of yeast tablets and no message. Indeed, there was no message pad.

The rest of the flat yielded nothing that could throw any light on that perplexing telephone call. She looked in cupboards and drawers, glanced at the files but uncovered only notes, his clippings, typescripts of his Lakeland series and what appeared to be the start of a novel.

The bedroom window looked out on Doomgate. The tapes had been removed from the entrance to Whelp Yard. She turned to the bed and drew back the duvet. She looked under the mattress and the pillow, inspected the contents of the wardrobe and a chest-of-drawers. She found nothing untoward. Rick was clean and no more untidy than was to be expected of a young man. Perry had left no clothes behind; he must have taken them to Whelp Yard.

Inside the front door she looked back, sensing something – something expectant; there was an object here which she should have found otherwise why had he telephoned?

There was a sound, a whisper like fur brushing wood. She froze. Inside the front door the passage was dim and cool as a vault. There was a faint creak. Her eyes focused reluctantly. She hadn't looked in the cupboard under the stairs.

She took several deep breaths, went quietly to the living-room, picked up the torch and advanced on the cupboard. She had no weapon, she remembered, as she flung open the door and projected the beam, flinching but her muscles tensed for a jump sideways.

The cupboard was empty. That is, there was an old vacuum

cleaner, brooms, a dustpan, two or three cardboard cartons which she eyed askance . . . rats? The creak came again: from above her head, and another, a little further away.

'Mrs Bland!' It was stentorian. Miss Pink had been badly frightened, and relief made her furiously angry. 'A word, Mrs Bland!'

She slammed the front door behind her and stamped round the corner to hammer on Edith's door. It was flung open and the woman was speaking before her face showed: contorted and as angry as Miss Pink's.

'That were you! I were just about to call t'police! All over the place: into cupboards and drawers, slamming – He'll be up here next, I were thinking, we'll all be murdered in our – It were you: all t'time?'

'Who did you think it was? Why shouldn't it be Mr Harlow?' Evidently there was no answer to that. 'You were running a risk,' Miss Pink went on, momentarily diverted but rallying: 'listening on the stairs, with a killer just the other side of a partition that he could have demolished with a kick.'

That struck home. 'Who's a killer?' Edith stared past her caller as if to spot one lurking in the yard.

'Wasn't that who you thought it was: the killer who – ' She remembered that the victim had been Isaac. ' – was in Mr Harlow's flat,' she went on lamely, 'coming for you next: isn't that what you were afraid of?'

'You reckon he's about?'

'Let's talk. Shall I come in?' Miss Pink advanced bulkily. They were both big women but Miss Pink had presence. Edith backed off and started up the stairs.

Settled in an easy chair that was too soft, registering the fact that she had not been offered refreshment (oversight or deliberate rudeness?), Miss Pink said, lying blatantly, 'I've come to offer my condolences.'

Edith's nostrils flared. In the face of such formal utterance she was unable to point out that the other had come to poke around the ground-floor flat. She waited. If she'd been a dog her hackles would have been erect.

'I hadn't realised that Blondel was your brother's farm,' Miss Pink said pleasantly. 'That was to have been the Thornthwaites' place.'

'I haven't offered you anything.' Edith was suddenly the soul of courtesy. 'Tea? Something a little stronger?'

'Why not? The sun's over the yard-arm.'

Edith's grin was unsettling. She brought a half-bottle of cherry brandy from a corner cupboard and two wine glasses. Miss Pink watched benignly as they were filled almost to the brim.

Edith sat down again, sipped and sighed luxuriously, giving an impression of bliss. She nodded and smiled. 'I didn't stay long at Blondel,' she said, 'I married Mr Bland and moved away.'

'Why didn't Mrs Fawcett take up the tenancy?'

'Did she not tell you that? No, she wouldn't. Once her man were gone she couldn't have managed on her own, and her in the family way.'

'So she handed the place over to Isaac.'

'That's right. It was a tenancy: Fawcett property.'

'Like this place.'

Edith nodded. 'Our local aristocrats.' The tone was naïve but the sentiment could have been contempt.

'Difficult to keep up appearances in these days,' Miss Pink murmured. 'Mrs Fawcett would like to sell this place.'

'She can do that.' It was a statement of fact, without feeling.

'Not while you're in it,' Miss Pink said.

'I'll be gone soon enough.'

'Glaucoma doesn't mean blindness. Your drugs will contain the condition, stop it getting worse.'

'You know everything.' Again a statement, neither sarcastic nor accusing.

Goaded, Miss Pink said, 'You weren't well disposed towards Mrs Fawcett when we talked before.'

'I've known her since we were bairns.'

'Hardly *known*. She's older than you. She was married when you were Joan's age.'

'I were older than Joannie. You're not drinking. Don't you like cherry brandy?'

She was getting nowhere with Edith, who could turn the sharpest of questions. 'Why would Isaac be calling on Perry?' she asked, letting the curiosity show.

Edith portrayed surprise. 'She were a prostitute!'

'He visited prostitutes with a loaded gun?'

The silence seemed to go on for ever and not once did Edith

take her eyes from her visitor's face. Miss Pink could feel those eyes as she lowered her own and sipped her cherry brandy.

Edith sighed. 'I've wondered about that myself. I can't think – unless he were afraid of that Rick. And yet I thought as, if the fellow was joined up with her like, in business, he'd become her – what d'you call it?'

'Her pimp?'

'She'd be walking the streets and he'd be taking the money. Is that a pimp?'

'But if Isaac was paying Perry, why would Rick mind? So why should Isaac need a gun when he went visiting?'

'I can't make head nor tail of it. I suppose it was his gun. The police can prove that?'

Could they? Surely there was no way that lead shot could carry a signature.

'Maybe there was another gun.' Edith was watching her closely. 'Isaac left his in the 'Rover but someone had another.'

'Someone?'

'Well, obvious, isn't it? They got him down at the station – he tried to put it on Mr Robson but he's a responsible married man – and *she* run off, the little whore – or did he kill her too? No more'n she deserved, the bitch. No knowing, is there, with a pair like that?'

The cherry brandy had released a sluice and the viciousness was seeping through. Miss Pink remembered something else. 'Was Walter gay?' she asked.

Edith jerked upright. 'Walter? Walter who?'

'Thornthwaite. Was he homosexual?' Edith looked bewildered. 'He preferred boys?' Miss Pink asked impatiently. She thought of Isaac and grimaced. 'Or men?'

'Never!' Edith checked. 'We'd have known,' she said thoughtfully.

'At your age?'

'I mean the village would have known, but there was never a suggestion of anything like that. The opposite: when he disappeared just after Joannie there were never no question in folk's minds. I mean, there wouldn't be, would there? No, Walter Thornthwaite were a fine figure of a man.'

*

'So what did you find?' Anne closed the door of Nichol House and faced Miss Pink, her expression defiant, even wild. She caught the other's glance at the stairs. 'There's no one here,' she snapped. 'They've taken the dog for a run. You've been an age. What on earth did you find there?'

'Oh, in the flat? Nothing. No yeast tablets – but Edith was listening behind that partition at the foot of the disused stairs. So I tackled her.' Miss Pink didn't add that in the short distance between Plumtree Yard and Nichol House she had come to the conclusion that Rick's intention had been just that: she should go next door and approach Edith. As it happened, Edith had initiated the meeting, however unwittingly.

Anne was leading the way to the kitchen. 'Drink?' she asked harshly, waving her guest to a chair at the table where she was preparing supper.

'Beer, if you have it, to get the taste of cherry brandy out of my mouth.'

'She was drunk?'

'She certainly lost her inhibitions.'

'Yes?' Anne put a bottle of Budweiser in front of Miss Pink who looked at it blankly. Anne found an opener in a drawer, opened the bottle and stared at it as if uncertain what to do next.

'A glass?' Miss Pink murmured.

Anne brought a tumbler, absent-mindedly wiping it with a corner of her apron.

Miss Pink poured the beer slowly. 'Is it possible that Edith could have been infatuated with your first husband?' she asked incuriously, as if advancing some unimportant theory.

Defiance faded but Anne was still tense and her eyelids drooped, masking the expressive eyes. 'It's possible,' she said coldly. 'Why do you ask?'

'She's fiercely jealous of you.'

'I married a Fawcett. Edith was always neurotic.' She paused, then continued: 'And she had no children. I suppose to a person of her calibre I have everything. What else did she have to say?'

Miss Pink shook her head as if to rid it of a thought, or a train of thought. 'Did you wonder why Isaac went to Whelp Yard with a gun, and loaded at that?'

'He meant to shoot someone.'

'That had to be Rick or Perry, or both of them. Why?'

'My dear!' Anne gave an angry laugh. 'How would I know?'

'I don't think anyone knows. I wondered if you have a theory. I'm sure Harald has.'

'Harald's full of theories.'

'But does he have one in this case?'

'I don't encourage him, not in that; not over the happenings in Whelp Yard. It's too close to home.'

The words hung in the air. Their eyes held until Anne looked away.

'There's a link between the two murders,' Miss Pink said.

'What – *two* murders? What on earth are you talking about?'

'Joan Gardner and Isaac.'

Anne's eyes wandered but she wouldn't look directly at the other. 'There'll be a number of links,' she agreed. 'Tenuous, but links all the same. Did you have something specific in mind?'

'Blackmail.'

'Oh yes?' The voice climbed and sank. 'Really.' Anne coughed. 'And who is blackmailing whom?'

'Both of them. Isaac prevailed on you to let him have Blondel; Edith has persuaded you not to turn the two flats in Plumtree into one house, which would have meant she'd have to leave.'

Anne's lips stretched, a grimace rather than a smile. 'And what would be the basis for blackmail?'

'They have some proof that your first husband was with Joan before she disappeared. Perhaps she told Edith that she was going to meet him – '

'That child was nine years old – '

'And – accustomed to men.'

'That's a foul suggestion.'

Miss Pink regarded her steadily. 'You implied Clive's visit was coincidence, but you sent for him after the bone was found.'

Anne licked her lips. 'I didn't send for him but he had to know. Walter was – is his father. And he could still be alive.' She took a deep breath. 'But I've always maintained his innocence,' she added defiantly.

'In spite of everything.'

Anne nodded. 'They do know something – *she* does, it's just Edith left now. It was only hints but it was enough – and yes, Joan had told Edith that Walter was – interested in her. Mind you, there was no truth in it; no way would Walter – '

'There's a suggestion that he was gay.'

Anne's hand flew to her mouth and now she did stare at Miss Pink who hid her surprise. After a moment Anne said weakly, 'Think of the scandal there'd have been in that little community forty-five years ago!'

'So that's why you say he wasn't interested in little girls.'

'No question of it. He'd steer well clear of her. And of Edith. She was the one with her nose into everything. And what she knew, she'd tell Isaac. Thank God there's only her to contend with now. I can deal with her.'

Quite. One blackmailer down: one to go. Didn't the woman realise that she had set herself up not only as a potential murderer but as an actual one?

'And you've never heard from Walter since,' Miss Pink said.

'Never. Except for the postcard of course.'

'Ah, that postcard. There never was one.'

At that point Anne should have shown her the door but she remained seated, her face empty, becoming relaxed. After a while she said quietly, 'When a man walks out on you, the first reaction is shock, then humiliation. No way are you going to let the neighbours think you've been abandoned. You're right, there never was a postcard.' She had herself well in hand now. 'You'll be thinking that my saying I had a postcard could also be a cover for murder.'

'It could be,' Miss Pink agreed. 'Getting in touch with home might imply he had nothing to fear but –' She stopped deliberately.

' – but he was gay?' Anne shook her head. 'However, he could have had a motive for that murder. Joan could have seen something she shouldn't, and taunted him, threatened to tell the neighbours.'

'What might she have seen?'

'We didn't lock our houses in those days. Children ran in and out. There was no stealing.' She smiled wryly. 'There was nothing to steal, nothing that would appeal to a child. However, Joan – or Edith, it's immaterial – one of them could have come in our house when I wasn't there, gone upstairs and found Walter.'

Miss Pink sighed. 'With a friend?'

'No! You've assumed he was homosexual. Not as far as I knew, and I'd have known. What he did was quite harmless.' She stopped. Miss Pink was racking her brains. 'He dressed up,' Anne went on, 'Oh, for heavens' sake, don't look at me like that! There are programmes on the TV, there are performers on the stage; no one thinks anything of it nowadays. It's legal.'

'Cross-dressing?' Miss Pink couldn't believe it, the innocuous nature of it. Then enlightenment dawned. Forty-five years ago – a remote community in the Lake District – a respectable farmer. 'Ridicule!' she exclaimed. 'He'd never have lived it down. But you were leaving anyway; you'd planned to go to Canada.'

'We'd talked about it but when Walter took off I had to reconsider. Harald's father had offered us Blondel and we'd decided in favour of that rather than emigrating. However, I had to pretend that we'd reverted to the idea of Canada after all and Walter would be sending for me. Actually that's what I hoped had happened, that something had snapped, he'd walked out but he'd come to his senses and we'd be together again.' Anne wouldn't meet Miss Pink's eye. 'So I let Isaac Dent have Blondel to keep up the subterfuge; I wouldn't be needing it because I was emigrating. Meanwhile old Mr Fawcett let me live in one of his cottages.'

'What did you really think – when Walter didn't send for you and there was no communication from him?'

'There was no time lapse. Shortly after Walter left, Isaac asked me to let him have Blondel. He said he'd been out late with the sheep and seen Walter leading a pony up the Corpse Road with a load on its back, at night. And Edith had told him Walter wore women's clothes. Joan had seen him. So he even knew why Walter killed her.'

'You've known all along!'

'And I've lied all along. Wouldn't you? Joan Gardner was a monster and I'm sure he didn't mean to kill her. He'd have struck out in a panic – or anger when she taunted him.'

'You were fond of him.'

'Of course I was! We didn't have a bad marriage. I knew what he liked to do – after all, it was my clothes he wore. Had to, didn't he? He couldn't shop for himself. He trusted me, knew I'd never say a word to anyone, knew he was far better off with me than he could be with anyone else. Our relationship was stable.'

'And he was the father of your baby.'

'I said: he wasn't homosexual; there was just this one little twist to him. He should have sent for us, you know; I came to think that he must have been prevented: robbed and murdered, maybe in some big seaport. The police may be able to trace his movements but I doubt it; they'll close the books, Clive says, although a case is never officially closed until the murderer is caught.'

'He can't be caught if he's dead.'

'Perhaps they'll assume he is. If he's alive he's too old to do any harm – and the police have another murder now.' She smiled grimly. 'They have to discover who was lying in wait for Isaac.' Miss Pink was expressionless. 'You left us rather late that night,' Anne went on, fixing her with those hawkish eyes, 'and afterwards none of us left the house.' She gave a sudden ravishing smile and in the face of it there was no need for her to add a corollary: that Harald and Clive would alibi her. 'That would leave Perry,' she said. 'And you reckon Isaac's death ties in with that old murder?'

'You come back to the question: why did he take a loaded gun with him to Whelp Yard? Perhaps Perry knew something about him? Blackmail again? But surely she'd had hardly any contact with him: just that day when she arrived in Orrdale and Bags found the bone – '

'Isaac's too old to be a criminal.'

'No one's too old. And someone was shot in the Hoggarths' kitchen. It had to be Isaac; there are the wounds. You can't shoot yourself beside the ear with a sporting gun.'

'There's Jonty Robson.'

'I'd forgotten him. You're suggesting he went there, after Perry, and shot Isaac by mistake. No, he wouldn't kill the girl because she'd stolen his sun-glasses and twenty pounds. Anyway, his wife will alibi him.'

'Naturally.'

Idle speculation: things were running down. Energy was running out. Miss Pink went home determined to have an early night. Waiting for her TV dinner to heat, sipping a modest shot of Talisker, she considered Anne's revelations which, if garbled at the time, made some sense in perspective. Anne was a woman of principle, but they were her own principles. She had lied in her teeth to protect her first husband, had succumbed to blackmail for the same reason, had even attempted to pull the wool over Miss Pink's eyes this evening, until cornered and forced to come clean. And all this for a man whom she hadn't seen for forty-five years, who was probably dead – but then he *was* Clive's father.

Clive knew his father had killed, but Miss Pink guessed that if Harald suspected, he would be too well mannered ever to broach the subject, and certainly he hadn't known about Edith's blackmail. Only this morning he'd been all in favour of her leaving Plumtree Yard. He could have known about Isaac's intimidation of Anne in respect of Blondel but there too, Harald being Harald, he could have held aloof. Not his business.

Someone knocked at her front door. She was immobile, all ears. She hadn't switched on a light, had been relishing the dusky shadows and the shining sky. She took a sip of whisky and waited, reflecting that no one could pose a threat in the centre of Kelleth – and then she recalled the blood in Whelp Yard.

'Melinda!' came Clive's voice below her window, pitched just loud enough to reach her if she were awake. She made no sign. After a while she heard a murmur and, standing well back from the window, she saw his heavy form plodding through the tombstones, Bags walking a few paces behind.

13

'They've charged him,' Dave Murray blurted as Miss Pink opened her door. 'No' – seeing her dismay – 'not with murder, but with sex with a minor – '

'He didn't – '

'I know, you know, but she slept at his flat, he visited her at the Hoggarths' place. Anyway it's only a holding charge, a ploy while they search for more evidence against him – or against them. As things stand it's too circumstantial; he swears he left his prints at the Hoggarths' the night before Isaac was shot. But there's Perry too. If Rick didn't shoot Isaac, was it her?'

'Isaac and Perry,' she mused, 'We keep coming back to that pair.'

'They weren't a pair! I'm not even sure they met.'

'Oh, they met – well, not to say *met* . . . Heavens! Jonty Robson!'

'He'd have killed Perry, not Isaac.'

'Where does he live?'

'You can't go up there. He's away in any case.'

'Rick got no answer when he went there. It doesn't mean they were away. And if they were, they could have come back.'

During the drive up the hill she felt stimulated, revitalised by the news of the danger looming for Rick. She was at her best in emergencies, rising to the challenge. True, the lesser danger might be more apparent than real, but Rick had put his head on the block by taking Perry into his house. Tyndale was within his rights to charge him on that score, except that if Perry could be found, she would surely deny that there had been any sexual shenanigans. The problem was that while Rick was in custody Tyndale was free to find evidence that might incriminate him in murder.

She stopped at a T-junction. Rick couldn't be incriminated if he were innocent. Oh yes, he could, said the voice of reason, someone else could lay false evidence. And even honest policemen made mistakes.

She looked left. Turn left, first house on the right, Dave had said. She found the place: the type that is termed 'luxury home' by builders, with nothing to distinguish it except size and a pool – the front where it would be noticed by callers. The door of the double garage was up and only one car inside, a Mondeo. So Jonty was home but evidently not his wife. Sunday morning: she'd gone for the papers?

Garden furniture and a barbecue stood at one end of the bright blue pool and a heavy fellow in floral trunks emerged from a slatted shelter roofed with plastic palm fronds.

She regarded him with interest. He had the vanity of the fat man who thinks himself attractive, but in the wet trunks the focal point of that appeal was over-shadowed by a pendulous abdomen. At sight of a woman, however old, he expanded his chest and blinked behind his Armani frames – which had evidently replaced the Ray Bans. He was trying to place her. Surely not Authority – on a Sunday morning?

She introduced herself as smoothly as if they were at a party. Somewhat disconcerted, he made a dive for a white robe on a chair. He liked white; it showed off his tan.

Miss Pink followed him to the chairs. She sat down and surveyed the roofs of the town beyond and below the pool. 'What a delightful situation,' she said, and meant it.

He seated himself gingerly. 'May one ask why – Should I know you?'

'We haven't met,' she said pleasantly. 'I'm a private investigator.'

His jaw dropped. 'Who're you working for?'

'The lost children.' She liked that; it had emerged spontaneously. Old age had many compensations – and people expected you to be barmy. 'I found the body,' she said.

Jonty clutched his robe to him like a shy adolescent. 'Whose body?' he whispered.

She was thinking fast. He was confused and she was playing it off the cuff. Having answered his questions truthfully – well, to some extent, anyone can call herself an investigator – she had side-tracked herself, but in doing so had put him at a disadvantage. She said chattily, her mind racing, 'It's tragic for accused men when the fault lies with the girls – children really: minors. Particularly when they take the initiative – what is a man to do?' Her brain kicked in. 'And to be robbed rubs salt in the wound. They took your fingerprints, of course?' It was a question disguised as an afterthought.

'Why should they do that?' His fear outweighed hostility.

'You followed her to Whelp Yard.'

He leaped up and took a few paces, then turned with a lurch. 'That blood was old Isaac's! He did it, he killed her. Fingerprints? I had nothing to do with it. Why would I have to give my prints? And no, they didn't ask for them. There – is – absolutely – no reason why they should.' He did a double-take. 'Who says I followed her to Whelp? I saw her in the churchyard and she ran off. I never saw her again!'

'Sit down, Mr Robson.' She was calm but firm, trying not to hurry, thinking that the wife could be back at any moment, and if she had any sense at all, the woman would immediately bring this conversation to an end.

'Isaac killed Perry?' she repeated. 'How do you know that?'

'You said she'd been murdered. You said you'd found the body.'

'Bless you, dear man! I meant little Joan Gardner – who was killed before you were born! I found her body in the peat.'

'Oh Christ, *that*! Yes, the dog brought the bloody bone down. That collie: I had it in the back of my car. That was before he picked up the bone of course, or they'd have said I had something to do with that, wouldn't they? Before I was born!' He gave a furious snort.

'It was a little girl's leg bone,' she pointed out.

'Yes, well, she probably asked for it too.' He was staring at the water and missed her sudden tension. 'You rattled me,' he muttered. 'I got the two girls mixed up.'

You were meant to, my man. Aloud she said, 'Isaac overheard your confrontation with the girl.'

He glowered. 'Not with her. It was the fellow – Harlow – who threatened me, told me he was from *The Sun* when all he is is some wannabe little wimp. Isaac overheard that; I noticed him when Harlow said there were witnesses. I was going to thump Harlow because there she was, getting away with my Ray Bans and my twenty quid, and here he's telling me she's fifteen – and how was I to know? She said she was eighteen. And he bundles her into his old heap, and the dog – and that's when he threw the bone out – and off he goes.'

'The bone?' murmured Miss Pink.

'Isaac picked it up.' He was morose, still bemoaning his losses.

A Fiesta turned in at the gate and came up the drive, passing Miss Pink's Renault.

'Was there anything else?' Jonty asked quickly. 'Have you got all you wanted now you know I don't go around killing people? And you won't find my fingerprints in Whelp Yard,' he added viciously.

Miss Pink believed him. She stood up, clutching her bag to her bosom as a thin woman advanced towards the pool. 'You've been a great help, Mr Robson,' she said, trotting out the formula glibly. She beamed at the woman and, not waiting for an introduction, continued gaily, 'I'm Melinda Pink. I'm writing a guidebook to the Border country. What a glorious place you have here. I'll leave you to enjoy your Sunday in peace.'

The only way to have stopped her retreat would have been by force, and her size and air of confidence would not permit of that. Christine turned blazing eyes on her husband.

Behind her Miss Pink heard the furious questions start. She reversed into the road, thankful that neither of them knew where she was staying.

On her way down the hill she recalled that her purpose in approaching Jonty had been to discover a connection between him and Isaac, but what connection there was had nothing to do with a motive for the old man's murder. Their paths had crossed however, even if they hadn't spoken to each other. Isaac had been interested in the confrontation between Rick and Jonty, and then there was the incident of the bone. At this point she back-tracked. Jonty would have been known to Isaac, the VAT man was a local figure, but did that have any special significance?

She didn't go back to the flat but drove to Orrdale House. A ride might clear her brain; it was still early enough for the woods to be cool, and repellent would take care of the flies.

She found Deborah finishing her morning chores in the stables. She caught a large black gelding for Miss Pink and saddled up, grumbling all the time, claiming she was exploited because she had to act as a guide in the house until lunch time. She was a responsible child however, and sent the visitor round the yard a few times before she'd allow her out on her own.

'You've got a choice of routes,' she said, holding the pony's rein and regarding Miss Pink fixedly. 'There are nice rides both sides of the reservoir. Go up the one beside the road while it's still fairly quiet and come back down the other side.'

Miss Pink's eyes strayed to the trees behind the house. 'Don't go in the woods,' Deborah said quickly, 'you'll disturb the pheasants. And there are man-traps.' Miss Pink looked grave. 'That's a joke,' Deborah said. 'Tell you what: I'll get off early and come and meet you: I'll circle the reservoir the other way round, then we can go up the Corpse Road. So I'll see you about noon somewhere near the old village.' Her eyes searched the other's face; the child was in deadly earnest.

'A neat arrangement,' Miss Pink said, and pushed the pony out of the yard on to the track that led along the back of the walled gardens.

The big house stood at the foot of a gentle slope that was clothed with hardwoods. Oaks, with a sprinkling of ash and sycamore, stretched north and east. This was private land and intersected by a number of tracks: dotted lines on the map that indicated rides deliberately laid out for pleasant exercise.

Near the end of the high wall, where an open door marked the back entrance to a potting shed, a wide grassy path forked right. A notice said 'PRIVATE' and there were old horse tracks in dry mud. Miss Pink needed to apply only the slightest pressure and the gelding bore right, accepting the diversion as if it were an accustomed route.

After half a mile of gradual rise she came to an intersection and turned right again, ambling on through the greenwood with never a sign of pheasants. Occasionally she consulted the map to make sure she wasn't missing any part of the woods. It was very quiet; she passed a pond with yellow water lilies and a family of coot, rabbits lolloped ahead of the pony and faded like shadows into the tall bracken. There was a smell of old garlic leaves and fungi. There was no breeze. Once movement on the periphery of her vision made her stiffen in the saddle. The gelding flicked an ear but paid her no further notice. She focused and saw a young deer framed in pink willow herb.

She must have been quartering the woods for an hour before she came to the building. It was a curious wooden structure, large and gabled with a stone chimney breast and wide windows. It was on the fringe of the trees and faced the fells, and it looked like something out of an old movie of the thirties: a pavilion on a village green or a squire's summer-house. It had the air of abandonment peculiar to large objects intended for human occupation (cars, churches) but the impression was fleeting; there was a lot of fresh dung at the end of the verandah where a horse had been tied.

She dismounted and fastened the gelding to the rail. She stood for a moment listening to the hum of insects in the tree canopy, wondering how they achieved such uniformity: singing on one note and that only a fraction above silence.

Inside the summer-house a door closed.

She licked her lips and mounted the two steps to the verandah. The planks were sun-bleached and dusty with drifts of leaves and twigs in the corners. She looked through a window, shading her eyes.

She saw old cane furniture: high-backed chairs, *chaises-longues*, brass Benares tables, an oil lamp on a nondescript sideboard.

There was a door opening on to the verandah. It was locked. She went round to the back, passing more windows, but these set too high to look through. She came to a back door with a thumb latch. It opened into a small dim room with a table and cupboards. On the table there were the remains of a quiche topped with bacon and anchovies, and a plastic bag containing oranges and bananas and a ripe mango. There was a whole baguette and the heel of another, an opened pack of butter and a cheap table knife, a wedge of Wensleydale and two two-litre bottles of Coca Cola, one almost empty.

She opened the door into the main room. Now she saw that there was a book on one of the *chaises-longues*, face-down. It was *The Kraken Wakes*.

There were two other rooms. One held an old camp bed and no mattress; the other, a foam mat and a sleeping-bag. There was a torch beside the bag and a rucksack. Thin, stone-washed jeans were draped over the rucksack.

A footfall sounded close by. She gasped and held her breath. Floorboards creaked under a heavy body. *This* was unexpected. The gelding was tied outside so her presence was obvious. She exhaled, swallowed, and stepped back to the big room.

Clive Thornthwaite regarded her sombrely. He was wearing Levis and a navy T-shirt, and a cotton sun hat that made him look no more ridiculous than an armed robber in a clown's mask.

'What *is* this place?' Miss Pink asked pleasantly. 'A summerhouse?' A mistake: in her effort to appear casual she had forgotten to greet him. Too late now.

'Exactly.' His lips stretched. 'What have you discovered?' His eyes slid to the doorway behind her.

'Perry,' she said.

'And what do you propose to do about it?'

She held his eye and said, almost truthfully, 'I'm sure she didn't fire the second shot at Isaac, so I'm on her side.'

'She didn't fire the first.'

'Tell me about it.' He had to now, either that or silence her. She had few options herself. If he proved hostile she had to talk herself out of the situation.

'Shall we get some air?' He moved to the front door and, turning the key which was in the lock, stood aside. She stepped out on the verandah and saw a second horse beside the gelding: a large animal, topping hers by inches.

'I didn't know you rode,' she said, surprised.

He emerged, carrying two of the cane chairs. 'I don't.' He placed the chairs facing the view. 'I climb on and trust that my weight will keep the beast down.'

She didn't believe him. He went back and returned with cushions. 'Isn't this nice?' he announced as he settled and regarded the hazy fells. 'We all love this place.'

'All?'

'They. They all love it: the Fawcetts. I'm an adopted Fawcett.'

After a moment she said, 'That's your quiche in the back. I didn't think it came from the supermarket or even the deli.'

'Perceptive lady. I baked it specially for her. She needs feeding up.'

'Deborah told you I'd come this way?'

'You guessed.'

'Not quite, but when she was so insistent that I should ride in the opposite direction, and to suggest I'd disturb the pheasants – in July! – the hints were too crude. Besides, I never thought Perry would go far, although I was looking for a tent. This place isn't even marked on the map.'

'The woods are private; we don't want to attract squatters. We have one now, but by invitation. Did you speak to her?'

'No. She was here when I rode up but evidently she doesn't trust me. She went out the back way. I heard the door close.' He was silent. After a moment she asked, 'Why is she frightened of me?'

'What? When she came back to the Hoggarth's that night and found the door open and all that blood in the kitchen? She had no idea who'd bought it but she knew she'd be the suspect. She's the kind who thinks the cops would always pick on her first.'

'She has no idea who was responsible?'

'None.'

'Nor why Isaac should have gone to Whelp Yard?'

'She thinks like everyone else: he found out where she was holed up and went along to try his luck.'

'And the gun?'

He shrugged. 'If he took that he wouldn't have to pay.'

'Rubbish!' Clive jerked back in his chair. He stared at her, nonplussed. 'It's not – not logical,' she protested. 'No, no way. Isaac's type don't go to prostitutes, not at his age anyway.' she pondered, then, doubtfully, 'Do they?'

He shook his head. 'What other explanation can there be? Jonty Robson tried it on.'

'Different age groups.' She was dismissive. She changed tack. 'How does Perry come to be here?' she asked. 'Did Rick bring her?'

'Lord, no! What happened was that when she bolted from the Hoggarths' place she didn't quite panic. She had enough presence of mind to grab her rucksack and stuff, then she made for the woods. Harald had told her about the big house and she knew there was a café. Deb found her at the back of the stables next morning, going through the trash cans for something to eat. Deb was fascinated. Believe me, those two got on like a house on fire. Perry told her the whole story, as far as I can make out, and Deb brought her up here. We've been looking after her ever since.'

'Who else knows?'

'Only me. I'm old Uncle Clive. We're pals, Deb and me. Rick doesn't know any of this. He'd give the game away: insist on coming up here to make sure she's all right, and you can bet your life the cops would be watching him – that's if he's out on bail. Deb and I are discreet – and we're not being watched.'

'You're going to be in trouble when Rick finds out.'

'I'm not bothered. Perry's safe; that's all that matters.'

She said slowly, wondering if he might know more than was apparent, 'I had an odd phone call from Rick yesterday – '

'My mother told me.' He regarded her shrewdly. 'So – you tumbled to the blackmail angles. A couple of rogues, weren't they? But Mum didn't kill Isaac, you know; nor me.' He smiled. 'Nor Harald. Mum says Rick reckons Edith knows something – which was why he sent you to Plumtree.'

'Rick's main concern is Perry. Could he think that Edith knows something about her – that might help?' She remembered the woman's savage denunciation of the girl. 'On the other hand it could be something dangerous.'

'Perry's said nothing about Edith.'

'Where was she when that shot was fired in the Hoggarths' kitchen?'

'You're not going to believe this. She was in the churchyard waiting for Rick to walk Bags but evidently the dog wouldn't come out. He's terrified of thunder.'

'Did she hear the shot?'

'No. Because of the thunder presumably. What are you thinking? Look, even if the first shot had been an accident and she was involved, no way can you believe she fired the second: the wound in the head.'

'Of course she didn't. No, what intrigues me is the reason Isaac went to Whelp in the first place. There has to be a link other than the obvious one. I wonder if there's something that she's unaware of. If I could talk to her...' She looked hopefully towards the trees.

'I'll mention it to her but she won't talk about it to me. That kitchen was a slaughter house. She told Deb – of all people – but then Deb's seen some ghastly sights herself: accidents and such to animals. So she told Deb and Deb told me.'

'Where's Perry now?'

'She won't be far away. I'll hang around to reassure her about you and see if she'll agree to meet you. I think you'd better go now. No need to hurry. Deb won't be at the village.'

'Yes, we arranged to meet there. How did she know – how did *you* know...'

'That you'd come up here? She nipped through the gardens and watched you take the fork opposite the potting shed. Then she phoned me. Now, what are we going to do about Perry?'

'We? It's you who are harbouring her.'

'How archaic. You have a choice: come in with us or tell Tyndale.'

She shook her head. 'She didn't fire that second shot, but you must realise that the most effective way of proving her innocence is to find out who did.' She held his eye. 'I need to talk to her before the police get any closer.'

She left him then and rode away, letting the pony take its own course, thinking about Isaac, about Perry and Isaac at the drowned village. *Was* that the only time that the two had met?

The pony dawdled and snatched a mouthful of grass. She

pushed him on automatically, not noticing where they were going, and shortly they came to the edge of the trees and a gate. The pony placed himself correctly and she opened it without dismounting, closed it too; the animal had been here before. Now they were on the open fell with the reservoir below on the left and the path dropping gradually towards the head of the dale and the old village.

There was a breeze from the west; it lifted the pony's mane and swayed the bracken, bringing a hint of autumn. Here and there a bracken frond had changed colour and all along the turfy ride the harebells danced like blue drops of dew.

She had brought sandwiches and she lunched by a beck, holding the reins, aware that if the gelding started for home she would never catch him. A hundred feet or so below and half a mile away the occasional car drifted by. The odd picnic party was encamped under gaudy umbrellas. She regarded them benignly, pleased that the tourists were having good weather.

The air was soft, her eyelids drooped – to snap open as the twisted reins tightened in her hand. The pony was straining to go home.

She placed him down-slope and climbed on. She headed up the dale and as she approached the village she saw that as usual there were people among the fallen walls. Someone was sketching, a couple were heaving stones aside. The crack of rock on rock sounded out of place above the muted voices and the murmur of tyres on gravel.

She circled the car-park and started across the dry mud, the pony stepping delicately between the tumbled stones. She drew rein behind the artist and saw that he wasn't sketching but drawing a plan. The fellow was young, shirtless, wearing faded jeans.

'Is this a project?' she asked curiously.

'Right. I'm interested in the history of hill-farming. I'm at High Barroc' – naming the local agricultural college – 'Mike down there, he found a clay pipe so he's looking for more stuff.' He nodded towards the two people shifting rocks. At close quarters Miss Pink saw that one of these was a boy. 'That's young James,' her acquaintance went on. 'His people used to own all this land before the dam was built. He's helping out.'

'They've found something.'

The two labourers had stopped heaving stones and were standing rigidly, staring at the ground at their feet. The man glanced towards his fellow student, saw the rider, hesitated, then waved urgently.

'Look!' Young James breathed as they came up. Everyone was wide-eyed. Someone exhaled loudly. At their feet, framed in a cavity just large enough to hold it neatly, staring yet eyeless, was a biscuit-coloured skull.

The man who had been sketching looked at the knoll where the church had stood. 'Washed down out of the graveyard,' he said, trying to sound casual.

'Oh come on!' – from his mate. 'It had tons of rock on top.'

'So how did it get there?'

'Let's shift the rest,' James cried. 'There'll be a whole skeleton under this lot – like there was in the peat.'

'No!' Miss Pink put in sharply. 'You have to wait for the police. Anyway,' she added, having caught their attention, 'the weight will have crushed the rest of it. The skull is whole only because the stones seem to have formed a kind of chamber and prevented its being damaged. What was this place?'

They were staring at her as if she'd appeared by magic. James said wonderingly, 'That's our Buck you're on. What are you doing with one of our ponies?'

'I'm Melinda Pink, a friend of your grandfather. You're James Fawcett, and these gentlemen?'

They introduced themselves weakly. Mike and Tim. She didn't press for surnames.

'Who is it?' James asked, satisfied with her credentials but his shock revealed in the silliest question.

But was it silly? This was a full-size skull, it had belonged to an adult, and it had been here before the village was flooded, and only one adult had disappeared around that time. At the same moment that Walter Thornthwaite came to mind Miss Pink wondered why one eye socket seemed larger than the other. Not quite so well preserved as she thought; one stone, in tumbling, must have glanced off the face.

The students had a car so she sent them to phone the police station, herself staying to guard the site and make sure no one disturbed it. The prime candidate for that was the excited James whom she hadn't a hope of sending home. He was still intent on exposing the skeleton he maintained was under the stones and she could restrain him only by colourful accounts of murders past. At first spellbound, eventually he caught the connection.

'You reckon this is murder too?' he asked.

'There's a doubt,' she acknowledged gravely. 'What do you think?'

'He's buried,' James said slowly, echoing her tone. 'That has to be foul play, doesn't it?'

'Not buried. He – or she – is under a gable-end, I take it.' They stared at the heaps of stones. 'Yes, I think that's a gable. Definitely a house, those flat pieces are roof slates. It could have fallen on him. On the other hand it might have been a barn.'

'They pulled down the gable-ends,' James said.

'They did? Why?'

'They were frightened that the ghosts would come back.'

'But the houses would be covered by the water. What ghosts anyway?'

'Yes, well. They were very superstitious.'

She thought of ghosts inhabiting a village under water and flinched. 'So,' she said loudly, 'he could have been pulling down the gable-end and it came too quickly, or too far.' She looked up at the Corpse Road and remembered the wall that had moved when she leaned against it. 'These old ruins are death traps.'

'It wouldn't take much.' He sounded pompous. 'He didn't jump clear.'

Their vigil was short-lived. Within half an hour a police car came speeding up the road, lights flashing, siren ululating round the fells. James giggled. 'A skull's not going to run away, is it?' he asked. Miss Pink wondered how long it would be before Tyndale arrived, and what he would have to say. What a load the poor fellow had on his plate: Joan Gardner's skeleton in the peat, Isaac shot – and now, this. She stared at the uniforms approaching over the dried mud, white shirts dazzling. Her brain had gone quite dead. Three violent deaths. Three coincidences?

When Tyndale arrived he was exasperated but clinging to a shred of hope. 'It must be an accident,' Mounsey said as they regarded the skull. 'Those students reckon it was a byre and this fellow was pulling down the gable-end.' They looked towards Miss Pink and her companion who were seated at a discreet distance. Beyond them a small crowd of tourists stood about: excited teenagers and self-conscious adults, all avid to discover the reason for the presence of uniforms and what could only be CID.

'We'll wait for SOCO,' Tyndale said. 'There've been too many violent deaths for us to assume it was an accident.'

Mounsey was startled. 'You never think this one's connected with the kid in the peat!'

'Why not? For my money they died around the same time. This chap didn't die after the village was flooded.'

Their attention shifted to the line of the Corpse Road. Miss Pink, simulating boredom, guessed someone was pondering connections, but if this skull belonged to Walter Thornthwaite and Walter had killed Joan Gardner, how had Walter met his death? Divine justice was seldom so punctilious.

Mounsey came over and asked her to go to the station to give a statement. James was affronted to be excepted; he was to go home, Mounsey said kindly, and his statement would be taken there. Furious, forgetting to say goodbye, he sped off on his mountain bike.

The pony stepped out smartly, eager for home. James was going to get there first and blurt out his sensational news. Thus he could be informing Clive – if he was at the big house – that his father had never left the dale but all these years had been lying under a gable-end in the drowned village.

14

There were a number of cars at the front of the big house, Tyndale's among them. It was past five o'clock and the last of the public visitors were pulling away. As the gelding clopped into the stable yard Deborah appeared at the door of the tack-room, stiff with excitement.

'I've been waiting ages!' It was an accusation.

Stung, Miss Pink retaliated. 'You should be glad it was me at the summer-house and not some nosy detective. I'm not going to talk, I'm on her side. Did Clive say if she'd agreed to meet me?'

'He's working on it. And keep your voice down, you don't know who might be listening. I told you not to go up – '

'You protested too much. You'll have to watch yourself if you want to become a successful conspirator.'

Scowling, Deborah held the pony while Miss Pink slid down, grabbing at the saddle as she hit the ground. Waiting for her to regain control of her legs, the girl said harshly, 'You don't want to go inside; the cops are here, grilling James. And they'll need to see you; you were there too!'

It was another cause for resentment; not only had Deborah failed to prevent her own secret from being discovered but her brother had created a sensation. 'They made me work all afternoon as well,' she grumbled. 'It's illegal. They'd be jailed if I told Tyndale.'

Miss Pink ignored this. 'How did they take the news?' she asked, following the other into the stable.

Deborah shrugged. 'How should they? They weren't as shocked as you'd expect.' She walked away with the bridle. 'You'd think a corpse rotting in our drinking water would get some sort of reaction, wouldn't you? I was disgusted.'

Miss Pink pulled off the steaming saddle and looked round for a peg.

'James made a meal of it,' Deborah went on, returning with a brush, 'but he would; he's only ten. Uncle Clive looked a bit sick. He's gone home; he'll want to tell Gran before she hears it on the News.'

'It's hard on them both, if it is Clive's father.'

'No doubt about it, Dad said; he was the only man who went missing at the time.' She caught Miss Pink's frown. 'I listened outside the door,' she added. 'The police will be finished with James soon, so you'd better escape while you can.'

Edith had installed the coveted hanging baskets. The wall was in shadow and pink and purple petunias made a flamboyant display against the dull sandstone. Miss Pink slipped quietly up to the side entrance, not wanting to be seen by Rick if he were home. The bookshop was closed; she had no way of knowing if he had been bailed or was still at the station.

Edith's face was set before she opened the door, and her expression didn't change at sight of the visitor. She grunted what might pass for a greeting.

'I have some news,' Miss Pink said. 'May I come in? We'd better sit down.'

Edith blinked once. You were told to sit down to hear bad news. She climbed the stairs heavily.

Seated at the table in the cluttered living-room, Miss Pink asked pleasantly, 'How well did you know Walter Thornthwaite?'

'I didn't – ' It could have been final but Edith thought better of it, ' – know him at all well. I was a bairn.'

'Just as well.' Miss Pink nodded. 'It appears he's been found.'

There was an empty glass on the table beside the inevitable bottle. Edith's eyes strayed to it and, devoid of expression, returned to Miss Pink.

'He's in Canada?'

'He never went away.'

Edith hesitated. 'So where is he?'

'Now that I can't be sure of exactly, but somewhere around the middle of the village, would it be? Not so far from the church. A byre, they say. How long did the search last?'

'We never looked for un.' The tone was flat, absent; Edith's mind was elsewhere.

'The search for Joan, I mean.'

'Oh, Joannie. Days. They searched for days. Weeks.'

'How many days did Walter go out with them?'

Edith reached for the bottle, and withdrew her hand. She stared at the chenille table-cloth.

'Walter did search for Joannie?' Miss Pink persisted.

'Aye, he were out with 'em.'

'For how many days?'

'Two, three, who knows?' The eyes focused sharply. 'He had to search, to pretend, didn't he?' She grabbed the bottle and filled her glass, spilling a few drops. She waved the bottle towards Miss Pink who shook her head. 'What's it to do with you anyway? You're always over here, asking questions.'

'I came to break it gently.' Miss Pink's expression was one of startled innocence. 'Tyndale will be here shortly.'

'Why? Walter Thornthwaite were nowt to me. I said: I were a bairn.'

'Well, ten years old? Even so it has to be something of a shock: to hear that the man you thought left the area was there all the time.'

'In a byre?'

'The gable-end had fallen on him.'

Edith drew a quick breath. 'They dropped the gables. They needed to destroy the homes.'

'Poor man.'

'I got no pity. You forget little Joannie.' The tone was saccharine.

'So he took her up to the peat cuttings on a pony,' Miss Pink said clearly, anxious that Edith should catch every word, 'at night. It had to be in the dark because of the neighbours . . . But Anne must have known.'

'Oh, she knew. She knew everything, thinks herself so high and mighty . . .' Edith gulped the rest of her drink and eyed the bottle moodily.

'She didn't know she was being watched,' Miss Pink said.

Pudgy hands gripped the edge of the table, the knuckles white. Edith's mouth hung open.

'You saw what you shouldn't have seen,' Miss Pink said sternly, 'and you waited all this time: forty-five years.'

'She *told* you?' Edith was incredulous.

'It doesn't matter now – '

'It's not true, I never asked for nowt, she can't prove anything. I told her I'd keep my mouth shut if only . . . you can't throw an old blind woman out on the street, live in a cardboard box, and her in yon great house with washing machines and microwaves and – and videos, and her with a bastard she allus swore were Thornthwaite's, and we all know why that was, don't us?' She was not quite beside herself because she managed to pause for a response.

It was as if a picture had fractured to re-form with different images, but there was no time to study it. Parts were missing. Miss Pink started to look for them. 'Clive could still be Walter's son,' she said reasonably.

'Is it likely?'

'You're talking about his cross – his fondness for dressing up.'

'He were one of them perverts. No way could Walter Thornthwaite father a child. So she went looking elsewhere – the old whore.'

'She'd be young then.'

'And made sure she got him, and got Walter out of way at same time.'

'Mrs Fawcett killed her husband – is that what you're saying?'

'Never! And you can't say as I did!' Edith glared at the closed window, the closed door to the bedroom. There were no witnesses. 'I never said nowt.' She drank and sighed. 'I can't help it,' she muttered, and Miss Pink knew that the cloudy mind was elsewhere, that even if she meant what she said, she was not referring to this conversation.

'Your voice is rather high-pitched,' she hazarded.

Edith seemed to shrink against the back of her chair. 'I got no more to say,' she whispered. She breathed deeply and hauled herself to her feet, armoured in the kind of fragile defiance that it would be dangerous to challenge.

Miss Pink nodded casually and, keeping the table between them, she left the room and descended the stairs, aware that there was no sound behind her and glad of it, glad too that there had been no knives lying around when she turned her back.

'What's she so scared of?' She glanced out of the kitchen window to make sure that Harald wasn't within earshot but he seemed to be dozing under the tulip tree, Bags stretched at his feet. Clive had gone out for some last-minute shopping and Anne was scrubbing tiny potatoes at the sink. She said drily, 'She'll be terrified of you.'

'No.' Miss Pink was puzzled. 'She took fright when I pointed out that her voice is high-pitched; she literally quailed: as if she'd been hit.'

'What was the context?'

Miss Pink sat down, the better to think. Fatigue was asserting itself after long hours in the saddle. She remembered the context, and played for time. 'She's unstable: early dementia perhaps.'

'She always was neurotic.' Anne turned back to the potatoes.

'I went there to tell her about James' discovery before the police should reach her.'

Anne's shoulders dropped. She was immobile, staring down the garden. 'They can't have identified it already.'

'There has to be an assumption. Did anyone else go missing before the flood?'

'No.'

In the ensuing silence they heard the front door open and close. After a moment Clive appeared with bags of shopping. His smile was wary but he spoke pleasantly enough.

'I was expecting you, Melinda.' He eyed her searchingly. 'You've had a full day.' He looked from her to his mother, evidently wondering what had been said. He saw Harald in the garden but he made no further comment.

Miss Pink studied his features. Yes, there was more than a resemblance under the flesh, not only to Harald but to Bob as well.

'She's been with Edith Bland,' Anne said, and addressed Miss Pink. 'I don't understand this. You didn't go there out of compassion, to break the news gently. What could she have to do with Walter?'

Miss Pink collected herself and concentrated on the business in hand. 'While we were waiting for the police, James and I, I thought of something that doesn't seem to have occurred to anyone else, at least I haven't heard it voiced. If Walter killed Joan, why didn't he disappear immediately instead of hanging around for two or three days?'

Anne said warningly, 'This is Clive's father you're talking about.'

'Is it?'

Mother and son froze as if a film had stopped, Anne clutching a paring knife, Clive with a bottle in one hand, the refrigerator door gaping. Miss Pink went on comfortably, 'As if it matters in these days! The resemblance is obvious, you must see it yourselves and' – addressing Clive – 'anyone can see you dote on Harald.'

Anne turned her back. Clive put the wine in the fridge and closed the door gently. He looked at his mother's back. 'We don't talk about it,' he said, and it was a warning.

'There's no truth in it,' Anne snapped, 'Edith's mad. She's always been jealous; she was probably drunk anyway.'

'She was drinking,' Miss Pink agreed.

'There you are!'

Clive looked dubious. Miss Pink wondered if they were all thinking similar thoughts, or was it only Clive who, more perceptive than his mother, guessed that Miss Pink knew exactly why Anne had always maintained that Walter was his father? Because if there was the slightest suspicion that it was Harald, it gave him – and Anne – a motive for killing Walter, should his body come to light. Which was just what Edith had alleged – before she retracted in a frenzy.

'Edith knows,' she said heavily.

Anne turned, pulled out a chair and collapsed into it. 'Of course she knows,' she cried. 'Why d'you think I let her stay in the bloody flat?'

Miss Pink nodded. 'The reason you gave me seemed a bit weak for blackmail.'

'What did you tell her?' Clive asked.

Anne was embarrassed. 'What?' he pressed. 'Something weak?' He glanced at Miss Pink, then back. 'If she knows you can tell me.'

'He dressed up,' Anne muttered.

Clive was bewildered. 'He was a cross-dresser,' Miss Pink explained. He gaped incredulously.

'It had to be an accident.' Anne ignored them and concentrated on the main issue. 'Everyone was pulling down houses and barns. Harald was with me.' She put her hand to her mouth, stood up and blundered out of the kitchen.

'It was an accident,' Clive repeated, holding Miss Pink's eye.

'I thought that myself.' She was equable. 'I know how unstable these drystone walls can be.'

He tensed and she followed his gaze to see that Harald was coming in from the garden. 'Does he know – about the skull?' she asked quickly.

'Oh, yes.'

'What was his reaction?'

Harald paused to peer at a bed of marigolds.

'Interest,' Clive said. 'No more.'

Bags came in, welcoming the visitor like a prodigal. He was

followed by Harald. 'Well, this is a nice surprise,' he told Miss Pink. 'And how many more bodies are you going to discover, eh?'

Clive rolled his eyes in resignation. Anne returned with a tumbler of whisky. 'Clive, love: will you do the honours? I'll carry on here.'

'I'm cooking.' He was firm. 'You stay here and talk to me. Bring the whisky, Harald; Melinda needs a stimulant after what she's been through today.' Was the tone barbed?

'What were you on, Mel?' Harald asked brightly.

'Buck. A nice smooth ride; one can relax and look at the scenery.'

'If you want something with a bit of spirit, next time – '

'Harald, our tongues are hanging out.'

'Oh, of course, dear boy, of course.'

He bustled out. Bags, sprawled under the table, lifted his head, decided Harald wasn't going far, and dropped back again.

'He's working on a new story,' Anne said urgently. 'Based on today's events, wouldn't you know? He'll be trying it out on you.'

'He's got the most vivid imagination,' Clive put in. 'He just lacks stamina. But he enjoys himself.' He sighed and smiled indulgently.

Miss Pink knew why she wasn't being entertained in the drawing-room. Clive was the chef and would stay in the kitchen and no way would he allow her to be alone with Harald, not even with both his parents. Clive was managing things. He caught her eye and nodded. He knew she knew what he was up to, and she tried to analyse her own reaction to being manipulated, because that was what was happening and not for the first time. Clive was a powerful presence.

'What?' he asked, returning her scrutiny.

Anne looked from one to the other, out of her depth, and at that moment Harald returned, without the whisky. 'Come into the drawing-room, Mel.' Anne wiped her hands. 'You stay here,' he ordered, 'I want to talk to Mel.'

Anne's nostrils were pinched, Clive was astounded, then angry. Miss Pink followed Harald cautiously. The clash of wills had been electric. In a different household it could have erupted in a scene but these three had too much at stake, at least two of them had, and there was Clive: determined to save them from themselves.

'They're terrified,' Harald said, handing her a glass. 'They reckon I'm for the high jump. Highly strung, both of 'em; a touch of the high strikes, you know?'

'It knocks you off balance when secrets you've kept for so many years are suddenly exposed.' He raised an eyebrow. 'Edith's been talking,' she explained. 'And Anne confirms what she said. So I know about Clive's parentage.'

He looked pleased. 'Good. Nice to be able to acknowledge it at last. Even if only to a limited circle,' he added cautiously.

'He's the elder,' she observed, and he was with her immediately.

'And born the wrong side of the blanket, m'dear. Besides, he's happy doing what he's doing, and he'll never have children. So young James will inherit, which is as it should be: carry on the line.'

'What's worrying them' – she gestured towards the kitchen – 'and me, is the construction Tyndale would put on your not acknowledging Clive. When Anne was pregnant with your child it gave you a motive for wanting Walter out of the way.'

'Walter would have let her go. He was fond of her in a platonic fashion; he wanted what was best for her. I could provide a good home and the baby would be properly educated.'

'You discussed it with him?'

'What? Er – no; I'm assuming – And their relationship wasn't *normal*. He realised – must have realised that.'

She was thoughtful. 'He did know that you and Anne were lovers?'

He hesitated. 'No doubt he guessed. The question is academic in any event. Everything turned out right in the end.'

'How can you say that? All his life Clive has thought that his father was a murderer.'

'Oh no, you're wrong there, Mel. We brought the boy up to understand that Walter thought the grass was greener in Canada and his sin, such as it was, was no more than walking out on his wife and baby. Clive came to look on me as his natural father; that's what I mean by its turning out as it should.'

She was uneasy but it wasn't her place to remind him that, as the elder son, Clive had been robbed of his birthright.

He divined the thought and smiled sweetly. 'The boy had love,' he assured her. 'That's more important than land or a big house.'

There was no arguing with that. However, with Harald now demonstrating a modicum of common sense, it should be pointed out that there could be trouble ahead.

'So you're adamant that Walter died by accident,' she pressed. He nodded. 'Then you should know that Edith accuses Anne of his death. She knows – or guessed – that you're Clive's father. Now that I know, and blackmail can't be effective any longer, she'll tell the police out of spite.'

Harald was stricken. 'She holds Anne responsible? Did you tell Anne this? What did she say?'

'I didn't tell her. My guess is that she'd say Edith's mad.'

'There is that, of course . . . Edith was a child – but sharp, very sharp. Between them they knew everything . . .' He was musing and he shook himself. 'That's all by the by. So she accuses Anne.' He stared fixedly at Miss Pink. 'The fact of the matter is I killed Walter. Oh, it wasn't intentional, I hit him and he fell on the stones and must have cracked his skull.'

'The stones came down after he died,' she pointed out, not turning a hair.

'Stone, he fell on a stone in the byre – or the wooden edge of a stall. Anyway, he died and I pushed the gable-end down on top of him.' He paused, thinking. 'I'd met him to discuss Anne, of course: to tell him she was carrying my child and to ask him to release her. He took it badly. I told you he was fond of her.'

'You're going to tell Tyndale this?'

'If he asks me. It's the truth.'

'Well, that's supper in the oven,' Clive announced, entering the drawing-room. 'You'll stay, Melinda: chicken stuffed with asparagus.'

He was followed by Anne carrying her empty glass. 'Finished your little chat?' she asked, too gaily.

'You could say that.' Miss Pink was cool. 'Harald maintains he's going to confess to Walter's murder.'

'Typical,' Clive said carelessly.

'Silly old boy.' Anne grimaced at Harald and held out her

glass. 'No water this time, sweetie; why you've started diluting single malt I'll never know. It's sacrilege. You will stay and eat with us, Melinda.'

Miss Pink cried off, pleading the need to soak her saddle sores in a warm bath. Anne accompanied her to the door. 'See what I mean,' she whispered, 'It's fantasy, fantasy all the time now, and I'll tell you another thing: he's getting his dreams confused with reality. The things he comes out with! You wouldn't believe!'

'He'll tell Tyndale.'

'I'm sure the police are accustomed to false confessions for all manner of crimes, particularly from the aged. Anyway, after nearly fifty years under water there's not going to be many clues left, are there?' She caught the other's expression. 'So Clive tells me,' she added airily.

Miss Pink was in the bath the first time the telephone rang and she ignored it. The second time she was heating soup, regretting chicken stuffed with asparagus but not the charged atmosphere of Nichol House from which she'd escaped. It had been a long day and she was feeling her age. She let the phone ring eight times before she picked it up. It was Mounsey, apologising for the late hour, saying he'd been ringing.

'I was asleep,' she said, as if dazed, 'I took a pill. Was it something urgent?'

Only her statement on the finding of the skull, he said, but they had those of the students and the lad James; it could wait until morning. She promised to go to the station at ten o'clock and returned to her soup, stirring it slowly. They were checking up on her whereabouts – and if Mounsey was doing the telephoning what was Tyndale doing?

He could be supervising operations at the old village. This late? But someone had to be there, guarding the site. All those stones would have to be moved to expose the skeleton – which must be crushed to splinters by now. As Anne said, no evidence could remain, although the skull might reveal some clue. She wondered if Mounsey might say something apposite tomorrow. She considered what she was going to say, but her statement would be confined to the discovery of the skull, and even then she was merely a witness to its being uncovered by someone else. I know nothing, she told herself, to realise immediately that they might all be under discreet surveillance. Heavens, she was becoming as theatrical as Harald! It was most unlikely that even one constable could be spared to haunt the churchyard, the police had more than enough to occupy them elsewhere; all the same, if it did come to their notice that this evening she'd visited first Edith, then the Fawcetts, Tyndale was going to speculate on the motive for those visits. And if Edith publicly aired her accusations, and Harald confessed, Tyndale would demand why she'd kept quiet. Simple, she thought impatiently, you don't place any credence on the ramblings of an alcoholic, nor on a poor old fellow's fantasies. I'll manage, she thought grimly, sufficient unto the day ... never dreaming what that day would bring.

15

'It was beige,' Miss Pink repeated. 'The same colour as the mud. It *was* mud, a thin veneer on the bone.'

Mounsey looked back at her statement. 'They're not words in common use,' he said stubbornly.

'The statement is in my words.' She was anxious to get away from the police station; there were things to do.

'"A thin veneer",' Mounsey read aloud and looked up as a plainclothes man entered the room to sit down before a computer. Mounsey returned to the statement but he was on edge, obviously expecting someone.

'Mr Tyndale must be run off his feet,' Miss Pink observed chattily. 'Which death is he concerned with today, or does he take turns like a builder: a bit here today, there tomorrow?'

'I don't know where he is,' Mounsey muttered. Anyone else he would have floored with a snub. Not Miss Pink.

'How did this one die?' she asked, indicating the statement.

'The wall fell on him, ma'am!'

She left and went looking for Clive. There was no reply at Nichol House and no barking when she rang the bell. It didn't need three people to walk the dog so it looked as if Harald had been removed, at least temporarily, to a place where he could do no harm.

It was Dave Murray who put her on the right track, beckoning to her from the door of the bookshop. 'It seems I'm the dead-letter drop,' he announced as she approached. 'Message for you from Clive. He suggests you go to the big house and ride. Deb will fix you up.'

'Bless you.' She beamed, then, casually, 'Where is Clive? And the others. There's no reply at Nichol.'

'I know. I saw you over there.' He looked past her shoulder. 'It's a gorgeous day – again; they'll have taken Harald for a drive.'

'You don't happen to have seen Tyndale?'

'Who he, dear?'

'The detective inspector. Have you seen any policemen this morning? Like sinister strangers hanging around?'

His gaze came back to her. 'Edith had a visitor. No, I tell a lie; I saw two men go along the walk towards Plumtree Yard and since Rick's away I assumed their business was with Edith.'

'What d'you mean: Rick's away?'

'He's out on bail. I came to the rescue: a small thing but – why not?'

'If he's on bail, shouldn't he stay in Kelleth?'

'I'm sure he will.' But the note of assurance was suspect.

'He'll be looking for Perry.'

Dave raised expressive eyebrows. 'I don't think he'll find her,' he said, 'but it keeps him occupied.'

Two ponies were in the yard at the big house, already saddled. 'I'm coming with you,' Deborah said, emerging from the stable.

'Do you know what this is about?' Miss Pink asked.

'Uncle Clive said you'd know.'

She was surprised. If Perry had agreed to see her why did she need an escort? 'Why – ' she began, to be checked immediately.

'We'll talk when we get going,' Deborah said, leading the gelding to a mounting block.

They didn't talk for quite a while because the girl led the way and told Miss Pink to keep back because her mare kicked. They went along the back of the garden wall, up the brae and into the woods, but at the top of the slope where she had turned right yesterday, Deborah kept straight ahead, puzzling Miss Pink until she recalled her meanderings before she came on the summer-house. All the same, when they had ridden another half-mile and, taking her bearings from the sun, she saw that they were riding north-west when she could have sworn that the summer-house lay to the east, she called to Deborah to stop. Watching the mare's haunches she eased forward gingerly.

'Where are you going?' she asked bluntly.

'We moved her.'

'You might have said!'

'You don't know who's listening.'

'Oh, come on!' Childish games were one thing but, like Harald's fantasies, carried too far they were an unlooked-for distraction, a sheer waste of time.

'It's unlikely,' Deborah admitted, watching her face, 'but there's murder involved and she didn't do it. So maybe the cops couldn't be near enough to hear what we were saying but you never know. We're safe now – I think – but I'm still not taking any chances. Perry's a suspect and if they thought she was in our woods they'd have dogs out here pronto. That's why we moved her from the summer-house. There were too many horse tracks.'

'*We* moved her?'

'Well – me.'

'When?'

'Last night, of course.'

'How was it your parents didn't find out? Your mother's so safety-conscious she makes you leave word when you take a pony out.'

Deborah sighed at such a display of tunnel vision. '*You* always tell the truth? And you didn't know how to get out of your house without your parents knowing?'

'*Touché*, but – did you take a pony?'

'I saddled up in the paddock so there was no sound in the yard. Not that it'd matter, they all sleep on the far side of the house.'

They were walking on now and ahead the trees thinned to the open fell. They stopped at a gate in the drystone wall. This gate was padlocked. They dismounted and lifted it off its hinges. Mounting again, they breasted an easy rise to a long whale-backed ridge. The path reached the crest and turned along it but Deborah continued over the top and, dropping a little, followed a route that was scarcely more than a sheep trod. Below, on their right, the tips of trees appeared above an unfamiliar dale.

They came to a little round sheep pen beside a gully. 'This is it,' Deborah said and slid down, coming to take Miss Pink's reins. 'Follow the water down to the wood until you come to where a rowan tree's fallen across the beck. On your left there's a crag and a cave. She's there.'

'This seems just a little over the top – '

'It's well hidden, right? That's all that matters. We're not playing games. Here, take these.' And she handed over her bulging saddle bags.

Miss Pink dismounted and started down the slope, grimacing at the lack of friction on the bone-dry grass. She came to the fallen rowan and looked left. Shadowed rock showed above a growth of brambles and nettles. She followed a trampled line through the undergrowth and saw the cave: more a wide slit than a roofed cavity, but still a dark and secret place.

'Perry?' she called softly, 'It's me: Melinda Pink. I'm alone. Deborah stayed on top.'

It was her hair that showed first, like a dandelion in the gloom. She came out slowly, looking just the same: thin, mouse-faced, the sharp nose and large eyes, the yellow hair now showing dark at the roots. The eyes searched Miss Pink's face hungrily but it wasn't food she was after so much as company.

'How long can you stay? Why didn't Deb come down?'

'She's holding the ponies. How are you?'

'I'm bored out of my skin. I got books though. Deb lent me hers.'

'Why did you come here?'

'They said the summer-house wasn't safe any longer. You found it – '

'I meant why didn't you go to Scotland?'

'Because they'd be watching the roads, and I don't know no one up there. Here I got friends. What's in the bags?'

Miss Pink handed them over and watched as Perry examined the contents, exclaiming at each item: chicken, sardines, a granary loaf, two cans of Coca Cola, Corbett's *Man-Eaters of Kumaon*. 'I love these people,' Perry said. 'They're risking everything for me.'

'The point is, they're sure you didn't shoot Isaac, and they're going to keep you safely out of the way until they find out who did.'

'How're they going to do that? Clive told me you reckon I know something. What?'

'If I knew that – Put it this way: it could be something you saw or heard and you haven't realised it was important.'

'Such as?'

Miss Pink spread her hands. 'There's a puzzle: questions and no answers. Why did Isaac come to Whelp Yard?'

'He knew I was there. He must have followed Rick.'

Miss Pink stared at the girl who, misreading the signs, turned sulky. 'How else would he know where I was?'

'Quite.' But Miss Pink wasn't agreeing, merely responding. She tried again. 'You had no contact with Isaac before then – '

'I *never* had no contact, not then neither. I come back – I'd been hanging around the churchyard waiting to see Bags but Rick wouldn't be able to make him leave the flat. He's scared of thunder. So I gave up and come back to the house and there was all that blood in the kitchen. I got out of there. Wouldn't you?'

'Did you hear a shot?'

'How could I: with the thunder, and buildings between me and Whelp Yard?' Miss Pink was biting her lip. 'So there's no way I can help,' Perry went on. 'I'm as much in the dark as you are. I never even spoke to Isaac. I saw him that one time when we come down to the drowned village where I met Rick, and I never saw him again.'

'He visited Edith. You didn't hear anything that passed between them? Rick's ceiling is thin.'

For a moment Perry was bewildered then she shrieked with laughter.

'Shut up!' The girl clapped a hand to her mouth. 'Sound carries,' Miss Pink hissed. 'Yes, I know there doesn't appear to be anyone about but there could be a shepherd or a hiker below. Never mind. What's so funny?'

'She's his sister, right? Edith and Isaac: they're brother and sister.'

'They were. Yes.'

'I said we could hear them screwing.'

Miss Pink was silent for so long that Perry's brain found the same track. 'That's *it*? He came to shoot me because Edith told him I'd said *that*?'

'It could be a motive. If it were true.'

'It's not true. I were just teasing her.'

'Why?'

'The old cow, she called me a trollop, didn't she? I said she were jealous because she were old, and I musta said something about her boy friend and she said he were her brother. I said that were all right, she couldn't get pregnant at her age.' She thought about this. 'Actually,' she said, more soberly, 'I don't think I said we could hear them in bed, I just suggested it like.'

'What did you say exactly?'

Perry frowned, trying to remember. 'You might have heard them talking,' Miss Pink prompted.

'You could hear her television – and her voice of course – she yells, don't she? On the telephone. No, I never heard him, 'fact, I don't know that he did come visiting while I were there. It were Rick told me.'

'You heard her telephoning.'

'Not what she said. Rick shut his bedroom door. The telephone's in her bedroom see, above his. So you can hear the noise like: her yelling, but not the words.'

Miss Pink reverted to the teasing. 'How did she react when you suggested she had a sexual relationship with her brother?'

Perry tried not to smile – and then she remembered. She hadn't liked that. 'She sorta dribbled,' she said.

A man was mowing the grass in the churchyard. DS Mounsey sat on a flat tombstone and contemplated a pair of blackbirds foraging in the wake of the mower. Coming home from Doomgate where she'd left her car, Miss Pink felt a sudden chill but she gave no sign that she'd guessed why Mounsey was there.

The male blackbird fluttered away with a chuckle of warning. Mounsey looked up and his eyes hardened. Miss Pink prepared her defences. 'The inspector's in the bookshop,' he said, his tone loaded. This interview wasn't going to be concerned with the skull.

From the doorway she peered into the shop to be met by weak smiles and sharp eyes. Dave was trying to convey something.

Mounsey was at her back and she felt crowded. Tyndale came forward, asking if they might have a little chat. Her eyes narrowed. He wasn't the man for little chats.

The men entered her flat with the alertness of their kind, eyes flicking to open doors: bedroom and kitchen, resting a fraction longer on the closed door to the bathroom. She filled the kettle and switched it on, went to the bathroom, washed her hands and emerged, leaving the door open. She wondered if they might consider looking for Perry in the roof space.

'What did Edith have to say?' Tyndale asked, sounding mildly curious.

'Edith?' The kettle started to scream. She filled the teapot and came back. 'She didn't say much; she'd been at the cherry brandy.'

Mounsey rose from his chair and went to sit by Tyndale on the sofa. 'Sit down,' he said, in the kind of tone he'd use to his aged mother, gesturing to the chair he'd vacated. 'You look tired.'

'I'm an old lady.' She retreated to the kitchen, poured tea into mugs and brought a tray to the coffee table. She sat down and regarded Tyndale expectantly. 'So you visited Edith,' she observed.

'What did she tell you, ma'am?'

Edith could have told them the truth about last evening's conversation. She hesitated, marshalling her recollections.

'What time were you there?' Tyndale prompted.

'Early evening. I went straight there after I returned the pony to Orrdale House.'

'You didn't come home first? Why was that? You'd be hot and thirsty after your ride, the first thing you'd want would be tea. Then a shower.'

Miss Pink returned his gaze. 'I'm fascinated by Joan Gardner's death. Aren't you? No, you have more recent matters on your mind. But I found Joan's skeleton.' She smiled shyly. 'I was born curious; I had to know how it got into the peat, or rather, who put it there. If the skull was Walter Thornthwaite's, you can guess my reasoning.'

'Not really, ma'am.'

She sighed inwardly. He was going to have her cross all the t's and dot every i. 'The accepted theory – except on the part of Anne Fawcett – is that Walter fled the country after killing Joan.

But if that is his skull he died shortly after Joan disappeared. It could be coincidence: that he met with an accident right then, but I was struck by the fact that he didn't go until some days after Joan vanished. I know some murderers do join the search for their own victims but that kind of man hangs around afterwards. If Walter intended to disappear why didn't he go immediately after he murdered the child?'

'His nerve broke,' Mounsey said.

Tyndale ignored him. 'What's your theory?' he asked Miss Pink.

'It is only a theory.' She was diffident. 'That someone else murdered Joan and, as soon as opportunity offered, killed Walter and concealed the body, intending him to be the fall-guy. Which he was, of course. Presumably there's a skeleton under those stones?'

'What's left of one,' Tyndale said: 'just fragments of bone.'

She nodded; it couldn't be anything else. 'So the timing of Walter's disappearance gave me a handle to question – to visit Edith,' she explained. 'She confirmed that two or three days elapsed before Walter went, and she accuses him – ' She stopped, rather too suddenly.

'She accused Walter of killing Joan?' Tyndale exchanged a glance with his sergeant. Miss Pink felt uncomfortable, blackmail and Harald's 'confession' bulking huge in her mind. She started to sweat; it was very hot in the flat.

'Did she say who killed Walter?' Tyndale asked gently. 'Because you'd have told her the skull had been found.'

'Of course I told her. She blames his wife.' She shook her head sadly. 'Edith's obsessed by jealousy.'

'Where does Harald Fawcett come into it?'

'Harald. She didn't make a lot of sense. I expect she mentioned Harald – yes, I'm sure she did.'

'And Isaac?'

'Everyone.' She went on wildly: 'Even Jonty Robson. Edith hasn't a good word for anyone.'

'What did she say about Isaac?'

She stiffened. They weren't concerned with the skull then, nor with Joan Gardner, but with Whelp Yard. 'She said Isaac went to the Hoggarths' that night because Perry's a prostitute. I said: the woman's unstable.'

'What did she say about Isaac and Joan?'

'Joan? Joan Gardner?' Stupid, what other Joan was there? She was bemused; had Edith mentioned the two in conjunction?

'She told us that Isaac killed Joan,' Tyndale said.

After a moment she said weakly, 'Why would he do that?'

'The usual reason in such cases: to silence her after rape.'

She nodded faintly. 'It's the only explanation.' It wasn't but she needed time to think about this. She sensed that he was disappointed in her.

'But she never mentioned Isaac to you?' he pressed.

'Not in relation to Joan.'

'Is there something you're not telling us, ma'am?'

'It's difficult to recall such a disjointed – I had to keep prompting – she must have been the same with you – exhibitionist. She has glaucoma and maintains she's going blind. And she forgets, but there: memory plays tricks in old age. So confusing: dreams and reality. I can remember every detail of the dinner I had on my twenty-first and I can't remember what I had to eat last night. Or whether I've taken my tablets . . .'

They were standing up. 'If you do remember more, you have my number.' Tyndale placed a card on the table. He smiled like a lizard. 'We'll go and see the Fawcetts, find out what they have to tell us.' He paused, waiting for her reaction.

'If I think of anything I'll give you a ring,' she assured him earnestly.

'Think she will?' Mounsey asked as they crossed the church yard.

'She'll tell us more when she thinks it's convenient. Like this lot here.' Tyndale nodded towards Nichol House.

The Fawcetts were home. 'It's all been too much for my husband,' Anne said, ushering them through the hall. 'I'm afraid of a stroke. Please don't say anything to upset him. He's very tired; I was just about to take him up.'

Tyndale didn't believe a word of it but he looked sympathetic and said they wouldn't be long, just a question or two, maybe Mr Fawcett – or any of them – might remember something. He was deliberately vague.

As they entered the drawing-room Harald and Clive turned from the french windows. In the rough grass outside Bags was attacking a stick with ferocious growls. Clive looked depressed at sight of the visitors but Harald's face was that of the polite host. He moved to the sideboard, asking what they would drink.

Tyndale chose Glenfiddich, Mounsey favoured beer. Clive went to the kitchen. Anne relaxed a little. You couldn't arrest a man for murder when you were drinking his whisky. In fact, police didn't drink on duty ... Did they?

Clive returned with a tankard of beer. Tyndale sipped his malt. They regarded him expectantly, except for Mounsey who was being pawed insistently by Bags.

'Edith Bland,' Tyndale began, 'how long has she been like this?'

Clive frowned. Anne was rigid. 'Like what?' Harald said.

'Accusing people of murder.'

Anne's eyes blazed. Harald said brightly, 'Since the first body came to light. The cadaver in the peat. Now there's a title! I'm sure it hasn't been used –'

'I've only noticed it recently,' Anne interrupted, adding in a rush, 'but we've never had a drought like this before, not for fifty years. That's what's disorientated everyone. That skeleton could have stayed hidden for ever if the peat hadn't eroded in the dry –'

' – and the village was exposed,' Tyndale supplied.

She flinched as if he'd hit her. 'Edith says Isaac killed Joan,' he said.

'Joan?' Anne repeated on a rising note.

Harald was frowning. 'She says *Isaac* murdered Joan?'

'Actually she said "killed". It could have been unintentional. That wouldn't be murder.'

'It's a fine point,' Clive said, speaking for the first time. 'He buried her; that implies guilt.'

'You can feel guilty if you kill someone by accident,' Tyndale told him.

Anne closed her eyes and turned away. Mounsey caught the movement but Tyndale was addressing Harald: 'There have been at least two murders.'

'The permutations are intriguing,' Harald observed. 'It could be three murders, or two, or one. It could have been three accidents; it's a novelist's conundrum.'

'Isaac was murdered,' Clive said firmly. 'You can't shoot yourself behind the ear with a shotgun.'

'You could if you wedged it,' Tyndale said.

'Really?' Harald looked fascinated. 'That hadn't occurred to me.'

'You'd thought he was murdered, sir?'

'Of course.'

'Who would be the perpetrator, would you say?'

Anne had been fussing at the sideboard. Now she turned and stared at her husband.

'I have no idea,' Harald said.

Tyndale gave the ghost of a smile. 'I thought you might have Edith in mind.'

'No.' Harald considered this. 'She doesn't drive. And why should she kill him?'

'Why should I suggest you have her in mind for the killer? Because she accuses you.' But Tyndale's eyes had shifted to Anne.

'Me?' She giggled hysterically. 'I killed Isaac?'

'Oh no, ma'am. Walter Thornthwaite.'

Whatever they might have expected at the start they had not expected this, and now. They were immobile, as if the slightest movement would betray themselves or each other. Then eyes flickered, shoulders dropped, Clive gave an angry laugh. 'We'll have to get Edith into sheltered accommodation,' he said harshly. 'Although she seems OK physically? I mean, she's not likely to burn the place down, or anything?' Anne said nothing. He tried again. 'The drugs she's on – for the glaucoma – and she's an alcoholic – maybe one of us should have a word with her doctor?'

'She says the gable-end was brought down on him while he was still alive,' Tyndale said.

'No!' Anne gasped.

'No, ma'am?'

'It couldn't have been – I mean, no one could have done that; he had to be dead.'

'Edith says – '

'What *is* this?' Clive shouted. 'Stop badgering my mother! That woman's crazy. For God's sake, my parents had a good relationship. 'Whatever happened, it had to be an accident – '

'It wasn't – '

Clive overrode him: 'So it wasn't an accident, then the most likely person who had it in for him – ' He stopped.

'Was me,' Harald said. 'I killed him and pushed the gable-end down. Poor fellow. Are you saying he wasn't dead when the stones fell? That's dreadful, dreadful – '

'He was dead!' Anne cried. 'Don't listen to my husband, he's tired, we've been out in the sun all day – '

'It's no good, my dear.' Harald stood up and, taking her hand, brought her to sit beside him. 'They know I'm not ga-ga, only somewhat eccentric when it suits. Now you keep quiet for a moment while we sort things out – '

'He's doing this for me,' Anne said wildly, snatching her hand away. 'Walter was nearly dead, just at his last – no, he was still alive. I pushed the wall down. It was the wall that killed him.' She glowered defiantly at Harald, then at Tyndale.

'It wasn't,' Tyndale said. 'Now tell me the truth.'

Clive thought: they haven't been cautioned, something's going on here. 'You know the truth,' he told Tyndale coldly.

'Yes.'

'Then why ask them?'

'I'm the one asking the questions, Mr Fawcett.'

'I'm not – ' Clive caught his breath. His mother looked stunned. Harald, in the eye of the storm, was again expressionless.

'Mr Fawcett – Harald – was the father of your baby,' Tyndale told Anne, 'and your husband wasn't prepared to release you.'

'Edith's a lying – '

'That's right,' Harald said.

'I'm addressing Mrs Fawcett, sir.'

'She can't tell you anything; she didn't know till afterwards. Oh, she knew I was going to meet him, but that was as far as it went. I met him in the byre and we had words. He was fond of her, d'you see; he didn't want her to leave him. So I told him she was carrying my child.' He looked fondly at Clive, then his face fell. 'He hated that; it was humiliating, a reflection on his manhood. One suspects he was sterile. We quarrelled and it came to blows. Neither of us was a fighter but I landed a punch and he fell and didn't get up. Must have hit his head on a stone. Perhaps he had a thin skull. Anyway the poor man was dead. So I pushed the wall down on top of him.'

'He's told the truth as far as knocking Walter down.' Anne had herself in hand now. 'But he thought Walter was no more than concussed, if that, and would come home, so Harald came running up to the house to tell me how Walter had taken the news about the baby, and I sent him home – to the big house. I said I'd look after Walter.

'I went down to the byre but Walter was dead. It was me who pushed the wall down on top of him. Of course,' she added quickly, 'it's possible he wasn't dead and the falling stones killed him after all.'

'He was dead, ma'am.'

'What?' Clive gasped. 'How can you tell after all these years?'

'There's a shotgun wound. It's scarcely visible from the front. He was shot through the eye; the exit wound's at the back of the skull.'

16

'You don't need me,' Miss Pink protested. 'Harald's in the clear. It had to be the gunshot that killed Walter. Someone else came along and shot him when Harald went away to tell Anne they'd had a fight.'

'The police appear to be thinking that way,' Dave Murray said, 'but suppose it dawns on them that Harald could have been carrying a gun that night, or was out rabbiting and the shooting was an accident – well, manslaughter? This is where you come in.'

He had come knocking on her door late that evening, dishevelled, breathing urgency and very wet. The rain had started an hour ago and showed no sign of stopping. A few more days and the skull might have been covered and concealed for another forty-five years.

Clive had telephoned Dave at his home after Tyndale left Nichol House, had given him the gist of the interview and asked him to inform Miss Pink. 'They need you,' he pleaded. 'Clive's frantic. He knows you've been involved with murder before – Harald told him. Clive says you'll be able to find out who shot Walter. He reckons the police are holding some cards close to their chest. They had this conversation with the Fawcetts and didn't reveal till right at the end that he'd been shot, although they did know that Harald and Anne were involved. They got that from Edith. That woman's a monster. When Anne wanted her out of the flat she threatened to tell the police that Harald killed Walter. And Anne thought he did! By accident certainly but it would only be his word. Imagine Harald serving a life sentence! You can't bear to think how those two must have suffered over the years.'

'Well, Edith's blackmail is recent, but Isaac – ' She stopped dead. After a moment she went on, 'I think I'll go across and speak to Edith.'

'Is that wise? Would you like me to come with you?'

'No, she'll talk better if I'm on my own – providing she's still capable of talking. However, you might care to wait . . .'

Edith's windows were tightly closed against the rain, that and the television must be loud enough to muffle shouts from below. Miss Pink turned back to the churchyard and, picking up lumps of damp soil, threw them at a window until it was flung up and Edith shouted in a fury: 'Clear off then! Louts, vandals, I'll set the dog on you – one more stone and I'll call police, I'll – '

'It's Melinda Pink. Let me in. We have to talk.'

Pale in the lamplight, Edith's face turned this way and that, trying to penetrate shadows. 'D'you know what time this is? You got the police with you?'

'I'm alone. I need to talk about Joannie.'

'What?'

'Joan Gardner.'

The face disappeared and the window was slammed. Miss Pink drew back, pulling the hood of her cagoule forward against the rain. She watched the windows. After a few minutes a light appeared in the living-room and then the door opened silently. There was no light at the foot of the stairs. She stepped forward. Edith said nothing, which was disconcerting. The woman had to be behind the door.

'You go first,' Miss Pink said. 'I'll close the door.'

There was no bottle on the chenille cloth but the room smelled of the liqueur and dust, and underclothes that had been worn too long. Edith had dressed in a hurry; her blouse was buttoned out of kilter. They sat on opposite sides of the table. 'This's got nowt to do with you,' she said, as if they were in the middle of a conversation.

'I found her skeleton.'

'So?'

'Isaac killed her.'

Edith put her elbows on the table, her hands under her chin supporting her head. Miss Pink thought she'd probably taken a sleeping pill on top of the alcohol. 'I already told the police,' she said.

'And you told them Anne killed her first husband.'

Edith's eyes opened wide. 'Have they arrested her?'

'Why wait till now before exposing her?'

'Didn't need to before. But she's not going to evict me: turn me out to live on some rubbishy estate with all them 'ooligans. What difference do it make when she done it. She can still pay.'

'How did she do it?'

'How?'

'How did she kill him?'

Edith glared. 'Her hit him with a stone and tumbled the wall down, like everyone knows.'

'How did *you* know?'

Edith's mouth opened and closed in astonishment that looked genuine. 'You found un! Under gable-end!'

'But you threatened to tell the police a week ago. How did you know then that he was there, in the old byre?'

Edith stared, then lowered her eyes. The lids flicked up again. 'Isaac told me, o' course.'

'How did *he* know?'

'You ask too many questions.' Miss Pink waited. 'He knew, didn't he?' It was spat out.

'How?'

'I don't know. Would I ask him that?' Another pause. She went on sullenly: 'He heard the stones come down then. He were out shepherding. He saw them running away. He moved the stones and found the body – dead. Nothing he could do.'

'Except blackmail Anne to let him have Blondel.'

'I don't know nowt about that. It weren't my business. I were only little.'

'You lived at Blondel until you were married.'

She shrugged. 'I kept house for un. Why not? He were my brother.'

'You said Anne – or maybe Harald? – hit Walter with a stone.'

'I don't know. I weren't there.'

'But you could blackmail Anne – '

'I never – '

'You can use any word you like, it comes to the same thing. Did they shoot him?'

Edith grinned. 'Never. Brutal, they was: stoned un to death!'

'Walter was shot.'

'He couldn't be,' Edith said.

'There's a gunshot wound in the skull. Isaac shot him.'

In the ensuing silence a sharp burst of rain lashed the window. Edith was breathing deeply. After a while she said, 'Now why would he do a thing like that?'

'Harald and Walter fought. Harald knocked Walter down and left him – alive. Isaac saw his chance and killed him because, if Walter disappeared, people would think he had murdered Joan. And it was Isaac who killed Joan.'

'I know that bit.' Edith was impatient and suddenly alert. 'So it were Isaac who dropped the stones on him?'

'No, Anne did that. She truly thought that Harald had killed Walter. The wound didn't show. He was shot through the eye and she'd attribute a little blood to a blow from Harald's fist, possibly a stone used as a weapon, certainly not a gun. The exit wound was at the back of the head and she wouldn't see it in the dark. Isaac could have intended to take the body away, to put it in the peat like Joan's, but Anne got there first and concealed it. She played right into his hands, in fact.' Miss Pink's tone changed. 'All this will have been a great shock to you.'

'It's one thing after another,' Edith said miserably. 'My own brother. What else? Is there more?'

'Why did he need to kill Perry?'

Edith looked as if she were in the depths of despair. 'He killed her too?' Her voice rose.

'Why? Why was he so obsessed with young girls, at his age – '

'He never! He never run after 'em. That Joan, she tormented un – ' Edith checked, fingering her lips.

'So why Perry?'

'She knew about Joannie,' Edith said.

Miss Pink sketched a nod as if this were common knowledge. 'She overheard you talking about the bone.'

'She taunted me! That phone call, when her dog found the bone: he phoned me. She heard. My fault, I talk too loud on phone. He were terrified. I were telling un to give over, no one knew except me; everyone thought as it were Walter killed Joannie. He were safe, I said, no one'd ever know, just keep quiet, go about his shepherding as if it were nowt to do with un, wasn't even on his grazing. 'Sides, they might never find the rest of it. She heard it all. Isaac, he went to Whelp to silence her for good an' all.'

'But she wasn't there.'

'What? 'Course she were. They fought and – what are you saying: she wasn't there?'

'There was a struggle but not with Perry. There are fingerprints.'

'There can't be.' Edith's eyes were fixed.

'They'll be matched. Everyone's prints will be taken for comparison. They have mine.' Miss Pink smiled benignly: the consummate liar.

'All right, I'll tell you. I followed him. She'd left doors open: one to back yard, and kitchen door. He'd gone in. She weren't there. He'd told me she were the only one as knew t'truth besides me and he blamed me for that, because of talking loud on t'phone. Got nasty, he did. I tried to take t'gun from him and we struggled like you said but he were only a littlun, tha knows. I could match un any day. And gun went off and wounded him. I thought it were just a scrape like but there were a lot of blood. Scared us, that did. He wanted out so I helped un to his Land Rover and he sent me home. Told me to keep me mouth shut. I said as he should go to hospital and he said he would. Wouldn't let me go with un. No sense anyways, I can't drive. Then he musta gone up the dale and shot hisself. He'd got a load of sin on his conscience: Joannie, Walter, what he'd intended for that Perry – he'd know the police would be after him soon as she talked. Which she would soon as she come back and saw the blood in the kitchen. So he decided to end it all.'

'How did he do it?'

'He musta wedged the gun down the side like' – Edith twisted and motioned to the right where the driver's door would be – 'put the truck in gear, one foot on – feet on them pedal things, and pulled trigger.'

Miss Pink nodded thoughtfully, trying to visualise it. 'Poor fellow. And so terrible for you. It's always worse for the ones left behind. Tell me, when he decided Perry had to be silenced, how did he know she hadn't already talked to Rick or Anne about the phone call?'

'I were protecting him all the way. I knew from how they spoke to me: Rick and that Anne, they didn't suspect nowt, so she hadn't told un. Perry were the only one to be feared of. Drive her away, I told him: frighten her off; 'sides, I said, it be his word against hers, who'd believe a little thieving whore, I said, but I never meant for him to *kill* her!'

'I was just about to come across,' Dave said, greatly relieved as she came up the stairs. 'You've been an age. Did you find out anything?'

She told him. 'Oh my,' he breathed at the end. 'So Isaac killed Walter. But she didn't know how he did it. What made you think he didn't tell her?'

'I know country people: the more isolated their lives the less communicative they are, even in the family, particularly there sometimes. Everything I heard suggested a dour taciturn couple. He might have told her Walter was dead, even boasted he was responsible, but there was a possibility that he didn't say how he'd done it. And whatever he said, it wouldn't have been at the time. Edith was ten years old at the time of the flood.'

'They were hardly a couple – at any time.'

She stared at him. He grimaced and changed tack. 'They seem to have been communicative enough when the bone was found. Can you imagine Edith shrieking away on the phone? Why didn't Perry tell Rick? Why didn't Rick hear that phone call himself?'

'Neither of them did. Perry teased Edith about her relationship with Isaac and implied the slightest sound could be heard below in Rick's flat. It was the old adage of that telegram: "All is known, fly at once." Half the recipients will take off. Edith assumed Perry had overheard that call.'

'Stupid woman. So she told Isaac and he – the old bastard!'

'The old murderer. He'd killed twice already.'

'Why did he go after Joan?'

She shrugged, exhausted. 'He liked little girls.'

'He had one already, don't you think?'

'Who knows?'

'Edith does. Do you think that Walter suspected incest? Do you think he *said*?'

'Oh no. It would never be mentioned. Isaac shot him to produce a fall-guy for Joan's disappearance. Although he wasn't slow to see how he could blackmail Anne and make her give up Blondel.' She yawned and apologised. 'I'm afraid I have to turn you out, I can't keep my eyes open.'

'So it's all wrapped up,' he said, turning back at the head of the stairs. 'Perry can come out of hiding, Rick will come home and complete his series, you'll write your book; everybody takes up where they were before Bags found that bone. You look dubious. Did I say something?'

She shook her head, her eyelids drooping. 'I don't think Edith loved her brother,' she said.

She didn't know what she was saying, he thought; she was half asleep.

17

The rain continued relentlessly through the night, to be augmented in the small hours by a sensational thunderstorm and a cloudburst over the high fells. The downpour tailed off before dawn and by the time the sun rose the sky was gentian blue with clouds piled above the Pennines like cauliflowers. Roofs steamed, birds sat on the ridges warming their backs, and Kelleth children were warned to keep clear of the river banks where the peaty water streamed past, the occasional sheep carcass rolling with the current.

At ten o'clock Edith breakfasted on tea and Alka Seltzer and went downstairs to see how the hanging baskets had fared in the storm. The petunias were a mess. She was in a carping mood when Miss Pink came round the corner, the collie's lead in one hand, a key in the other.

'I've been searching his flat,' she said, as if no night had intervened between the two encounters.

'Searching for what? I didn't hear you in there.'

'Evidence. I'm wondering where Perry is.'

'You was looking for her there?' Edith's eyes slewed sideways as if they could penetrate walls.

'We must leave no stone unturned – and she has to be somewhere.' Miss Pink sounded mystified. 'Or her body is.' She leaned against the sunlit wall, prepared for a neighbourly chat. 'I've been thinking. Obviously Isaac didn't shoot himself despite what the police say – wedging his gun and so on – because he was in the passenger seat, so Rick had to be driving – well, Rick or Perry . . .' She paused, blinking. Edith was poker-faced. 'No, that doesn't fit,' Miss Pink murmured – and repeated it loudly for Edith's benefit, 'because I'm thinking that he killed her and then – buried her? Threw her in the river? In that case the body might never be found. Have you *seen* the river? It's full of drowned sheep.' She shuddered, looking down at Bags sitting at her feet. 'I'm walking the dog for Harald,' she gabbled on. 'We usually take the river walk but the water's over the path. And he would go in, he loves the water; he'd be swept away. I'd have no chance of getting him out, I can't swim. What was I saying?' It was rhetorical; she was merely drawing breath to plunge on, but Edith took it for a question.

'About the girl in his flat.'

'The body.' Miss Pink nodded. 'I have a theory. It must have occurred to you too. I don't think your brother went to the Hoggarths' to see Perry but to find Rick.'

'Why would he do that?'

'Because he'd killed Perry.'

'Who had?'

'Isaac. You told him to frighten her off. He did more than that. You think so yourself.'

Edith was fidgeting with her hands, pleating her apron, scowling with concentration. 'You was in this flat.' She was looking for firm ground in the quicksand that had appeared.

'He could have killed her here – or at the Hoggarths' – or she could have visited him at Blondel. Did you think of that? Of course you did; you've maintained all along that she was a prostitute. How well have you searched Blondel?'

'I never searched. She weren't there.'

'In a wardrobe perhaps, or the barns. In a pool below the waterfall? She's been missing for five days. There's a country-wide alert for her. If she were alive she'd have been found by now. She can't hide that yellow hair.'

'It don't make sense.'

'It does when you know that Isaac didn't commit suicide. Rick's fingerprints will be in the Land Rover.'

'They won't then. It were under the water!'

'That makes no difference with modern technology.' Miss Pink was dismissive. 'There'll be prints on the gun too. Unless he wore gloves, of course.'

'Do the police know all this?'

'No. Tyndale is certain it was suicide: says that, with the truck bouncing and toppling as it went down, Isaac would have floated out of the driver's seat. He wasn't wearing a seat belt.'

'Never wore one in's life!' Edith was contemptuous.

'So they won't be looking for fingerprints.'

'You said they took yours.'

'That was earlier – and there was all that blood in the kitchen at the Hoggarths'. She spent a lot of time with me. Nasty minds these local police have.' Miss Pink bared her teeth. 'Probably expected me to make a run for it – or commit suicide.'

'They didn't believe you when you said Isaac were murdered?'

'I'm not going to mention it just to be laughed at. I go my own way: poking in odd corners, interviewing suspects – '

'What d'you suspect me of?'

'Suspects *and* witnesses. You didn't let me finish.'

There was a pause. 'I could do with a ride to Blondel,' Edith said, visibly relaxed now. 'I need to sort the furniture for Age Concern.'

Miss Pink looked doubtful. 'I did tell the Fawcetts I'd go along the river – but that was before I saw the flood. Still, it's immaterial. Yes, I'll run you out to Blondel. I'd like to look over the place myself.'

'You won't find nowt.'

'There may be something you've overlooked. I'm a trained investigator, and quite good at it if I say so myself.'

Edith went back indoors to emerge wearing a cagoule and gum boots. They walked to Doomgate by way of Botchergate to avoid passing Nichol House. 'No need for Anne to see us together,' Miss Pink said with a hint of amusement. 'It's nothing to do with her where I'm going nor who I'm with.'

Edith said nothing. She didn't understand half of what the old fool was saying but she was in command of the situation; they were going to Blondel. Belatedly she wondered if this Pink woman were right and there might be some trace of the girl at the farm. Not that it would matter, she had it all worked out.

Miss Pink reversed out of her garage and Edith closed the doors unasked. She got in beside the driver, the collie monopolising the back seat. They didn't say much on the short drive, Miss Pink concentrating on the road, Edith lost in thought, giving no assistance at junctions, but then she'd admitted she didn't drive.

No dogs barked at Blondel now that Bainbridge had removed them but it wasn't quiet. Below the birdsong there was a persistent rushing note from the direction of the waterfall, while higher up the slope white water marked the course of the full beck.

Miss Pink grabbed at the dog as they left the car but Edith said sharply, 'I don't want him in the house. Let him off the lead; he'll come to no harm.'

They went inside, shutting the door on Bags who gave a low whimper before turning away to explore the barns.

There seemed to be nothing sinister in the house, only dirt and dust and rat droppings. Miss Pink wandered in a distracted fashion from room to room looking for any place large enough to conceal a body. It was an old man's home with clothing draped on chairs in one bedroom, and the only decent garments a heavy dark suit on a wooden hanger in a wardrobe. The furniture was basic. 'He sold the good pieces,' Edith explained, but Miss Pink doubted that he ever had any.

They paused on the landing under a trap door. 'There's a ladder somewhere,' Edith said.

'No. He wouldn't have gone to the trouble. For my money, if she is dead, she's in the peat – like Joan – or the river.'

'Of course,' Miss Pink went on, descending the stairs ahead of Edith, looking back, her hand on the banister, 'Isaac buried Joan, whoever killed her.' She opened the front door and stepped out into the sunshine.

'He buried her but someone else killed her? Is that what you're saying? Different folk?'

'Oh yes. Walter killed Joan.' Miss Pink was preoccupied, looking around. 'Bags,' she called. 'Here, boy! They were in league.' Her eyes searched the yard. 'You must have realised that yourself – no, you were only ten. It had to be two people who were very close: one to kill, the other to bury; two people who could trust each other implicitly. Walter and Isaac.'

'Them trust each other! You don't know what you're – Where are you going?'

Miss Pink was crossing the farmyard. 'To the waterfall,' she called back, adding something Edith failed to catch. She hurried after the older woman.

'What was that? You said what?'

'The body could be caught up in wire in the bottom of a pool. Isaac wouldn't be bothered about dumping old fencing. Out of sight, out of mind.'

She was hurrying across the pasture, panting, stumbling a little. She came to a halt, clutching her chest. 'Too fast,' she gasped. 'I've a weak heart and high blood pressure – should slow down, take it easy – '

'That's right.' Edith eyed her shrewdly, assessing her condition. 'You take it easy.'

The fall was thundering down the rock face like a miniature Niagara, a rainbow arching the spray. Sunshine filtering through leaves chequered bright wet rock in a confusion of colour and light. Down in the shaded chasm the black water was streaked with foam.

Dangerously close to the edge Miss Pink said something. Edith leaned closer, holding a branch, straining to hear.

' – makes me dizzy,' Miss Pink shouted. 'Give me a hand to get back – '

'Look!' Edith commanded, gesturing across the chasm with her free hand. 'What's that?'

Miss Pink turned to look, felt sudden pressure, and fell.

*

Bainbridge surveyed his flattened barley dismally. If it wasn't one thing it was another. Mad cow disease, sheep scab, lodged barley. Next thing he knew, he'd get bit by one of Isaac's glumpen dogs – and what was that – barking its head off? His own little bitch was interested, and she knew where t'noise was coming from: Blondel. One of them animals had got loose and run home maybe. So why bark? It certainly wasn't killing sheep, sheep killers work in silence. Trippers at Blondel? Broken into the house and shut their dog outside?

He hurried home and looked in his pens. All the dogs were there: Isaac's and his own. Taking the little bitch he drove to Blondel. No car, no people, no dog, The barking was coming from the direction of the beck and now he guessed what had happened. Some dog was cragfast: washed down with the flood, it had survived the waterfall and hauled itself out onto a ledge some place.

The bitch led him to the edge of the ghyll way downstream of the big fall and not far above the lower cascades. The trees seemed to choke the chasm here but above the black rock face was a small turfy ledge where a big fat collie was barking at something below.

Bainbridge told the bitch to stay and lowered himself gingerly to the ledge. The collie had stopped barking and looked eagerly from him to the water below. Bainbridge spoke quietly to the animal and it moved back and sat down.

He put one arm round a young oak tree and leaned over the edge. 'Oh, my God!' he breathed.

There was a tiny cove of black pebbles washed by the water. Lying across it, hips and legs submerged, arms outstretched, the hands still clawing into the stones, was the body of a large woman.

Edith came downstairs with the second hanging basket as Tyndale appeared at the open front door. She nodded to him and asked him to put the basket on its hook for her. Mounsey stood in the yard, watching. She wondered what they'd come for this time.

'We were here this afternoon,' Tyndale said. 'Twice, in fact.'

'I've been in Carlisle. Had to buy more flowers. First lot were ruined in t'storm last night.'

'Did you drive to Carlisle?' Tyndale asked.

'I would if I had a car, and if I could drive. I took the train, o' course.'

'What time did you leave Miss Pink?'

'I've not seen her today.' Her tone changed. 'You don't want to stand around out here. Will you come inside?'

'No, we're looking for Miss Pink; we were told you went out with her. Must be a case of mistaken identity. If you see her perhaps you'll ask her to give us a ring at the police station.'

'I'll do that.' Edith was equable. A thought struck her. 'She did say something last night about going to Carlisle.'

'Did she say anything else – about her intentions?'

'No, she just looked in, see if I was all right. After me brother died like.'

'Of course.'

They turned away. Edith looked critically at the new petunias, nipped off a wilted blossom and went indoors. As she climbed the stairs she felt a pang of hunger. She would have liked to eat immediately but the thought of chips, deepfried and succulent, was too tempting. She lit the gas and put the chip pan on to heat the oil and then it was time for the first drink. She hadn't had a drink all day. Her face relaxed in anticipation as she went to the corner cupboard.

She was sitting in the easy chair in her bedroom watching *Neighbours* when someone knocked on the front door. She let them try again – folk who knew her knew she was deaf and shouldn't expect an answer; strangers could go to hell. Then the caller started to hammer as if he'd break the door down. This was no stranger.

She'd had two glasses of cherry brandy and should have felt good; indeed, she had been feeling good until this madman came battering on her door. She went downstairs furious, prepared to blast him off the step. She opened the door to Miss Pink.

She looked just as she'd looked *before*: neat slacks, shirt, denim jacket, hiking boots. Her hair was dry, she was in command: powerful, pushing her way in; Edith retreating, turning, groping her way up the stairs.

Miss Pink followed, ignoring the crab-like progress, treading lightly, inexorably, to the top, following Edith into the living-room, watching blandly as the other sank on to a chair at the table to stare at her visitor with chattering teeth.

Miss Pink settled herself on the far side of the table. 'Where did you go?' she asked curiously.

Edith was massaging her chest. She looked towards the stairs as if expecting more people.

'Yes?' Miss Pink asked, like a teacher with a tongue-tied pupil.

'Carlisle,' Edith whispered.

'Where's the car?'

'I dunno.' A long pause while she stared at the table-cloth. 'I dunno what you're talking about.'

'You drove to Carlisle – ' Miss Pink prompted.

'I can't drive.'

' – and left the car in a back street with the keys in the ignition. You were seen – '

'I weren't in no back street!'

'Where were you this afternoon?'

'I were in the town centre. I went and come back on t'train.' The sentences emerged in spurts. 'I bought plants. I got the receipts.'

'You drove Isaac's Land Rover to the reservoir and put it in the water.'

'I can't drive.'

'You shot Isaac.'

'We was struggling for the gun – '

'The second time. Your fingerprints are on the gun.'

'They can't be – '

'Why wipe it if he was shot by accident? And the Land Rover. You may have wiped the gun – but you missed a thumbprint. You forgot to wipe the Land Rover – '

'I didn't then – '

' – forgot to wipe it everywhere. Your memory's going. And something's burning.' Miss Pink stood up and went to the kitchen, switching off the gas under the chip pan. She returned and sat down.

Edith said shakily, 'I didn't kill him. He died in the truck as I were taking un to infirmary. So I shot un again, make it look like suicide, and I drove to the lake and put t'truck in the water like you said, with him inside. It weren't murder.'

'He was a threat. He was dangerous.'

'He couldn't do me no harm.'

'You always threatened each other.'

'He were my brother! You said police says as it were suicide, you said Walter killed Joannie – '

'What's Joan got to do with Isaac?'

Edith bit her lip and her eyes wandered. 'Why was she killed?' Miss Pink asked.

'How would I know?' Edith reddened, hesitated, then said heatedly, 'She asked for it.' She stared at the window. 'We was friends once but she were no better'n she should be.'

'She was nine years old, a child.'

'Huh! Joannie were more grown up than . . .'

'More than Isaac?'

'Never! Never, never!'

Edith pounded the table, overcome with rage. Miss Pink looked round quickly, seeing nothing she could utilise as a weapon, flexing her muscles.

'She never come near un,' Edith hissed. 'She'd never dare! Her were too feared o' me!'

'Not all that feared,' Miss Pink said, adrenalin surging. 'She got you on the raw.'

'I tell you – Listen – ' Edith leaned over the table, dropping her voice like a conspirator. 'Folk as didn't know her said she looked like an angel, but in truth she were a devil.' She sat back and smiled. 'She were lovely: blonde, and big eyes the colour of violets, and a voice like a bird. She could make 'em do anything . . .' She trailed off.

'Like a movie star,' Miss Pink said: 'beautiful, seductive – '

'But not Isaac.' Edith shook her head vehemently. 'She told me and I said as she were a liar. She laughed at me. She said he were tired of me, what he wanted was a pretty little girl.'

'But you wouldn't blame him – even if it were true.'

'No, it weren't his fault.' They spoke like women in a dream.

'No more than it was with Perry. He never meant her any harm.'

Edith frowned. 'He were always on at me: shouting too loud on t'phone, drinking too much, and like when I told that Anne I'd go to police – but I can't help going blind and being deaf and talking loud. That little trollop shouldn't have been listening.' She grinned slyly. 'Another one as were asking for trouble.'

Miss Pink said nothing, concentrating on the words, letting them sink into the sponge of a brain, making a record.

'Taunted me,' Edith said viciously. '"You got a carrying voice, we can hear every word you say"' – grotesque mimicry of Perry's southern accent. 'I coulda finished her for good only Isaac, he had to follow me there, the stupid gowk! An' all he got for his pains was to go and shoot hisself!'

'He followed you to the Hoggarths' to see you came to no harm. He must have known you'd taken the gun.'

'That would be what brought him back from Blondel. He'd been with me that evening and I took the shotgun from t'truck. He never missed it until he got home and then he come straight back. He knew where I'd have gone. I told un I'd seen Rick go out and through churchyard and I saw him come into Doomgate and cross to Whelp. My bedroom looks over Doomgate. I'd guessed *she* were there. Isaac knew where he'd find me. Everything happened just like I said.'

Except that Isaac had been trying to take the gun from his sister, not the other way round. 'I wonder,' Miss Pink said, 'if the police had questioned him about Joan, would he have admitted it, perhaps saying that she died by accident?'

'Joannie?' Edith considered the point carefully.

'You never thought about it?' Miss Pink seemed only academically interested.

'Hard to say. No, I never did think about it.'

'On the other hand, you could have taken the blame. You could have led the pony up to the peat cuttings and buried her. You're a powerful woman.'

'I were only ten, but you're right, I coulda done that. I could harness the pony.'

'I doubt if you had the strength to lift her on to its back.'

'Oh, he done that.'

'How did she die?'

'Strangled.' Marginal surprise that the question had to be asked. As if that were the obvious way for one little girl to kill another. Her hands were on the table now and she glanced from one splayed thumb to the other, slowly, in slow motion. 'She were a wee slight thing.' A long pause. Miss Pink held her breath. 'I hated her,' Edith said. 'I never asked him; all these years and I never asked. You wouldn't, would you'?'

'But you believed her.'

'Aye. That's why I killed her.' She was silent for a long time, as if cataleptic. At length she sighed deeply and focused on Miss Pink. 'You thought Walter killed her.'

'I said someone close to Isaac killed her.'

'You know. You've known all along. You shouldn't be here. How did you get out?'

Miss Pink shrugged as if it were of no consequence. 'I swam down the gorge and hauled out on a gravel beach. The dog found me and barked until Bainbridge came with a rope.'

'You said you couldn't swim!'

'I lied.'

Edith regarded her sleepily, then she smiled. 'You got no witnesses – to anything. What are you going to do?'

'I don't need to do anything. Miss Pink was quite calm. 'Tyndale's here – I left the front door ajar.' She raised her voice: 'We're in here, Mr Tyndale!'

Edith didn't move. She heard the steps recede and the front door close. She realised she'd been tricked, and then why: the old fool was frightened of her! She giggled and went into the kitchen and lit the gas under the chip pan again. She turned the jet high because she was suddenly very hungry indeed, then she went in the bedroom and switched the television on. She lay down on the bed and slept a while.

There was a sound in the flat. That woman was back again? Edith staggered into the living-room and saw a shape fade through a blue haze. Objects in the kitchen weren't clear but even blind she'd have known where everything was – except that she must have missed something because there was a hard sound, some kind of sensation and a brilliant light against the smoky cloud.

She fumbled for the chip pan and pulled it off the gas.

Oil slopped and ignited and tresses of flame reached out to her and she saw that the visitor was Joannie with her long blonde hair and violet eyes.

18

'Her neck was broken when she fell,' Tyndale said. 'The skull was badly bruised.' He touched the back of his head. 'She must have cart-wheeled down the stairs. Death would be instantaneous. Just as well: she wouldn't want to live with those burns. Chip pan fires are the devil.'

Rick, coming home that evening, turning into Plumtree Yard, was just in time to see the top flat's kitchen window explode outwards, followed by smoke and flames. He glanced at Edith's door, knew that if she could get out she would have done so, rushed into his flat and dialled 999. He shouted the address, and then tried to break down the partition in his hallway, but plywood is difficult to smash. By the time he'd prised it away with a poker and dashed up the disused stairway the fire in the kitchen had spread and he had to retreat. His attempt at rescue would have been useless anyway for by that time Edith was dead. The firemen found her inside her front door at the foot of the stairs.

At first the neighbours watched the fire in horror: Rick and the Fawcetts and Miss Pink – it was she who told Tyndale that Edith intended making chips for supper – but as soon as the firemen found the body the initial horror was over. At least she hadn't suffered – not for long anyhow. Not as long as Joan Gardner did, Miss Pink thought grimly, wondering how long it took for one little girl to strangle another. Time was relative. How long would she have taken to drown this morning had she not been able to swim?

She spoke to Tyndale that night but it wasn't until next morning that she told the story to the rest of them. They sat in the garden at the back of Nichol House while Bags chased butterflies and Rick listened, interested despite himself, despite his frustration at having visited every travellers' camp in the Borders without finding Perry.

Tyndale arrived, in a clean shirt and washed, but haggard. He drank coffee gratefully, saying it would keep him going.

'You should go home and get some sleep,' Miss Pink told him. 'It's all over now.'

'Ma'am, it hasn't started! Now there's the paperwork, not to speak of your own statement.'

'The investigations are over,' Harald pointed out. 'All of them. Three,' he added as Tyndale glanced at him morosely. 'Joan, Walter, Isaac.'

'And Perry?' Rick put in angrily. 'What happened to her?'

Clive raised his eyebrows, looking to Miss Pink for help. She smiled neutrally. They were grown men, they must sort out the problem of Perry between them.

'She can come back now,' Rick persisted. 'Edith's dead, there's nothing to be scared of – although she never knew what it was.' He looked mystified himself. 'Did you find out?' he asked Miss Pink. 'I meant you to go to Edith – '

'It was the bone,' she told him. 'Edith must have said – shouted rather – something revealing on the phone, like telling Isaac to keep quiet, that everyone thought Walter had killed Joan, that she was safe as long as Isaac kept his head.'

'But Perry didn't hear anything like that, she'd have told me – '

'Edith thought she did. Guilty conscience.'

'I wouldn't say that Edith Bland had a conscience,' Anne put in coldly. 'She shot her own brother – or are you suggesting that he did die from the first wound like she said, and she shot him again to stage a suicide?'

'No,' Miss Pink said. 'If she was driving him to hospital why not continue? How would she know he was dead? In any event, why stage a suicide if he died by accident?'

'I still can't see her walking back to Kelleth after she'd put the Land Rover in the water,' Tyndale said. 'She was a heavy woman.'

'Oh, come on!' Miss Pink protested. 'Four miles?'

'When did you start to suspect her?' Clive asked, going for the nub of the matter.

She thought about it. 'Not to say suspect, but one had the feeling that something was out of kilter, a word or a look that jarred, or someone acting out of character. Little things like her saying she couldn't drive but knowing how Isaac might have shot himself in the driver's seat, and how he'd have placed his feet at the same time to get the truck rolling.'

'You did a crazy thing,' Tyndale said: 'setting a trap for a woman you suspected had already killed once, if not twice.'

'A calculated risk, and it worked. She did push me into the gorge – and I'd looked at that spot before; it was a clean drop into deep water. And she did drive my car to Carlisle, confirming that she knew how to drive. *You* couldn't have incited her to do that. No' – seeing he was affronted – 'I mean, you're bound by the rules. I could – and did – lie, and I used innuendo and generally confused her. I deliberately muddled the murders, the victims, even the pronouns, until she didn't know where she was. I'm talking about last night, in Plumtree, although even there she still had enough sense left to point out that there were no witnesses.' A thought struck her. 'Have you found my car yet?'

'No, but we found a witness on the Bigrigg estate in Carlisle who saw a small boy open the door and look inside. Correct registration: it was yours all right, and she must have left it unlocked, the kid didn't have to break into it. No doubt the keys were in the ignition too. Next time the witness looked the car had vanished.'

'She wasn't clever but she had a streak of cunning. She was single-minded to the point of recklessness. It was that that made her dangerous.'

'For you.' Tyndale was determined not to let her off the hook.

'For anyone who came in contact with her, given the right conditions. Isaac knew that. They were two of a kind, a team, right from the start.' She paused, considering. No one else spoke. 'Remote communities,' she mused, 'the Lakes, the Pennines, probably any country you care to name. Old sins, old crimes, family secrets – '

'Not confined to the countryside, Melinda,' Harald said firmly. 'There's child abuse in urban areas.'

Tyndale coughed and glanced at Anne, embarrassed.

'Actually that's how it started,' Miss Pink said, alert now. 'Edith being so possessive about her brother, Joan knowing the relationship between them, teasing her plain friend, flaunting her own charm – two little girls sexually initiated but with no control over their emotions. And once Edith had strangled Joan in a jealous rage Isaac had to dispose of the body because otherwise everything could come out, not only his sister being a killer but the incestuous relationship.'

'Poor Walter,' Rick said, and flushed, throwing a glance at Clive. No one had seen fit to enlighten him, least of all Clive himself. His parentage didn't concern Rick.

'Yes,' Anne said, easing an awkward moment, 'he was totally innocent. As was my old man here,' she added quickly, taking Harald's hand and glaring at Tyndale. 'All those two ever did was fight.'

'But my blow knocked him down,' Harald pointed out.

'So Isaac came along,' Rick said. 'And got his fall-guy for Joan's murder.'

'And a handle to make me give up Blondel,' Anne said drily. 'Isaac was an opportunist.'

Clive said wonderingly, 'He could blackmail you but he didn't trust his sister to do it.'

'Exactly,' Miss Pink said. 'He didn't trust her. She didn't have his self-control. Isaac would guess that Edith's comparatively innocuous blackmail to counter what she thought of as eviction would lead to harder demands. She was prodding sleeping dragons and he was worried. That's why he followed her to the Hoggarths' place that night, when he discovered his gun was missing. Edith was being crowded by events, she was close to breaking point – and she could destroy both of them.'

'I never liked her,' Anne said, 'right back to the old days. Joan was nothing: a precocious silly child who enjoyed being naughty, but to Edith sin came natural.'

Tyndale stood up. He was uncertain of the distinction between sin and crime in this context and didn't want to be drawn into any discussion on it. 'Statements,' he told Miss Pink heavily. 'Shall we say two o'clock?'

Anne escorted him indoors. Clive and Harald started to talk about rebuilding the house in Plumtree Yard. Miss Pink accepted Bags' insistent paw. Rick stared into the distance, frowning. Anne returned with Perry.

The others broke into smiles, all except Rick who leapt up and made to rush towards her.

'Hi, everyone,' she said, nodding round the circle, avoiding eye contact with Rick. She stooped to maul Bags who was welcoming but not beside himself with joy. Bags was Harald's dog now.

'Clive, let's make a start on lunch,' Anne commanded, and he trotted indoors with her obediently.

'We have to talk,' Rick said, bewildered by Perry's lack-lustre greeting.

She glanced at Harald. 'Why not?' he responded kindly. 'You have to tell him your plans – and everything.' She looked sulky. 'He's been searching the Borders for days,' he pointed out. 'And in the dark. You could have been dead for all he knew.'

Miss Pink got to her feet. 'We'll leave you to chat,' she said. 'Come along, Harald, we have business to attend to.'

'Better to have them in sight in your garden,' she added as they entered the kitchen. 'We don't want them going off on their own. There's been enough trouble.'

'Trouble?' Clive looked up from the chopping board. His eyes went to the figures under the tulip tree.

'There won't be any trouble,' Anne assured them. 'I'll see to that.'

Harald and Miss Pink went to the drawing-room where the french windows were wide to the garden and the sun. Bags wandered in and sat by Harald's chair. 'Here's one who's accepted the situation,' Miss Pink said approvingly. 'Poor Rick.'

'Rites of passage.' Harald smiled. 'Who am I to talk? I was never disappointed in love. Of course what's going to rankle with Rick is that everyone else knew where she was, and they allowed him to go off on a wild-goose chase in the Borders, and all the time she was in Orrdale's attics.'

'Deborah brought her down to the attics only because of the storm – and most of the time only Deborah and Clive knew. But the point was she was a murder suspect and Rick was so besotted that if he'd known where she was he could have given the game away. Look how easy it was for Edith to follow him to the Hoggarths.'

'I doubt he's looking at it logically.'

Under the tulip tree Rick was gesturing wildly, Perry half turned from him, looking down the garden.

'Relationships!' Harald sighed. 'Jonty Robson came back.'

'Who? Oh, him. I didn't know he'd been away.'